THE
LORD
OF
DARKNESS

THE HORIZON CHRONICLES

————•◆•————

BOOK 4

KIM RICHARDSON

The Lord of Darkness, The Horizon Chronicles Book 4:

Copyright © 2018 by Kim Richardson

Book cover by Damonza

www.kimrichardsonbooks.com

ISBN-13:978-1986070867

ISBN-10:1986070867

First edition: February 2018

BOOKS BY KIM RICHARDSON

SOUL GUARDIANS SERIES
Marked

Elemental

Horizon

Netherworld

Seirs

Mortal

Reapers

Seals

THE HORIZON CHRONICLES
The Soul Thief

The Helm of Darkness

The City of Flame and Shadow

The Lord of Darkness

DIVIDED REALMS
Steel Maiden

Witch Queen

Blood Magic

MYSTICS SERIES
The Seventh Sense

The Alpha Nation

The Nexus

THE LORD OF DARKNESS

THE HORIZON CHRONICLES

BOOK 4

KIM RICHARDSON

CHAPTER 1

ALEXA SAWED THE TOP DOOR hinge of her prison cell with a piece of jagged rock she'd kicked loose from the wall weeks ago. The shard slipped in her wet fingers and she hissed at the stinging pain as the sharp edges cut into her skin. She wiped her sticky fingers on her pants and went back to work.

She'd managed to cut three millimeters through the steel hinge after working nearly every minute of every hour, taking only short breaks to let her hands heal before going back to work. Her skin would stich itself back together, leaving nasty white scars, which had now split open again after only an hour's work. At this rate, she figured she would cut through the hinges in ten years.

She didn't have ten years. Milo didn't have ten years.

Alexa swore. Her ears rang, and she could taste terror in her mouth, like bitter metal.

"Keep going, Alexa," she urged, willing herself to calm down. "Don't ever stop. We keep going. That's what we do. We can't stop."

Soft white light emanated from a hovering globe, illuminating the black stone in warm golden tones. It had shone brighter when Alexa first arrived in her cell, inside the angel prison Tartarus, but now it seemed her only source of light was growing fainter each day, mirroring her hopes of ever getting out. The globe flickered, its light dimming. Soon it would burn out, leaving her in impenetrable darkness.

Alexa shook the thought away. Although time had an altogether different meaning in Horizon, she continued to mark the floor with a thin line each time she felt a day had passed. If her calculations were accurate, she'd been in her cell for about a month, but it felt like years. She had had no visitors. Not a single soul came to see her. Not even the prison's own guards, the giant eagles, ever bothered to check up on her.

During the first week of her confinement, Alexa perked up whenever she heard a scratch or the sound of nails scraping on a hard surface, hoping to see a white German Shepard bursting through the door.

But Lance never came. No one came. She was utterly alone.

The moans and wails of the other prisoners were her only companions, and most of the time she'd hum and sing just to keep their despairing cries from interfering with her work. She knew if she stopped, if she didn't keep herself busy, she would fall into despair, succumbing to their cries just like the thousands of angels locked up with her.

"Damn it."

Pain shot up her arm. The piece of broken rock, covered in white liquid, fell to the ground next to Alexa's feet. She examined her right palm. White essence poured from a large cut in the soft flesh and dripped down her wrist onto the floor. The citrus smell rose up to her nose, so unlike the metallic scent of blood from her mortal life.

"What's the point of being supernatural if our hands are completely useless?"

Alexa cursed again as she picked up the rock with her left hand and cut two long strips of cloth from her jacket. She then wrapped them tightly around both wrists.

"I don't have time to wait for these stupid hands to heal," she whispered and began to cut through the hinge again. "Milo doesn't have time."

Milo was all she could think about since her imprisonment—especially his kiss.

It had been such a passionate, desperate kiss and had taken her by surprise, filling her with warmth and an overwhelming sense of joy.

Joy. It was strange to feel such a sensation when locked away in a dank cell. But whenever she thought of his lips, his closeness, the look of longing in his eyes, butterflies fluttered inside her.

Milo cared for her. That much was obvious. She had never realized just how much she cared for him until she saw him disappear through the black mist.

It was a terrible ache, a searing pain that felt a lot like being stabbed by a death blade in the gut. The only way she could describe it was as an unbreakable bond—a bond that went beyond the realm of death and angels.

At the very beginning of her training, Alexa had learned that love was forbidden in Horizon. Relationships that went beyond friendship were grounds for a visit to Tartarus. Angels were soldiers, and soldiers didn't have intimate feelings. They obeyed orders. They obeyed the angel code.

"Screw the code," Alexa hissed as she dug harder. "I'm not a mindless robot. I have feelings. I care about things."

Milo was her mate, and she wouldn't abandon him. She *would* see him again. She dug harder.

But the flutter of fear stayed with her, just under her rib cage, along with an unexpected twinge of pain. What if she never got out?

No. She would break down the door somehow. Whatever it took, one day she *would* be free.

She sawed more fiercely.

She was alone and now in the complete darkness.

Alexa was also in the dark about events in Horizon and the mortal world. Whatever the Legion told themselves, she knew the balance hadn't been returned.

Lucifer was free.

In her stupidity, she'd freed him. It wasn't the first time Alexa had screwed up, but this was the royal screw-up of all time. She'd freed the devil, the Lord of Darkness, the Morning Star—Satan. He had played her, and like a fool, she'd fallen into his trap.

That night in London, at the Victoria Gate in Hyde Park, Alexa had witnessed firsthand what Lucifer was capable of. She had seen archangels and angels on the ground, thrashing in pain as their insides burned. She remembered it well because she'd felt his power too, her mind swallowed up by darkness.

Milo had saved them all with a selfless act, a noble one—one she didn't think she could have managed. The pain Milo felt at leaving her was evident in his eyes, but she also recognized another pain. He was about to join his daddy dearest, the devil.

Alexa didn't know much about Lucifer, apart from what she'd read and studied in Demonology 101. He was cruel to mortals and angels, but what of his sons? Would he harm his favorite son? She'd briefly met Milo's brothers in another reality in purgatory, and from that experience alone, she'd recognized Lucifer's love for his children.

But what if purgatory changed him? What if his hatred of the Legion went beyond fatherly love? Milo had joined the Legion of angels, the very organization Lucifer despised and hated above all else.

If Lucifer killed Milo out of spite, it would be her fault. Worse was the thought that she might never know. She might live out her days in this dank hole and never know what had befallen her Milo, her warrior, her golden angel.

Then there was the chaos and apocalypse that would soon follow Lucifer. Alexa was certain Lucifer wouldn't just go his merry way and live out his immortal life somewhere away from the Legion. She had seen the fury in his eyes, the anger at the Legion for being imprisoned in purgatory. He had said he would let the angels live—for now. And that meant his revenge would soon follow. Alexa was sure of it.

Even worse, Alexa didn't know if Lucifer and his army of fallen angels had already attacked the Legion. There was no way of knowing what was happening outside the walls of her cell. What if the Legion had fallen and she and the rest of the prisoners were left to rot in Tartarus for all eternity?

If Lucifer hadn't already taken his revenge on the Legion, it was coming. With the desertion of so many angels, the Legion would need all of the remaining souls to fight. But they'd thrown her in prison, and rightly so. If not for her, Lucifer would still be in purgatory.

She could still see the archangel Sabrielle's face as she lied to them about the so-called bone sword. If only she'd listened to Milo when he'd tried to warn her, none of this would have happened.

Alexa slammed the rock against the hinge, pretending it was Sabrielle's face. "I'm such an idiot."

Grinding her teeth, she hacked at the hinge with all her strength, creating a miniscule, barely noticeable dent. It was too late and completely useless to wallow in self-pity. The worst was done. All she needed now was to make things right again, to rectify her colossal mistake.

Alexa had also regained her memories while incarcerated. Images rose up suddenly in her mind's eye, like fountains of water pouring forth visions of her mortal life. She remembered an ordinary, plain girl with no real prospects, who had an absent father and a drunk mother. At first, as the panic set in, she took sobbing breaths, but then she realized her angel body had no need for such. Once she stopped retching, the crying began. When she stopped crying, the pain settled deep in her soul. Buckets of it. Until she collapsed to the cold stone floor in shivers.

As crazy as it sounded, even to her, she missed her mother. More importantly, she feared her mother wasn't eating properly and wasn't taking care of herself.

Alexa had been gone a long time. And once the memories came spilling back into her mind, she had an overwhelming desire to see her mother, if only to make sure she was okay. The mortal Alexa hadn't been much in life. She had been ordinary. But in death, she *would* be extraordinary.

With Hades' death, the connection between them died as well, as did her soul channeling abilities. After her burst of emotions had passed, Alexa had felt that her special gift had been erased. It was as though she'd shed a layer of herself, a layer of skin, like tossing a new coat for the old one.

She had stood up in shock at first, trying to home in on that familiar light, the pulsing of power in the compartment inside her soul. She found nothing. She couldn't help but feel angry that she'd lost the part of her that made her different. It had made her special, stronger than the other angels. As much as it had scared her in the beginning, she'd come to understand her gift and had come to admire and even enjoy it a little. It had made her feel unique in a giant sea of angels.

But now it was gone.

A part of her had also thought her gift might have been the only way she'd get out of her cell. She hadn't figured it out yet, as there were no souls in here but her own, but it had still been some false sense of security that she wasn't beyond help.

Without her abilities or anyone else's help, Alexa had to rely solely on her ingenuity. That's when she'd decided the only way out was through that door. If she could remove the hinges, she could then leave her cell.

But how would she get off of Tartarus? It was a giant floating black cube in the middle of the sky. The only way out was to either jump and die or hitch a ride in an eagle's talons, which she'd sworn was an experience she never wanted to experience again.

"How the hell am I going to get off this cube?"

A sound split the air, and Alexa's hand froze in midair.

It was a high, shouting cry, a sound of pure excitement. Nothing like the shouting wails of terror she'd gotten used to. This was a happy cry, almost too happy.

Dust and pebbles fell on Alexa. She stared at the door of her cell as the ground trembled below her feet.

"Now, that's never happened."

And just when she went to take a peek through the small window above the door of her cell, there was a deafening boom… and then the door blew off its hinges.

CHAPTER 2

ALEXA WAS THROWN WITH VIOLENT force across her cell. She hit the wall with a crash and slid to the floor as the door slammed against the wall next to her. Her ears rang as she blinked through the layers of dust and debris. It took a moment for her eyes to adjust to the abnormal amount of light that shown through. Why was there light and where was it coming from?

Through the clouds of dust, Alexa could see the shimmering curtain of light from beyond her cell. She blinked several times, her eyes now watering at the continued brightness. She'd forgotten how bright the outside world was, how glorious the color of the sky was with its puffy white clouds.

What the hell had just happened?

For a moment, Alexa contemplated lying there on the filthy, damp cell floor, savoring the free air around her and feeling the breeze against her face. Finally, she heaved herself onto her feet, her legs unsteady. It took only a few seconds before the sounds of boots scraping on stone floors reached her, and then she saw a figure move past her doorway, disappearing into the brightness of the light.

Is this a raid? she thought.

Closer now, she heard more rushing footsteps and shouts followed by the unmistakable high-pitched cry of eagles.

Excitement pounded through her limbs as she crossed the threshold of her cell.

When Alexa had first arrived inside Tartarus, the eagles had ushered her through a doorway onto a small platform. Beyond the platform there was nothing, only a bottomless black pit in front of her. One false move and she would fall into the abyss. There was no walkway. No stairs. There was only darkness between the rows of cells.

But now she could see a solid walkway spread out in front of her. And there were angels everywhere.

Light streamed through a great hole where the north wall used to be. It was as though Tartarus had cracked open like the shell of an egg. Through the giant gap, she could see the glorious blue sky and puffy white clouds. The sight lifted her spirits and she almost smiled. Almost.

Alexa stepped onto the walkway and grabbed the wrist of the first angel who rushed past her.

"What's happening? Is the Legion attacking us?"

The angel, a disheveled redheaded and bearded middle-aged male, looked at her with wide eyes. "Attacking us? Are you stupid or something? The Legion's not attacking us… we're *breaking out!*" With a wild and crazed expression, he shouted, "The Order of the

First! The First creations! The First shall rise and kill all the flawed creations!" And then he dashed down the passageway and jumped, disappearing below the ledge.

"Wait! Stop!" Alexa shouted. "There's no ground below! You'll die!"

She knew there was nothing but air below the cube. The ground was not for many, many miles. Down meant instant death.

"He just killed himself," said Alexa bewildered.

Another figure, a female angel with a long flowing white dress and golden tresses, reached the ledge in a mad dash and shouted, "The Order of the First!" She jumped, spread eagle as though she had leaped from a plane with a parachute.

Alexa looked around. "They've all gone mad."

As Alexa made her way carefully across the walkway towards the north wall, angels spilled through the open doors of their cells by the hundreds, scurrying around like rats released from their cages. The closer she got, she saw their dirty, encrusted, shredded clothes hanging over their bodies like ribbons. It was as though the cloth had simply withered away with time, leaving only the immortal angel body intact. Lots of naked bodies rushed past her, and she tried hard not to stare.

Then she spotted the giant-like angels. Their skin glowed as though they were illuminated by tiny lights from the inside. Archangels.

Alexa stared at the two big male archangels. Both wore ancient-looking armor, similar to what she had seen on Lucifer. Their features weren't delicate and handsome like the other archangels she'd come to know. They were hard and weathered but still a good deal more appealing than Metatron. Thick and heavily muscled, it was obvious these two were warriors. The larger of the two caught her staring and frowned at her with pale, watery eyes and huge gnarled hands made into fists.

Months ago, she would have cowered at his scowl, but now she stood her ground and stared right back until the archangels moved away.

The archangels and the angels were all here because they had committed crimes against the Legion and the angel code. She knew these were probably some of the worst, most evil angels that had turned as bad as they could go. There were no belphegor demons that she could see—only angels and the two archangels. For some reason, that made her feel worse.

What could they have possibly done to end up in here like her? And why were they all jumping off the ledge in an apparent mass suicide?

Alexa rolled her tight shoulders, shaking loose the knot in her chest, and crossed the walkway. Each step brought her too quickly toward the great big gap in Tartarus' wall where the angels leapt to their deaths.

She swore and hissed at the angels that crashed into her as they came plowing down the corridor towards the light and their death. The last thing she needed was for one of them to accidentally push her off the edge. She wasn't ready to face her true death. She wasn't done yet.

As Alexa moved forward, she could feel the heat of the sun against her cheeks, a far cry from the damp, cold, and black cell walls she'd grown accustomed to.

More angels rushed past her shouting, "The Order of the First." They all jumped in midair and disappeared below Tartarus' jagged ledge.

On it went until every single angel in Tartarus had barreled past her to end their lives. Perhaps this was what they wanted. Perhaps taking control of their deaths was better than spending eternity in Tartarus. Perhaps if she'd been in here for a hundred years, she too would be jumping off the ledge like the rest of them.

All but one.

By the time she'd made it across the walkway, a single angel stood on the right side of the opening. His skin was the color of oil, a sharp contrast against the bright white of his clothes. A quiver of arrows was strapped across his shoulder, and leather bracers sheathed his arms from wrist to elbow. A long, wicked-looking sword hung from his waist.

But that wasn't why she reached out and gripped onto the slick black rock.

Five giant eagles, as white as snow, were perched just below the opening, their yellow eyes gleaming in the light of the sun like jewels. They were massive, the same size as the prison guard eagles, but white in color. Somehow it made them seem more mystical to her, more celestial.

And sitting on top of the white birds were eight to ten angels. Together, the great white birds pushed off and glided westward towards the sun, taking the last of the angels with them. Alexa stared until her eyes burned from the sun's rays.

A harsh wheezing sound caught her attention. Lying far below the edge of the opening was one of the prison guard eagles. Maroon liquid oozed from deep gashes on its back and neck, spilling over its golden feathers and onto the black rock. One of its wings lay open, the long feathers spread out like fingers reaching for help. Its eyes were closed, and Alexa couldn't tell if it was alive or dead.

"I don't recognize you amongst our brothers and sisters," said a deep, but rich and pleasant voice. "You must be a recent addition to the black box. What's your name, angel?" The stranger had a deceptive smile like a smooth-talking car salesman trying to close a deal.

Alexa watched him carefully. With his eyes narrowed slightly, he stood too straight and stiff to pass as being relaxed. His bearing appeared far more apprehensive as though ready to put an arrow into her chest before she could make the slightest move. She knew he'd waited for her. Not to help escape on one of the eagles, but rather, to figure out who she was. Or maybe even to kill her.

"Alexa," she said and immediately put her guard up. "You blew this hole in Tartarus, didn't you? To free your friends." *And me. Thanks for that.*

The angel seemed to lose his composure for a half second before becoming all business again. "To free friends that were *unjustly* imprisoned," he answered, "and perhaps, *new* friends. We owe you a great debt, Alexa Dawson. Yes, I know who you are. We all do. You freed our lord. You helped return him to us, and we thank you."

"It wasn't exactly my idea," she said and noticed how fast the smile faded from his face. She didn't care. "I never wanted to free him. I didn't even know he was in that damned place. I went to get a weapon to defeat Hades."

"Hades has been defeated by our lord," answered the angel. "Even Greater demons as powerful as Hades are no match for our lord."

"Yes, I know. I was there," said Alexa, feeling some of that familiar anger returning. "But the weapon was the only reason I went in the first place. I never wanted to free Lucifer. I would never have gone if I'd known he was there." She paused and then added. "I'd take it back if I could. I wish I'd never gone." Alexa saw the flicker of anger flash across his features, and she moved ever so slightly away from the ledge and the angel.

"I see you have been misinformed, as virtually every angel in the Legion. It's not your fault, of course, and so I will not take what you say too seriously. The Legion has taught you falsehoods about our lord. He is not the evil creature you were coached to believe, but a lord of love and devotion, a just lord, the only true lord the angels should serve.

"But when you are as old as I am, you remember the truth. You remember the old ways before everything was changed, the ways that should be. Before the Legion turned its back on the angels and favored the mortals. We do not answer to the Legion, nor shall we abandon our ancient practices."

17

The hair along the back of Alexa's neck was prickling, her every nerve screaming.

"I gave you my name," she said, keeping the anger from her voice. "How about you return the same curtesy. Who are you?"

"My name is Nathaniel."

"That explains it."

Nathaniel frowned. "What does?"

Alexa felt a pressure under his dark stare. "Nothing." She knew he was an ancient angel and probably leading the deserted angels, which meant he was probably equipped with ancient power or ancient battle moves. Either way, it was not good.

A long silence followed. Alexa could feel Nathaniel's gaze rolling over her, probably debating whether he should kill her now and toss her over the edge.

The sound of beating wings made her turn just as another great white eagle perched itself on the exterior prison wall. Its golden eyes moved to Nathaniel and waited.

"You can't get off this rock without the eagles," said Nathaniel.

Alexa's gaze moved to the dead or injured eagle guard, and she felt sorry for it. The massive creature had never harmed her. It had only followed its orders like a good soldier when it brought her here. It didn't deserve to die like this.

"Even if it lives," said Nathaniel, noticing her eyes on the giant bird, "it won't help you. It's programed to keep all prisoners in Tartarus. It will kill you if it can't put you back into those cells. It's a stupid beast. It's rather big and powerful, but stupid. It talks, but only as well as a four-year-old child."

Alexa recalled a very developed conversation with the so-called four-year-old vocabulary. "Where's the other one?"

"Dead," said Nathaniel impatiently. "Your only chance is if you come with me. Come. And let me open your eyes to the truth, away from the corrupted Legion and their lies. Come with me and meet the others. I'm sure they'll be very pleased to meet the angel girl who freed our lord. They'll have many questions for you, I'm sure. We are all very interested in your recent trip to purgatory."

Alexa dared to look over the ledge and then wished she hadn't. She could barely make out the tiny specks of land from the clouds that obscured the view. She couldn't even fathom how high they were.

She pulled back, feeling a little dizzy. "I think I'll take my chances with the Legion. They'll probably be here any minute now. You should go."

"As you wish," said Nathaniel. "But if they can't put you in their prison anymore, what do you think they'll do to you? The one who released Lucifer? Don't think for one minute that your precious Legion will let you live."

Alexa scowled. "They wouldn't do that."

"They would, and they *will*. And you know it to be true. I can see it in your eyes. They can't let you live after what you've done. I'm surprised they even bothered to put you up in this place. Goes to show how soft they've become and what meddling for generations with mortals did to them. But it matters not. The Legion is full of lies. If you seek the truth, come with me and let me show it to you."

The white eagle ruffled its feathers, eager to take flight. Alexa surveyed Nathaniel. He was all smiles, but she could see the underlying fakeness of it. It was in his eyes and the way his face twitched whenever he smiled like it pained him to do so. She trusted her instincts, and right now, every part of her screamed *no!*

"It's like you said." Alexa remained as calm as she could. "No offense, but I don't know you and you don't know me. And right now, the last thing I need is to get mixed up with another group. You're part of The Oder of the First, right? I don't even know what that means. It's just a lot for me to process right now. I still need time to figure out some stuff on my own." Which was true. She wasn't about to leave with a stranger, an ancient angel who she knew despised mortals and the Legion.

"Where will you go?" Nathaniel shook his head, his black eyes flicking back and forth. "You can't stay here. Surely you want to live? You must know that the days of the Legion are over. Why fight for the losing team when you could stand with us? There is so much you don't know, so much you can learn. Believe in the order and your future will be bright."

Alexa's gaze fell on the injured eagle again, and she felt her temper rise. "Like I said, I'll take my chances with the Legion."

Nathaniel watched her for a beat longer, and then he whistled. The great white eagle pushed itself off the stone wall and, with a great beat of its wings, hovered just below the ledge.

Alexa's hair and clothes flapped in the strong gusts of air from the bird. She watched as Nathaniel leapt effortlessly off the edge and landed on the beast's back. The great bird gave one last great flap of its wings and banked left, sailing westward and away from the great prison.

"There is a place in The Order of the First for you, Alexa," called Nathaniel over his shoulder. "Should you ever want it."

Alexa didn't know how long she stood there, watching Nathaniel as he and his eagle became smaller and smaller until they were no larger than flies as they flapped westward on the horizon.

The eagles were the only way to and from Tartarus, and now as she watched her only ride disappear into a speck of dust, she wondered if she hadn't made a mistake.

The Legion would arrive soon, and then what? Would they believe her? Would they think this what *her* fault? Her doing? That she was involved with this? Her punishment had been swift and harsh. Alexa knew once the Legion saw that all their prisoners had escaped, they would unleash their fury on her.

Maybe even kill her…

"It took courage to refuse the angel Nathaniel," said a guttural voice.

Alexa flinched, slipped, and had to catch herself before falling over the edge. She gripped the corner of the left wall to steady herself and stared at two large golden eyes.

"You're alive!"

The eagle guard stretched his right wing, rotating his shoulder as though trying to loosen a stiff joint. "I am."

"You were pretending to be dead?"

"I was regaining my strength," said the eagle as he folded his right wing against his body. "I'm not a fool. I am in no condition to fight another eagle."

Alexa's eyes traced the amount of blood splattered on the rock and was amazed that the creature was still alive. "It wasn't courage," she said finally.

The eagle stretched its neck, and Alexa saw a bit of blood around its beak. "What wasn't courage?"

Alexa turned back and looked out towards the west again. "Why I refused Nathaniel. It didn't matter what I had heard about him. There was something off about him, you know. The way he looked at me made my skin crawl."

"I have no idea what you mean."

Alexa sighed. "He creeped me out. He felt wrong somehow. And he smiled *way* too much. Never trust someone who smiles all the time. It's like my instincts told me this guy was bad news."

"Then your instincts were right to warn you about him." The great bird stretched to its full height and beat its wings, as though testing them for the first time. It turned its eyes on Alexa. "Do you know what was locked up in here... for centuries?"

"I'm guessing very bad angels."

"The very worst. Angels gone rogue, angels who spilled each other's blood. Some I cannot say for sure if there is even angel left in them. They are corrupted to the core, twisted, not demons, but something else, something more vile. And this Nathaniel just let them all out."

"To join his crazy cause." Alexa bit her lip. "Who were the two archangels?"

The eagle's eyes lowered into slits. "The archangels Barakiel and Sorath. Once upon a time, they were Lucifer's lieutenants. They helped him as he tried to overthrow the Legion. But when Lucifer was finally vanquished and sent to purgatory, the Legion sent them here."

"But not Lucifer," guessed Alexa, "because he could have easily blown his way out as soon as he got here."

"Exactly."

Alexa thought of Milo and her spirits sank. "What happens now?" She wondered if the eagle would lock her up in one of the cells that wasn't damaged by the blast.

The eagle cocked its head to the side, and a gust of wind ruffled the feathers above its eyes in tiny ripples like waves. "I must inform the Legion of what happened here. They must know the angel Nathaniel was responsible for the breakouts. I will fly to the High Council and speak to Jeremiel. There will be sky raids. The other guards and I will search Horizon for the escapees before they have a chance to escape to the mortal world. Then we cannot help them."

Alexa swallowed, her throat tightening as though hands were pressing around it. "And me? What happens to me?" She doubted she could fight off the creature. Even though it was injured, it was massive with a razor-sharp beak and talons the size of long swords.

The eagle was silent for a long while. "What do *you* want to happen?"

"To put Lucifer back in his cage." The words came out before she could stop herself. When she looked at the bird, its eyes seemed to pierce through her, into her mind. It reminded her of Metatron for a moment.

"Then I will help you."

Alexa's mouth fell open. She couldn't believe her luck. "You will? You won't put me back in one of those cells? Why would you do that? I thought you had to obey the Legion? I'm a prisoner—I was tried and convicted—same as all the others."

"As far as I'm concerned, the prison is gone. I'm a guard of Tartarus, not a minister on your council. I won't meddle in those affairs." Its golden eyes gleamed. "I know what you've done, but I can also see that you're sorry for it. I'm loyal to the Legion. Your refusal to leave with Nathaniel and the others is proof to me that you're still loyal to the Legion. But without a prison, I see no reason why you must stay here."

"You must have graduated top of your class," smiled Alexa.

The eagle chuckled, and it sparked something bold inside Alexa's chest.

"I will take you back to the Legion. Level six, preferably," it said. "You won't be noticed there. After that, you're on your own, angel."

Alexa kept her face blank, though her insides were bouncing around like rubber balls.

The eagle crawled up the side of the wall and pressed itself right next to the opening, so close its feathers brushed her legs.

"Sorry, but, what do I call you?" asked Alexa, realizing that she wanted to thank it properly. Yet it didn't sound decent without the creature's name.

"Albatross," said the eagle proudly, and Alexa could feel the honored smile in its voice.

"Albatross," whispered Alexa, her excitement mounting.

And with a grin that matched her exhilaration, she leaped off the edge.

CHAPTER 3

"**T**HERE ARE MANY DIFFERENT WAYS to attain the levels, but you know of only one way. That's with the elevators," Albatross had told her just before he'd landed on the platform on level six. The small platform was surrounded by clouds, propped with a single elevator. "We need to be able to access them, like you. But not through elevators. We wouldn't fit."

Alexa had never known there was a back door to the different levels in Horizon. She'd always thought the only way to access the levels was through the internal elevators.

After Alexa had said her goodbyes and thanks, she climbed down the eagle's back and stepped into the waiting elevator. She saw a flash of golden wings flapping in the blue sky before the elevator doors slammed shut.

It took a second for her to realize something was wrong.

The elevator looked exactly as it always did—elegant handcrafted cherry panels decorated with golden-wing crests, a brass control panel to her left, and all seven buttons to the seven levels. It even had the familiar smell of mothballs. Everything seemed in order, and yet something was missing…

There was no operator.

Alexa whirled on the spot, expecting one of the operators to be hiding behind her. The operators were unpleasant little creatures, and she wouldn't be surprised if one was waiting for the perfect opportunity to pester her.

But there were only walls, air and her. She was utterly alone.

Alexa had never been in any of the Horizon elevators without the company of an arrogant primate. They were the operators, but they were also the keepers in a way, making sure only the right kind of angel or supernatural being stepped into the elevators.

However, it now dawned on Alexa that the breakouts from Tartarus she had witnessed had something to do with the disappearance of the operator.

Staring at the panel, Alexa rolled her eyes from the brass number seven to the number one. She couldn't return to the Counter Demon Division on level five, not unless she wanted the archangel Ariel or any of the angels to arrest her.

Was Nathaniel right? Without an angel prison, would they kill her?

The news of the breakout had spread, that she was sure of. Why else was the elevator empty? Or was it unrelated and the operators' disappearance was something else entirely?

She didn't have time to dwell on that. She needed to act fast. Where should she go? Anywhere in the Legion was a risk. She was a fugitive. An escapee. She had no friends in the entire Legion apart from Lance and Milo. The oracle Mr. Patterson had helped her a few times, but would he now after all she'd done?

Making up her mind, Alexa pressed her finger on a brass button. The number one button flashed, and with a jerk, the elevator began its descent.

Alexa stood awkwardly behind the doors, her chest compressing inward, as though she was running out of the breath she didn't even need. She wondered what would happen when the doors swung open. Would there be an army of angels waiting for her? Would they eliminate her now to avoid more mishaps? Each time the floor indicator dial pointed at a new level, a cold sweat slid down her back.

Alexa had been near tears when she'd suffered her sentence. She'd never been so humiliated. All those archangels thought those terrible things of her. Every angel did too. Now there was nothing left to humiliate her with. She'd been to her lowest. There was only one way left to go, and that was up. She *would* make this right.

As the elevator descended, she felt a wave of nausea hit her hard. Her mind was so dizzied by the thoughts that she could no longer trust she was thinking straight.

She reached out and pressed a hand on the wall to steady herself, fighting the dizziness. She took a deep, unnecessary breath to try and calm herself. It didn't work. She pushed off into a fighting stance, fists up, although it did nothing to hide her shaking.

"You won't take me," she whispered, her teeth chattering.

When she thought she might pass out from the dizziness, the floor dial pointed to the number one, followed by a slight *ting*, and then the doors swished open.

With a cry, Alexa flung herself forward—and landed in an empty chamber.

The walls of Orientation threw Alexa's cry back to her, amplified and echoing.

She stood, her hands still clamped into fists, as her own voice died down until there was no sound at all but the elevator's doors closing behind her.

Orientation—the place where all newly appointed angels from around the world were gathered to be sorted. The enormous chamber was the size of ten football fields. She had found it intimidating and had been overwhelmed by the thousands of people. Now, it was deserted.

There were no chaotic noises of thousands of voices speaking at the same time, no happy cheers from the recently deceased, or unhappy moans from those who still couldn't grasp the fact that they were dead. It was like stepping into a ghost town where the remnants of people were still in the air. You could feel people had once been here.

Alexa felt her nerves pounding through her body. What the hell happened here? Where were all the angels? The oracles?

"Hello?" she chanced and waited for her echoing voice to subside. But the silence that followed was eerie and unnatural, causing the hairs on the back of her neck to stand up as sharp as nails. For a moment, she felt like she was back in her cell, and a flutter of fear spiked through her again. But she would not panic.

She only let herself feel a sense of relief at the familiar humid air and the smell of the ocean. The pools were still there.

Her boots echoed on the hard floor as Alexa made for the score of office buildings nestled in the middle of the chamber like the remains of a village on a deserted island. Now that the chamber was empty of people, she could see the buildings more clearly—haphazard office buildings sandwiched together in too tight a space. Through the windows she saw beige walls and carpets with many doors leading to many offices. It always made her feel like she was walking into a bank.

Finally, Alexa reached the door fit for an elephant with the brightly lit neon sign, which read: *Oracle Division # 998-4321, Orientation.*

With her nerves hammering inside her, she grabbed the handle, turned it, and pushed in.

For a panic-filled instant, she focused on the hundreds of scattered papers covering the ground and littering the desks. The filing cabinets that twisted all the way to the ceiling looked just as she remembered, just as messy, as though a bomb of papers had gone off from within them.

"Hello? Jim? Mr. Patterson?" she ventured and stepped through the threshold. "Anyone? Hello?"

It was quiet, too quiet. The only sound was the papers crunching under her boots. She could see them in her mind's eye—the tiny old men who ran balanced on top of crystal balls, like circus acrobats, their silver gowns and long white beards flowing behind them.

She pushed open the first door on her right and saw nothing but an empty desk littered with papers. No oracle. She ran to the next one and, with her shoulder, plowed open the door. Piles of papers were stacked in dangerously tall and teetering columns, but no oracle.

Every door she tried gave her the same result. The oracles were gone. When she came at last to Mr. Patterson's office, she heard a cry escape from her own throat as she pushed through.

His half-moon, mahogany desk was empty except for one single sheet of paper. As she stepped into the room, the raised salt water pool was her only comfort. At least she could use it to go to the mortal world. But where would she go? Where would she start? How would she find Milo when she didn't even know where he was? Maybe he wasn't even in the mortal world. The last she saw he had disappeared into a portal of black mist to another dimension. Milo could be anywhere.

She was alone, really alone. When she was in her cell, at least she could fool herself into believing that once she was out, she would find her friends again. Someone could assist her on her journey. She'd been wrong. Orientation was deserted. She felt her eyes burn, but she wouldn't let herself cry.

Alexa paced the room, her mind swirling with questions. Broken images raced each other through her mind—Lucifer escaping from purgatory, angels and archangels writhing on the ground, the breakouts from Tartarus, Milo's kiss...

31

Alexa sat on the edge of the desk and hung her head. "I can't do this…"

"Not with that kind of attitude, you won't."

Alexa flinched and slipped off the desk, landing with a hard thump on the ground. She whirled around and blinked up at a large white, long-haired dog.

"Lance?"

"Do you know of another, white-furred, dangerously handsome canine devil in the Legion?" The Scout trotted in the room, his tail wagging behind him. "Please tell me you don't."

Alexa got to her feet and brushed the hair from her eyes. "What are you doing here?"

"Looking for you," said the dog. "When I heard about the breakouts, I came straight here. Everyone else thinks you took off with Nathaniel, but I knew you didn't. I figured you'd come see your oracle bestie. Clever girl—made everyone think you were somewhere else so you could come here and move ahead with the plan right under their noses. That's something I would do. I hummed all the way over here."

Alexa's spirits sank even lower. "When you say *everyone*… everyone as in Ariel and Metatron and the rest of them… the rest of the Legion?"

Lance sat on the floor. "Well, I don't have all the facts, but it's clear they think you're gone with Nathaniel and the prisoner escapees. I do remember hearing the archangel Ariel speaking up for you, saying that she thinks you probably *had* to, that if you didn't follow Nathaniel, he would have killed you."

32

"He didn't."

"I can see that."

Alexa leaned on the desk. She was so happy to see her friend, and part of her wanted to reach out and hug him. But she couldn't help the sudden sick sense of dread that crawled inside her mind, heavy and ill-fated, as though she would never be happy again.

"Lance. What's happened? Where are the angels? The oracles? I took the elevator and there was no one in there. No operator. That's never happened before, and I've taken *lots* of elevator trips."

"Well, *lots* has happened since you've been... you know... gone," said Lance carefully, his brows low.

"Like what?"

"Well, for starters," said the dog, "Metatron went a little ballistic after Lucifer showed up. Not to mention Sabrielle's betrayal. He grabbed an army of angels and arrested every angel he suspected had something to do with The Order of the First. They were tossed in Tartarus, just like you, but without even a trial. I'm sure some innocent angels got caught up in this."

"There's nothing we can do about that now." Alexa thought of how persuasive Nathaniel was. "Nathaniel will have no problem luring the innocent angels to join him after they'd been wrongly imprisoned in the first place. But the real issue here is that he got all his buddies get-out-of-jail-free passes."

"Yes," Lance said, his voice uneven with rage or fear, "all new recruits for his army. The Legion suspects their numbers to be about ten thousand."

33

"Ten thousand?" said Alexa incredulously. "But that's an enormous amount."

"It gets better," said the Scout. "After our friend Hades was destroyed and the Hellgates closed, the Veil began to repair itself—and then it stopped."

"It stopped?"

"Yup," said the dog. "It's like the layers of protection, the invisible skin that keeps the supernatural from penetrating through, is super thin and weak. The Veil is sick. Too sick to repair itself. There's some anomaly shifting inside of it, but no one knows what it is. It's infected with a darkness that has nothing to do with Hellgates."

Alexa's jaw tightened. "Lucifer."

"Exactly. It's as though he's infected the Veil with a virus. I don't know when, but it will eventually crumble."

Alexa shifted uncomfortably. "Can the mortal world survive without the Veil?"

"Think about it," said Lance. "Not only will every single mortal now *see* the supernatural—demons, devils, imps, and the like—but all the demons from the Netherworld will be able to come through into the mortal world. They won't need to wait for a rift or a crack in the Veil because there'll be nothing to stop them from entering. It'll be like the gates of the Netherworld are open. Once that happens, it won't make a difference how many angels there are to fight them. It'll be too late. The humans and their souls will be fair game. The demons won't stop until there's nothing living in the world. Until they've devoured every last human soul."

Alexa felt another wave of dizziness and grabbed the edge of the desk until it passed. "What about the Greater demons that escaped from the Hellgates?"

Lance blinked. "The reports I've seen say that Lucifer's killed every god, goddess, or demon that wouldn't submit to him. *Every* single demon. Which means, he controls both the Netherworld and The Order of the First."

"He's got demons *and* angels pinned against the Legion," said Alexa, "and that would make a very large army, wouldn't it?"

"A hundred to one is what I heard the archangels say," answered the dog. "With odds like that…" Lance didn't finish, as though what he was about to say would only make things worse and he'd decided against it.

The memory of the thrashing angels and demons at the mercy of Lucifer's power sent a lick of cold up Alexa's spine. "But it doesn't explain why everyone's gone."

"While Nathaniel was busy bailing you out of Tartarus—"

"He didn't *bail* me out."

"—word reached the Legion that The Order of the First were planning an attack on the Legion, Orientation to be exact."

"Why would the order want to attack Orientation?"

"It was said they wanted to put a stop to the forming of new angels," Lance added quickly. "And what better way to hinder us— to stop the wheel from rolling—than to destroy the first level and kill thousands of innocent angels and oracles. Orientation is where everything starts. Remove it, and the wheel stops. Levels one and three are the most vulnerable levels with barely any protection and all newly appointed angels. The High Council decided to move everyone to levels two and five. And to shut this one down."

"Shut it down?" exclaimed Alexa. "But isn't that exactly what Lucifer and his followers want? To stop the Legion? To break it?"

Lance hung his head, his eyes glimmering. "Yes. But we can't risk the lives of all those angels and all the other creatures that work for the Legion. The High Council really didn't have any other choice. It's not safe for them here." He paused. "It's not safe for anyone. They shut it down until they can figure out their next move."

"Which is what?"

Lance clamped his mouth shut and shrugged. "No idea."

Alexa shook her head and stared beyond the open door to the piles of papers scattered in the hallway. "So, who's protecting the mortals if there's no more Legion to protect them?"

"We are?" offered Lance and gave a small wag of his tail.

Alexa gave him a feeble smile. "Then, I feel bad for the mortals." She felt a deep pain inside her chest, as though her ribs were caving in on her. She couldn't stop shaking.

"It's not your fault," said Lance gently, but Alexa wouldn't look at him. She knew if she did, she would lose it.

Her lips shook. "It is. It's *all* my fault. I let him out."

"Not willingly. He tricked you. Sabrielle tricked you. You can't blame yourself."

"I can." Alexa moved off the desk and rubbed her eyes. "Tragedy followed me as a mortal, and it's followed me as an angel." She turned and looked at Lance. "Everything I've done or touched turns to crap. Ever since I've been an angel, I've created disaster after disaster. Haven't you noticed? I thought I was special with the soul channeling ability. I thought *this* time, I could make a difference with this gift. But now I realize this gift, this *thing* I had, whatever it was, was never meant to do good. It was *evil*. I used it to release the most powerful, malicious being that ever was."

"Alexa," began Lance, "you can't say things like that."

"It's fine," she said, her voice raw and her eyes burning. Guilt pushed down on her shoulders. Her face burned with shame under the cool mask. She'd felt regret that night when Lucifer stood in place of the boy demon Markus. Regret and shame for acting on blind defiance and for her insubordinate behavior towards the Legion.

The consequences of her actions were catastrophic. Without the Legion to protect the mortals...

Death. There was only death.

Her wrath was a song in her essence as she said, "I can't change what happened, what I did, but I can try to fix it. Or die trying. But first, I need to find—"

"Milo."

Alexa raised a brow. "Am I that predictable?"

"No. Yes." Lance's gaze was intense. "I'm a Scout. It's my job to know things. Besides, I think whatever you're planning on doing, he's a big part of that. And... I kinda miss the tall brooding blond."

The corners of Alexa's mouth twisted. "Good. The only problem is I have no idea where he is. He could be anywhere. He could be in Horizon or the mortal world or some other dimension with his father."

Lance got to his feet and stood next to Alexa. "I think I might know where he is."

Alexa's insides rushed to her throat. "You do? Where?" She tried and failed to hide the emotion from her voice.

"With his brothers," said the Scout. "Nephilim have been spotted in the mortal world."

"But I thought the Nephilim were destroyed."

"They were. But this is Lucifer were talking about. He can raise the dead or create more of these creatures on a whim. I don't know how he did it, but I can assure you, the Nephilim have returned."

Lance moved towards the desk. He lifted himself on his haunches and rested his two front paws on the surface.

"What's that?"

"What's what?" said Alexa, snapping her mind out from her thoughts of Milo.

Lance rolled his eyes. "It's right in front of you. That piece of paper there. What is it?"

Alexa glanced at the sheet of paper she'd barely taken notice of. She leaned over and slid it closer so she and Lance could both read it.

Words were scribbled over the piece of paper as though the person who wrote it was in a hurry. She smoothed it out.

Dear Alexa,

If you've found this letter, then what I've seen in the crystals will come to pass. I cannot abandon my obligations as an oracle in good conscience without leaving a little something behind. First, I must proclaim—all is not lost. Where there is light, there is a way. And your path is illuminated in light. Let me explain.

The oracles and I have tried to persuade the Legion with our findings, but our efforts were in vain. Alas, our hopes rest in you.

The only way to vanquish Lucifer is to reopen a doorway to purgatory and trap him back inside. To do that, you need to create a vacuum rift, which will open a doorway to purgatory. Three special ingredients are required to open a doorway to purgatory.

First, you will need to bind Lucifer. Otherwise the vacuum rift will be useless as he can use his portal abilities and get away unless he's in a closed environment. Therefore, you will need Holy Fire. A circle of burning Holy Fire is the only way to trap a celestial being.

Second, you will need the help of a celestial weapon—the Staff of Heaven. The staff is imbued with supernatural power. It was created by the archangel Michael to use against Lucifer. Since then, the staff was stolen from the Legion, but we know it is hidden somewhere in Horizon.

Third, you will need the blood of a demon. A demon sacrifice. The blood must be offered willingly. The blood from a compliant demon with a slam of the staff will create a shockwave and open the doorway to purgatory.

Alexa turned the paper over, expecting more, but it was blank.

"He wanted you to find this," said Lance. "He knew you'd come here. It says he saw you in one of his visions. Their prophecies don't always come true, which I'm guessing is the reason the Legion didn't listen. Or they were just too busy trying to save the angels before Nathaniel's attack. But he felt strongly enough to risk his post by leaving you this note. He's got some big crystal balls, if you know what I mean."

Alexa flashed him a smile. "This is it." She waved the paper excitedly. "This is what I needed. *This*," she waved the paper again, "is how we're going to defeat Lucifer."

She read the note again and felt a quickening sense of excitement rise within her. "He's left us the tools to destroy Lucifer." Her hand shook as she read the paper again. "Holy Fire, the Staff of Heaven, and the blood of a willing demon. I have no idea where to start, but the one thing I do know—we can't do this alone. We need to find Milo."

"I agree," said the dog, wagging his tail happily. "Let's go get the handsome bastard."

Alexa folded the paper carefully, which took some effort with her hands still shaking uncontrollably and stuffed it in her pocket. "So," she said turning back to the dog, "how do we find the Nephilim?"

Lance pushed off the desk, his eyes bright. "Just follow the crazy."

CHAPTER 4

ALEXA AND LANCE FOLLOWED THE crazy to Las Vegas, Nevada. The sun was a glowing yellow disk in the blue sky. The air was hot and dry, and Alexa knew if she wasn't protected with her M-suit, she'd be sweating buckets.

The hot weather didn't seem to bother Lance at all as he bounded next to her, his ears up and alert and his white fur glimmering like pearls.

Giant glass and metal buildings rose up on either side of them, disappearing into the blue sky as though they wanted to reach Horizon. Hotels and restaurants lined the streets. Alexa read the signs: all-you-can-eat buffets, pool parties, and too many Vegas clubs advertising to remember. It gave ordinary people with moderate incomes a chance to live the five-star lifestyle of the rich and famous for a few days.

Despite the fact that Alexa had never actually been to Vegas, it was very different from what she remembered seeing on television. There was none of the loud, fast, flashy and energetic atmosphere she knew the Vegas Strip ought to have.

The Vegas Strip was a charred desolation for miles around. The shops, hotels, and casinos were all blackened shells. Alexa felt like she was walking through a zombie apocalypse movie without the zombies. Empty cars, trucks, and buses were piled onto the sidewalks, their doors open as though the mortals had left in a hurry. The hot air smelled of carrion, blood, and rot.

Savagely slaughtered, mortals lay scattered across overturned cars and rubble, sprawled in pools of congealing blood with their insides spilling out into a liquid mess around them. Some had lost limbs and even heads. A body hung upside-down, strapped to the hood of a black Range Rover. As she neared a body, it was too decomposed to tell if it was male or female. The skin was wet and engorged with white maggots. Alexa retched at the smell, her eyes watering.

She could feel the dead. The chill of death was close by. A cold shiver rippled over her skin despite the hot air. But the dead and the sheer number of bodies weren't what had Alexa fuming with anger. It was with the way they were displayed, like art in a gallery.

Another rotting corpse hung on the side of the brick wall of Chase Bank. A piece of metal pierced through the head was holding it in place and hundred-dollar bills were tucked in the mortal's mouth. Severed heads topped spikes in a circle. Alexa smelled the burnt bodies before she saw them, impaled on sharpened stakes next to the street signs with their hands drawn up in front of their faces as if an in attempt to fight off the flames.

There were piles of severed hands and feet. Some of the hands still clutched cell phones, keys, and other hands. She saw tiny fingers, hands of children, and then she wept.

Alexa had thought she'd seen the worst in purgatory, but somehow this was worse. She felt her fury—her total, immeasurable hatred for the Nephilim—rise in her hot like a fever.

Lance was looking at the pile of severed limbs, muttering hotly, but Alexa couldn't make it out.

Trash, vehicles, and shopping bags were all laid down in a haphazard fashion as though a great hurricane had blown through, leaving a tangled sea of dead bodies. Alexa and Lance picked their way carefully amongst the tangle. Warm air, heavy with drought, carried the fetid decay. A fog of flies followed them as they went— the few things still living as far as Alexa could tell.

Lance was right. Whatever had happened here could only be described as crazy.

"You think the Nephilim did all this?" she asked between coughs and fits of rage.

"Sure of it." Lance lifted his head in the air and sniffed. "It's them. They've got a distinctive smell. It's not quite demon but has a little mortal and angel in the mix. It's hard to follow their scent with all the dead, but the signs don't lie. Nephilim were known to put their dead, their *kills*, on display in ways to intimidate the mortals and the angels. It's a scare tactic to terrify and shock their enemies with their madness, to show them just how far they'd go. They're psychotic killers that should never have existed."

Alexa flinched as she thought of Milo. He had been born Nephilim, but he was so different than his brothers. Milo would never have murdered the innocent and put them on display like this. These Nephilim were the essence of evil.

She gripped the soul blade she'd found when rummaging through the oracle's desk. She knew the evil that they would soon come across and would have to fight.

Alexa hadn't shared all the accounts of purgatory with Lance. She had kept the parts that had involved Milo to herself. She felt it was too personal, and if Milo wanted Lance to know, he would tell him.

Her chest heaved with pain at the memory of Milo's face, the way he had looked at her with total confusion when he'd first seen her with his brothers. He had not remembered her. If Milo was with another group of Nephilim now, she prayed he would remember her and be himself, not the confused young angel she'd found in purgatory with his brothers.

"It's like we're following a trail of bread crumbs," Lance's voice cut into Alexa's unpleasant reverie. "But instead of bread crumbs, we've got human remains and body parts."

"I'd prefer the bread crumbs," said Alexa as she wiggled around two mangled corpses whose eyes and mouths were sown shut. Alexa hoped the stitching had been postmortem.

"Yeah, well… who wouldn't," said Lance as he jumped over a pile of rubbish. "I hope golden boy is here at the end of this feast of bodies."

Alexa thought of something. "These Nephilim... can any archangel create them if they, you know... spend time with a female mortal?"

Alexa could swear she saw the dog smile as he said, "You mean share a bed with them?"

"Yes. And?"

"Well, there are other *rare* cases of male angels who've fallen in love with mortal women, usually their charge—which is totally forbidden by the way. If, incidentally, that relationship results in an offspring, they're called Elementals."

"Elementals," repeated Alexa. "Yes, I remember reading about them. They're powerful because they have the best of both worlds—supernatural energy from Horizon, and natural magic that comes from the Earth."

Lance sniffed the ground as he walked and then raised his head. "But not all are powerful, and not all are even aware of their supernatural abilities. It all comes down to genetics. Sometimes you get more of the father. Sometimes you get more of the mother. It really depends."

"How are Nephilim different?"

"Nephilim are Lucifer's creations, *his* very own children. Elementals are more human whereas the only human in the Nephilim are their human shells. There's nothing else like them."

"Milo is different," said Alexa before she could stop herself. "He's nothing like his brothers. Nothing at all."

"No, he isn't. And that's why we like him."

"Why do you think Milo was Lucifer's favorite if he was so unlike his brothers? He hated what he was."

"Maybe that's why," answered the dog. "Milo was the youngest and the most troubled son. Perhaps what made him different made Lucifer love him more? Who knows. Lucifer *is* psychotic."

As they walked through the strip, Alexa marveled at the size of the buildings that rose up on either side of them. She saw buildings on fire and the crumbled remains of what looked like a spa resort. Yet they saw no humans—no one alive.

They came upon a murder of crows, feasting on the corpses, and the birds cawed furiously at being disturbed. Alexa tore her eyes away and followed Lance.

"What do you know about Holy Fire?"

"If my memory serves me correctly," said the Scout, "it's actually an *oil* that burns. The oracles created it to bind angels and archangels who turned against the Legion when they couldn't control them anymore, specifically Lucifer and his followers."

"Do you know where we can find some?" Alexa asked.

"Well, knowing a little bit about how oracles operate, I would have to guess they'd probably keep some hidden somewhere in their offices."

"But we checked Mr. Patterson's office together. Nothing was there except for the weapons we found and the letter."

"That's true," said Lance, "but I didn't mean *just* in Horizon."

Alexa cut a look at him. "You mean here? Somewhere in the mortal world?"

"That's exactly what I mean. I think the oracle, or Mr. Patterson as you call him, wouldn't have mentioned it in his letter if he didn't trust you would find it. If it wasn't in his desk in Horizon, it's here. The oracles must keep stashes of it in their safe houses. Be that as it may, I happen to know of a safe house right here in Vegas. We can check it after we find golden boy."

Alexa felt a pang in her chest at the mention of Milo. "Well, that's one ingredient we can tick off the list. At least we have an idea where to find it. What about the Staff of Heaven? He said in his letter that it was stolen from the Legion and hidden somewhere in Horizon. Any ideas where?"

"Hmm..." Lance seemed thoughtful. "That's going to be a bit of a problem."

"Why?" Alexa glanced at the dog. "Because you *don't* know where it is?"

"I don't know where it is," repeated the dog. "It could be anywhere, but my guess is it's with—"

"Nathaniel." Alexa glowered. "Yeah. I bet he has it, or one of the members of The Order of the First. And I'm willing to bet he's the one who stole it in the first place. So that no one could use it against his beloved Lucifer."

"That's exactly what I think. Which is the bigger problem. If he *does* have the staff, it's not like he's about to hand it over either. Even if we ask nicely."

"So, we don't ask nicely," said Alexa as a plan formed in her head. "We steal it."

"I like the way you think, girl," said Lance as he trotted next to her and swerved to avoid stepping in a large red puddle.

"We agree Nathaniel has it," said Alexa, "but that still leaves us with a problem. Where are they? Where are The Order of the First?"

"Horizon, that's for sure."

"How can you be so sure? They could be hiding out here, in the mortal world. It would be harder to find them if they were."

"Nah." Lance shook his head. "They're in Horizon. I'd bet my nine lives on it."

"Cats have nine lives."

Lance shrugged. "Same difference. To these angels, the mortal world and its mortals are a waste of space. They hate it. They despise anything to do with the mortal world. To them it's dirty, packed with filthy mortals and other living creatures. They want nothing to do with it."

"Which is why hiding it here makes perfect sense," said Alexa, feeling excited at the prospect of finding the two missing ingredients for the vacuum rift right here. "Think about it. It's the perfect hiding place. That's what I would do, anyway."

"The only reason these angels would ever come here, to this neck of the woods," said Lance, "would be to *slaughter* the mortals. Trust me. Don't forget, to them humans are the *flawed* creation… the mistake that never should have been. They want to rectify that mistake. It's not here. I'm sure of it."

Alexa couldn't argue with Lance's logic, but it still annoyed her a little. There was a sudden quiet as they walked. And then Alexa asked, "What about the—"

"The blood of a *willing* demon?" Lance glanced around, as though he had missed the scent he was following, and then moved to the right as though he'd caught it again.

"Yeah, that." Alexa jogged to catch up. "What do you make of it?"

"Well, for starters, it's not going to be easy... maybe even impossible to get a demon to change sides, to sacrifice itself for us angels."

"Great. That's not helping. Don't you want to get rid of Lucifer?"

"Of course I do," snapped Lance, his voice harder than Alexa had ever heard before. "Of course I don't want his supreme unholiness to take over the worlds—ours and this one. But to find a *willing* demon—a demon who's willing to bleed for us—they're not a dime a dozen. Our chances of finding one are...remote. Why would a demon want to help us? The very creatures that hunt them?"

"They could have had a change of heart? Of conscience?" offered Alexa.

Lance stopped is his tracks. "Demons don't have a conscience. They're *demons*."

Alexa threw up her arms and kept walking. "I don't know. Angels turn bad. Why can't the opposite happen? Demons... growing a conscience? It could happen?"

"No it wouldn't. They're psychopaths. They don't have any moral qualms. They don't and never will have that little voice inside of us all that tells us when something is wrong. It just doesn't exist. Demons weren't programed that way. They were created for one single purpose—to kill us and mortals."

"Are you saying there's never been an incident, no record ever, of a demon changing sides?"

"Never."

"So, all demons are mindless automatons programmed to eat humans and kill angels."

"You got it."

"You can't think of *one* demon that could help us. One?"

"Nope."

Alexa kicked a can out of her way. "Doesn't the Legion have spies inside the demon armies? Informants?"

"You watch too much TV."

Alexa rolled her eyes. "I'm serious, Lance. I'd bet Metatron does. He probably has a handful of demon spies working for him. Of course, he's giving them something in return. Mortal souls for a few favors?"

"Stop that," said Lance. "Metatron can be a jerk, but he's true to the Legion. He'd never sacrifice the souls of mortals for information. There are other ways."

"So, I'm right."

"They don't have *spies* as you say," said the dog, glancing at Alexa. "But I'm aware of the Legion doing a few favors for demons in return for information. And what I mean by favors, I don't mean

50

in souls, but more like an all-inclusive vacation package—a seven-day trip to Hawaii."

"Demons take vacations?"

"You'd be surprised. They'd do just about anything to get out of the Netherworld."

After an hour of following the dead, they crossed a few streets made for a tall concrete building with rows of windows. It rose high before them, its gleaming roof pointing to the sky. Alexa saw a sign high above written in bold red letters that read Marriott.

Carefully, Alexa followed Lance inside the hotel and through an arched entryway flanked by giant palm trees on either side. Despite the bright sun, it was gloomy inside. But the darkness glowed with the richness of the paintings hanging on the walls.

The light polished floors were slippery with blood, and Alexa had to slow her pace to keep from ending up on sprawled on the floor, sticky with human blood.

A massive crystal chandelier lay in pieces in the middle of the lobby. The sound of her boots crunching the glass echoed around them. Lance picked his way carefully around the sharp fragments, his nails scratching the tile floor.

"There's blood but no bodies," remarked Alexa, inspecting the blood. "Did we take a wrong turn?"

Lance stilled and sniffed the air. "I don't think so. The Nephilim trail led us here. I can still smell them, the stink of them—"

"And here I thought it was the angels that stank," said a familiar voice next to her ear.

Alexa froze, her hand hovering over her weapons belt. She blinked at the tip of a sharp sword pointing at her face, and then her eyes moved to the snake sigil on his neck.

From the corner of her eye, she saw two tall and broad-shouldered men pointing swords at Lance. Even from her limited view, she recognized them—the harsh grim faces, the same tailored trousers and white shirts buttoned up under dark vests, with heavy black capes brushing against their boots.

"Hi, angel darling," purred Anagar. "How I've missed you."

CHAPTER 5

AFTER ANAGAR CONFISCATED ALEXA'S SOUL BLADE, he began to search her for more, his hands patting over her body a little too slowly. For a moment she feared he would find the piece of paper hidden in her pocket as his hands moved over her hips. If he discovered their plans, all would be lost…

Her pulse raced as she felt his hands brush her pocket, felt the warmth of his fingers through her clothes—and then he pushed her forward.

"Move."

Alexa let out a breath she didn't know she had been holding and did as she was told.

The three Nephilim led Alexa and Lance past the lobby and into a large room with plush red carpets lined with tables and soft, high-back chairs. The air smelled of alcohol, blood and rot. She tried to catch Lance's attention, but the dog's focus was on the room.

She followed his gaze and faltered. Sitting at the tables were mortals. They sat slumped, as if they were drunk, their heads lolled to the side and their eyes wide with vacant expressions. Their skin was pale and covered in lesions, split apart with the beginnings of decomposition. Blood stained their lips and throats. String was tied around their hands and fingers and then wrapped tightly around beer bottles and glasses. It was a horrid scene, dead mortals set up like mannequins enjoying happy hour.

The scene fanned Alexa's rage. Her nails dug into her palms until she felt the skin tear as she thought about the ways to kill the Nephilim.

A low growl escaped from Lance's throat. His was head bowed with the whites of his canines gleaming. Alexa had never seen him look more like a wolf than he did at that moment, a very angry wolf ready to tear into the Nephilim to protect his pack.

Alexa swore under her breath. She whirled around. "You sick bastards—"

Anagar laid a stinging backhand across her cheek. "Mind your tongue, angel. You are not in Horizon now. There is no one here to protect you."

Alexa tasted something metallic in her mouth and felt the lingering sting of his strike on her cheek. "I thought all the Nephilim had been destroyed. How is it that you're alive? Didn't the Legion kill you miserable bastards."

Anagar slammed a fist against her back and she stumbled forward again. "They tried. They might have succeeded in destroying our mortal bodies, but we are part archangel. Immortal

54

creatures born of the most powerful archangel that ever was. The part that was from Father lived on. We cannot die."

"Your daddy's not an archangel. He's the devil."

Anagar smiled brightly as though she'd just given him a compliment. "That he is. The mighty Lord of Darkness, The Morning Star, lord of all lords, the true lord. He will bring about the death of this world."

"Not if I can help it," Alexa heard Lance mumble.

"What was that, dog?" said the one with the shaved head and covered in demon runes. Alexa remembered his name was Hadaz. He combed the top of Lance's back with one of his axes as though it were a brush. "I could use a new pelt like this one. I've never had a white wolf before."

"White German Shepherd, you half-wit," growled Lance.

With a flick of his wrist, Hadaz sliced the top of Lance's back. Lance yelped as droplets of pale pink liquid trickled down his side.

"I'll kill you!" Alexa hurled herself at Hadaz, but she was yanked back hard as something caught her arm and sent her crashing into the nearest table.

She landed on something soft, and the smell of rot filled her nose. When she looked up, she blinked into the sagging, rotting face of a woman and gagged. The woman's eyes were wide, her mouth slightly open. With the frown still on her brow, Alexa could almost see the fear and pain she'd felt just before the Nephilim had killed her.

Alexa picked herself up. Lance was shivering, and he didn't look at her. She thought of Milo and her chest contracted. What if he was responsible for some of these deaths? What if he had *turned* the way he had begun to in purgatory? If Lucifer had the power to bring these creatures back to life, did he have the power to manipulate his youngest son?

Yes, her feelings for Milo had surprised her. They were strong, and ran deep, so deep into her core, it ached. She cared about him more than she'd ever cared before—even for Erik.

Was it love? Perhaps. She had no idea. But she did know if Milo was turned, she would bring him back. Just as she did in purgatory. She would not abandon him to this life of horror and killings, a life he hated. Never.

Her chest hollowed out, but she kept her face blank. She could feel a thin trickle of her own essence running down her left leg, but she barely noticed. Her cheek was still ablaze with pain. If she were human, her facial bones would have shattered.

"The next time you go and try something like that, Alexa dear," said Anagar as he twisted his sword in her face, "I will cut out your pretty eyes… one by one."

Not if I cut yours first, Alexa thought. She wacked his blade from her face as she moved past the table. "How do you know my name?"

"We met in purgatory," he said, sounding a little confused.

"But you were an illusion. A figment of Lucifer's imagination. You weren't real."

The other Nephilim laughed at that.

"Did you hear the angel, brothers?" laughed Anagar as he grabbed Alexa's shoulder, spun her around, and then shoved her forward again. "We are *not* real. We're ghosts."

Their laughter only increased Alexa's hatred of them. She looked over at Lance, who was walking slowly, his lips pulled in either a grimace of pain or a snarl. She couldn't tell.

"I've always said angels were inferior," voiced Ruthus. Long strands of oily black hair stuck to his face, looking almost wet, and Alexa doubted it had ever been washed. "Weak bodies and weaker minds, these angels." He widened his eyes, and the whites stood out against the thick black kohl, making him look like a crazed killer. "Wolves exist to eat sheep, and the weak exist for the strong to play with."

Alexa glowered at the all-yellow, decaying teeth of the smile Ruthus gave her.

"In purgatory," she said as she picked her way around another table with two dead mortal women, their hands stitched with pink thread around martini glasses. "You were just part of a test—a trial—all created by your father. You were but a figment of his imagination, a memory."

"But we *weren't* an illusion," said Anagar. "The Inferno Trials *weren't* an illusion. They were real. It was all real. As real as you are here now. As I am."

Alexa turned and shot him a dark glare. "That makes absolutely no sense. Purgatory is the realm of monster and demon souls. Only the dead live there, if you want to call that living. There is mortal in you, and I can see that you're alive." She didn't want to tell him that she had felt his warm-blooded fingers. "Though it disgusts me to say it, you're part of the world of the living. Not the dead."

"I've already told you," said Anagar, "our bodies were destroyed, but our souls lived on. Our father is most powerful, more powerful than your precious Legion will ever know. When Father was beaten and trapped in purgatory, our souls followed. We are connected in ways that you will never understand. You can't understand."

Alexa just shook her head. "Can't be."

"It's like your flesh suits that you wear—"

"Mortal suits," spat Alexa.

Anagar chuckled. "Are you real when you are wearing your human guise? Yes? Well, we were real in purgatory. It's the same thing."

"It's not."

Anagar answered her with another hard shove forward, but her mind was still trying to wrap itself around what he'd just said. If what he said was true, how many more Nephilim had returned to the mortal world? Hundreds? Thousands? The chill that she felt went deep into her bones.

But then she thought of something else that dulled the chill, replacing it with a growing sense of excitement. If the Nephilim were connected in the way Anagar suggested, then logically, if Lucifer were vanquished, that would solve the problem of the Nephilim.

They hauled Alexa and Lance to the back of the room towards a large bar lined with stools and a polished wood surface topped with bottles. A bear-like man sat at the bar with his back towards them. But at the sound of their approach, he set down his drink, stood and turned.

"I see it's the same angel whore," said Baruk.

Alexa flinched. It was obvious that whatever had happened in purgatory, the Nephilim standing before her now were in fact the *same* ones.

"I told you the angels were predictable," mocked Anagar. "They can't stand a little disorder."

"Is that what you call the murders of all those mortals?" growled Alexa, heat pumping up her neck and into her face. "Disorder? You're even crazier than I thought."

Anagar licked his lips, smiling in the same way a serial killer might smile at his victim just before killing. Alexa shivered and looked away.

"And the beast?" inquired Baruk, staring at Lance as though he were looking at something that disgusted him.

"It's an angel, disguised as a beast," said Ruthus elatedly. "Must be one of the shape changing ones Father warned us about. The watchers."

Lance's ears perked on his head, and he looked happy for the first time since their encounter with the Nephilim.

Baruk stared at Lance for a moment longer. "No matter. If the girl angel is here, he will come for her."

Alexa's blood chilled. She felt the eyes of all the Nephilim on her. "Where's Milo?" She looked around the bar but saw only more dead mortals tied to their chairs and drinks like puppets. She felt no sense of relief at Milo's absence, but rather a pounding in her head. Her throat tightened as though she were choking, running out of the air she didn't need.

What if he was still with Lucifer?

"Funny you should ask that." Anagar leaned forward and poured himself a generous quantity of Jim Beam whiskey into glass and drank it. Then he poured himself another. "He's not here. Or should I say… not here with us."

This time Lance glanced at her, and she saw the same look of confusion on his face that she felt.

"What have you done to him?" Alexa took a step towards Anagar, who flashed her a smile that would have scared the average woman. She stood her ground. They might have taken her weapons, but she could do some real damage to his head with those bottles.

"We," he said, pointing to each of his brothers, "didn't *do* anything. Our little brother left us. Just like he always has. Sneaky little bastard."

"He could never handle it, that's what," said Hadaz as he swung his sword up on one of his shoulders. "He has the weak heart of a woman. Can't stand the sight of a little blood."

Alexa glared at him. She couldn't help it. She opened her mouth, but Baruk cut her off.

"Once again the life of the Nephilim proves to be too hard on his weak mind and body. Father entrusted us to shape him up again for the war that's coming. And once again, our little brother disappeared when the killings started."

"Smart man," grumbled Lance.

"Father will not be pleased," continued Baruk, as though Lance hadn't spoken.

"By the looks of it, I'm guessing Daddy doesn't know, does he?" quipped Alexa, her eyebrows raised.

Baruk stared at her, the muscles in his jaw contracting, and for a split second she thought he was going to hit her.

"Milo *will* be punished," said the big male. "It's only a matter of time… and what punishment we choose."

Alexa felt elated, and it was hard not to smile. Milo was himself. Milo hadn't turned, but rather he'd turned on his brothers. But where was he? And why hadn't he returned to Horizon?

Alexa looked at each of the Nephilim, feeling bold, defiant and strong. "So, what do you want with us?" If only she could reach the whiskey bottle…

"Simple." Anagar raised his brows. "I know my little brother. I know him very well and much better than he thinks. I know he's soft, weak." He moved so close to Alexa that she could smell the alcohol on his breath as he said, "I saw the way he looked at you. The way a man looks at a woman when he desires her."

"And you speak from experience?" said Lance in a disgusted tone.

Hadaz growled and struck Lance with a violent kick. Lance flew in the air and landed hard on the ground with a whimper.

Alexa tightened her hands into fists, but she stayed where she was.

Anagar didn't stop smiling as he looked at her. "He will come for you. I knew if we caught you, Alexa the angel girl, Milo *would* come."

Alexa felt the blood drain from her face. "You're setting him up. You're using us as bait."

Anagar clapped his hands. "Exactly. Do you like games? I like games. We're going to play a game, you and me."

Alexa looked around her. "But you said he was gone. He doesn't even know I'm here. He's probably out looking for me. He won't come back—"

She cried out in pain as Anagar's fist collided with her chest and she collapsed to her knees, her vision plagued with black spots.

"He will come," came Anagar's hot breath against her ear. "Because I'm willing to bet that our dear little brother is never too far away from you. And you better hope he does because if he doesn't, you and the mutt will die."

CHAPTER 6

ANAGAR WHACKED ALEXA ACROSS THE face again and her nose made a crack like a branch breaking. She heard him laugh, and then his boot caught her in the chest. She only felt pain as her back made contact with the floor.

Spitting out essence, Alexa rolled over and got to her feet. She wasn't about to let this abomination keep beating her like she was some mortal who couldn't fight back. She *could* fight. She was *trained* to fight.

She lowered herself into a fighting stance, bringing up her only weapons—her fists.

The Nephilim roared with laughter, but their laughter wasn't what sent a spark of rage through her. It was the amount of essence that puddled around Lance and the way his eyes drooped.

Anagar grinned, but Hadaz moved past him and stood before Alexa, tossing his axes on the ground. "I've never beaten a girl angel to death with my bare hands before," said Hadaz, his voice high with excitement. "Perhaps today will be the day."

"Go to hell." Liquid filled her mouth as she struggled to get to her feet. She shook with the rage storming through her.

"But I've killed many human women. Squished their heads until their eyes popped. Their wails were music to my ears."

"You're a monster," said Alexa. "You're all crazy. Even if you kill me, there's no escaping what you've done. The Legion knows and they're coming for you. For all of you."

"Not this time." Hadaz flashed her a smile of yellow teeth and sprang, swift as a shadow. He moved with incredible speed for such a large man, faster than Alexa had anticipated. Before she could raise her arm to block his attack, a giant fist made contact with her temple. It was like being smashed by a boulder. Alexa swayed, black and white spots playing in her vision. She stumbled back, blinking the spots from her eyes. A whistle sounded in her ears just as a shadow moved.

She let her instincts guide her and ducked. She felt the air move over her head as she spun around and kicked out as hard as she could. She heard a satisfying crack followed by Hadaz's curse. The big brute stumbled as he fought to keep the weight from his right knee.

"She can fight," came Anagar's voice from behind. "For a woman, that is."

"She's not a woman," argued Ruthus. "She's an angel. It's not the same."

"Well, she looks like a woman to me."

"She's not."

"Will you two shut up," growled Baruk.

Alexa straightened. She felt a stiff soreness in her chest, and her head still pounded where Hadaz had hit her. She should have been afraid, but all she felt was anger and hatred. Her pain was forgotten as she stared down the big male. She hated the bald ogre more than anything at the moment. So, she flashed him a smile.

With a growl of rage, Hadaz slammed Alexa aside, lifted her by her hair and struck her with his fist. She fell back, knocking chairs to the floor with her. Before she could get up, she felt strong hands grab her from behind.

Hadaz pushed her hard into Anagar and Ruthus. They shoved her back and forth among them, slapping her, hitting her in the face, and spinning her around roughly until she was too dizzy to stand. She fell from one pair of arms to another. Alexa cursed and swung her fists at them, too disoriented to make contact.

They all laughed even harder.

"Not much you can do without your weapons, eh, angel?" mocked Ruthus. "You're nothing but a bag of bones and meat."

Alexa followed the voice and swung her fist again. Her knuckles cracked as she hit something hard. As her eyes focused, she saw blood dripping from Ruthus' nose and fury in his eyes.

"What was that you said again?" Alexa ignored the pain in her hand as she stood in the middle of the ring of Nephilim, feeling small and frail compared to these armored beasts. She knew they enjoyed beating her, never too much, just enough to keep her standing in pain. They loved the pain. This was their favorite game—to play with their prey before they killed it.

She knew she was outmatched and out muscled. Her only comfort was that they'd temporarily forgotten about Lance. Good. She wanted to keep it that way.

Movement caught her attention and she saw Ruthus unsheathe his sword. "It looks as though our little brother abandoned you." He twisted his blade. "We were wrong. He cares nothing for you. He cares only for himself. Always has. He's left you to die."

"You're wrong." Alexa knew it wasn't true, but somehow the words still stung. The Milo she knew had always been selfless in every way. "Maybe he's smarter than you think and knows what you're playing at. He won't be a part of your game."

"He *will* play," said Ruthus. "Eventually."

"Milo's clever, a lot cleverer than you, which is why your father loves him more. Isn't it?" From the corner of her eye, she saw Lance turn his head her way. She knew she was asking for it, but she couldn't help herself. She hated these guys.

A growl escaped Hadaz as he said, "Can I slit her throat now? She's practically begging for me to kill her—"

"No," ordered Baruk. "We stick to the plan. Rough her up, but don't kill her." His eyes met Alexa's as he said, "Not yet."

Alexa felt a chill roll over her despite the warmth in the room. She wiped her mouth with the back of her hand.

"So, where's your father now? It looks to me as though he's abandoned you as well. Where is he? Is he hiding? Away from the battle so he won't get his hands dirty? That sounds a lot like a coward to me."

Ruthus' careful composure faltered. "Our father's plans do not concern you, angel."

Alexa felt her strength returning slowly, enough to give her a little more courage. If Milo wasn't coming, she had to figure out a way to get herself and Lance out of here. She saw her soul blade tucked inside Anagar's belt. She moved casually to the left, closer to him, until she could almost lean over and grab it.

"What would happen if Daddy found out you've lost his *favorite* son? A spanking? Does he do it with his hand or does he use his belt? I bet it's the belt—it *is* the belt. I knew it. I can see it in your face."

Ruthus advanced. "I'm going to cut out that tongue of yours. No. I'm going to reach in that big mouth and pull it out."

"Milo's with your father, isn't he?" Alexa leaned over ever so slightly, talking fast. "He played you. He's not coming. He's not coming because he's with your father right now, having a good laugh at the lot of you—"

Ruthus shot forward, but Alexa had already leaped and snatched up her soul blade. She heard Anagar curse as she broke through their circle and came up from behind them, swinging.

She cut Anagar on the arm as he reached out to grab her. He pulled back, blood seeping through his leather bracer. The look on his face was pure hatred as he lunged at her.

Alexa sidestepped and felt him fall past her, to where she'd been standing a half second ago. She never stopped moving. She brought up her arm as Hadaz came swinging with his axe. The look in his eyes was murderous. He wanted to kill her. His axe met her blade, and she felt a sharp pain in her wrist, the muscles in her arms straining. She dropped low and kicked him hard in the kneecap.

Her pain paused for a second, long enough for her to see Hadaz hit the ground and rise again.

But someone sprang up behind her back and caught her wrist before she could move. Swinging around, she brought up her other fist to hit him, but he snatched it and clamped her wrists together with one hand. With his free hand Anagar stabbed her hand, pushing the tip of his sword all the way through it.

Alexa screamed and dropped her blade.

Anagar threw a kick that caught Alexa square in the chest and slammed her against the wall. She crumpled to the floor, dazed and senseless.

She felt her bones shattering as her body rose and then slammed onto the hard floor. Anagar kicked her again and again and again. She was crushed beneath a continuous wave of torturous agony.

She tried to fight him off, but he was too big, too strong. Even with her M-suit, she was no match for the large male.

Anagar stood above her. His face was red and covered in sweat, his features contorting until he looked beast-like. "I will beat you till he comes. Did you hear me, angel girl? I will. And if you die… I will still beat you."

Alexa's head snapped back as his boot connected with her face. She tasted blood in her mouth as the world around her blackened. She fought against the dizziness. She would not pass out. She felt as though she was she was being ripped apart from the inside out, and she thrashed, unable to out-scream the pain.

"If you kill her," said Lance, "your brother will kill you. All of you."

Anagar looked down at the dog, a gruesome smile spreading on his face. "Milo couldn't even kill the rat that bit him once. He would never hurt his brothers."

Through the throb of pain, Alexa knew she couldn't leave. If there was a chance Milo would show up, she had to endure the beatings. She needed his help. She needed him…

"Milo," she whispered before she could stop herself.

The beatings stopped suddenly.

"I knew she fancied him," said Anagar, looking smug.

"She can't fancy him, you fool," said Ruthus. "She's not a woman. She's an angel." He turned to look at her, his wide eyes rolling over every inch of her. "Everyone knows she doesn't have the parts that the other women have. You know, the important bits."

"Excuse me?" coughed Alexa, feeling suddenly exposed and totally grossed out.

Anagar's face flushed as he grinned. "How do you know? Have you ever seen one without clothes? Maybe there's nothing there… but maybe there is…"

Just when Ruthus made to move towards Alexa, Baruk stood in his way.

"Enough of this," Baruk commanded. "We have more important things to do—"

"I couldn't agree with you more," said a voice behind them.

Brushing the hair from her eyes, Alexa turned her head and saw a tall, strong and imposing male angel standing next to Lance. His handsome face was set in a mask of cold.

"Touch her again, brother," said Milo, as he unsheathed his spirit sabers, "and I'll cut you to pieces and feed you to Father's hounds."

CHAPTER 7

BARUK TURNED. "OUR LITTLE BROTHER HAS finally decided to grace us with his presence." His smile was cold and vicious. There was no brotherly love.

"Took you long enough." Anagar glanced at Milo with disinterest.

"I was busy trying to clean up your mess," Milo pointed out.

The warrior angel was still as strikingly handsome as ever—his strong jaw, angled cheekbones, and the richness of his golden skin. He wore the black CDD gear, the cloth cut close enough to his body to reveal broad shoulders, which flowed into lean, muscular legs.

Alexa hadn't seen him since he'd walked into the black mist, right after he'd kissed her. She felt the flush rise up from her neck to her face at the thought of his soft lips crushing hers, of the desperation and passion that had been in that kiss. She would never forget it.

Milo's mouth was pulled tight, and Alexa could see the barely suppressed anger in his stunning gray eyes under the thickness of his blond locks. She could sense something else in the angel warrior, a nervous tension that came perilously close to fear.

Alexa shared his unease. His clothes were torn and stained with blood, mortal blood. Then she noticed he favored his left leg and had thin white lines across his forehead, cheeks, and neck like cuts that had only just healed. He looked like he'd been in a fight.

Carefully, Alexa struggled to her feet. She felt the skin around her wound pull and stitch as her M-suit repaired itself. Lance was sturdier on his feet. Either his body had healed, or Milo's presence gave him courage.

Alexa gazed around the Nephilim. They all shared the same loathing in their eyes for Milo. She tried to get his attention, but he wouldn't look at her.

Baruk reached out and grabbed Alexa by the arm, hauling her forward with the tip of his sword pressed hard against her back.

"I knew you would come for her, little brother. You were always so predictable when it came to matters of the heart. Softer than a mortal, you are. Soft, sentimental, weak."

"Being compassionate and caring for the well-being of others isn't a weakness," said Milo simply. "It's strength. The mistreatment of others ignites a fire in me. It's something you'll never understand."

"Perhaps not." Baruk squeezed Alexa's arm until she hissed in pain. "But from the look you gave this one in purgatory," he said and shook Alexa, "I knew you'd come. I knew you couldn't stay

72

away while we *played* with your little pet. You haven't changed, little brother. Even in death, even as an angel, your feelings get in the way. Your sentiments will get you killed."

Milo's lips became a hard line. "And I knew, since I was old enough to *know*, to really know, that I never wanted to be your brother."

Baruk's eyes darkened. "Such harsh words for your own family. You disappoint me, little brother."

"Glad to disappoint you." Milo was still, and his face showed no emotion. The only thing that moved was the glint on his spirit sabers from the ceiling light.

"I see that our punishments still haven't healed." Baruk's voice was hard. "There is no remission without punishment. You should have killed that mortal child, and none of that would have happened. You could have been spared."

Alexa's eyes moved back to Milo, but he still wouldn't make eye contact with her. *What had they done to him?*

"I'll live," answered Milo, "if that's what's worrying you."

Baruk's lips twitched into an ugly smile. "Oh, I'm not worried about whether you'll live."

Alexa thrashed in Baruk's grasp. "Let me go, you beast—" she cursed as Baruk pushed the tip of his sword farther into her back until she felt warm liquid trickle down her spine.

"Feisty little thing, for a dead girl," laughed Baruk, his eyes on Milo. His brothers joined him in the laugh.

A hard scowl darkened Milo's face. "Let her go." He crossed his sabers in front of him like giant scissors and then uncrossed them, taking a step forward.

The other Nephilim all moved around Milo in a semi-circle, surrounding him, and waited.

Baruk smiled faintly. "Such a disappointment to Father," he shook his head. "You were needed here, but you left. You abandoned your family to join the angel Legion, the deceivers, with all their ministers and archangels. There is only the need for *one* leader. A very great one, and you lied to him, to all of us. You never intended to fulfill your promise to him. To join him. It was the only reason he didn't kill all your beloved angels when he could have— because you had *agreed.* You made a promise, and you broke that promise when you refused to kill the humans and raised your swords against us. If Hadaz hadn't been foolish enough to let his guard down, you would have never escaped."

Hadaz's face reddened as anger flashed across his features. He seemed about to scream. "It was just for a moment," he said with scarcely contained rage. "It's not like you were busy doing anything. Why didn't you look after him? Why is it always me?"

"Because it was *your* turn," argued Ruthus. Hadaz snarled at him but left it at that.

"It doesn't matter that he escaped," continued Baruk. His breath, hot and sour, brushed against Alexa's face. "Father knew you were going to betray him. He told me so, you see." He squeezed Alexa's arm painfully as if she was the cause of the betrayal. "Still, as his son, he wanted to give you one last chance. A last chance to prove your loyalty to him, to us, your kin."

Alexa watched Milo as flashes of cool disdain and rage traveled to his eyes. Still, he wouldn't look at her. She felt a cold, piercing pain inside that had nothing to do with the sword penetrating deeper into her flesh.

Despite herself, Alexa felt her mouth open, and the words tumbled out. "He's nothing like you. You're monsters. Freaks of nature," she spat. "Milo doesn't slaughter innocent mortals for pleasure. He's not a killer."

"He *is* a killer," said Baruk, with iron certainty. "Just a different kind."

"He's not."

"He kills demons, doesn't he? Creatures of the Netherworld? And you kill demons too. You're both killers."

Alexa could feel Baruk's anger bristling and sense his disgust, but she blocked it out.

"It's not the same thing. We protect the world of the living from monsters like you." She could feel the sharp coldness of the sword's metal, her wound aching. The warm stickiness of her own blood dripped down her back and into her pants.

"Call it what you like, but it is the same." Baruk cut a glare in Milo's direction. "We're predators. We hunt and then we kill. There's nothing more gratifying than the sensation that comes with watching someone breathe their last breath. And Milo is no different. He's a killer, our little brother. He just likes to hide behind his angel Legion to do it. He enjoys killing, just like we do. It's because of his Nephilim blood. You can't hide from what you are."

A deep-throated growl rippled from Milo. "I was never like you."

"Yes, you were, and still are, little brother, because the blood of our father is still in you. Even now, even in death, his essence runs through you, his favorite son."

"When he hears about what you did," interrupted Ruthus with just the hint of a smile, "you won't be his favorite for much longer."

"He can't be his favorite when he's dead," added Anagar, showing his teeth and running a finger across his throat.

Milo's voice was strained as he replied, "Like I said before, I won't kill the innocent. Not for you. Not for Father. For no one. I will never be one of you. I despise what you are. I despise everything about you."

Ruthus and Hadaz swore, Anagar's face went taut, but Baruk laughed without humor and said, "You misunderstand me, little brother. We're not here to try and persuade you. We already tried that. And quite frankly, I'm tired of trying. You see, little brother. We're here to kill you."

Alexa flinched. Her eyes traveled to Milo, who finally met her gaze. She could tell by the calm, solemn expression that he'd known all along this was no method of persuasion. He was aware they intended to kill him. But she also saw fear—not for himself but for her. He looked away.

She glanced at Lance, who gave her a tiny nod, the kind he always gave to encourage her to get ready to fight.

But Baruk's grip on her was iron hard. With his sword still impaled in her back, there wasn't much she could do. With the slightest movement, he would run her through with his sword. She needed to think. She had no idea where her soul blade was now, and it wasn't as though she could turn around and look for it. Still, she couldn't let Baruk run her through either.

"You can try," said Milo, his voice cutting into Alexa's mind. His confidence almost made her smile.

Baruk sneered derisively. "I won't just try, little brother. I *will* kill you."

Then everything happened at once. Baruk's fingers tightened on Alexa's arms, and she felt the blade inching forward into her body. She knew she had only seconds to react. So she did.

As Baruk made to impale her, Alexa flung her head backward as hard as she could. There was a *crack*, followed by a howl, and the hand that gripped her loosened enough for her to wiggle out of it. She felt the sword's blade slip out of her back as she fell forward, and she pushed off with her feet.

She stumbled into a table and chairs, and her head knocked on the hard surface. Alexa felt the presence of someone, and nearly at the same time, she spun around and sprang to her feet, fists in the air. Ruthus stood right before her, his sword coming down in an arc above her head.

Alexa dove to the side, and she felt the stinging pain as his blade cut through her shoulder. But she never stopped. Stopping meant death.

She didn't have a weapon, but Alexa was slim and quick on her feet. Ignoring the pain, she came up and twisted around, her shirt already sticky with her essence.

"I'm going to cut up that sweet angel body of yours," said Ruthus, "and then stitch you back together, my angel doll." His blade glimmered in the dim light. He was so close, she could smell the alcohol on his breath and the stink of his male perspiration. Sweat trickled down his forehead.

He lunged. As the sword came at her again, she ducked under it, coming up and around him. She hit him as hard as she could in the ribs, and Ruthus yelled as he backhanded her with his sword hand. Alexa fell back, the hit muddling her vision for a second. Ruthus hesitated, wincing in pain with his free hand on the spot where she'd hit him.

Alexa took a moment and darted a quick glance around. Lance scurried back and forth at Hadaz, chomping in quick succession at his ankles and legs while the big brute howled in fury. Hadaz swung his big axe at the dog but never touched him. She saw Milo heave Anagar and Baruk back, his swords swinging in lethal vengeance.

Alexa ignored the tumult around her and seized the calm within. The cacophony faded away as she focused on her training. She homed all her energy, her angel sense and instincts, towards Ruthus.

She saw only him. Not the man nor the mortal, but the monster and the killer. She realized at that moment that she wanted him dead. She was focusing her innate drive to protect all life and her deep hatred for demons towards the Nephilim.

With every fiber of her being, she wanted nothing else but to destroy them all. Some savage part of her wanted to kill. Perhaps Baruk had been right. She *was* a killer.

With a scream of fury, Ruthus sprang towards her, swinging his long sword in a great big arc over his head. In a cold calmness, Alexa unleashed her wrath.

The tip of Ruthus' sword whistled as it came down, the blade mere inches from her head. Alexa feigned right and whirled towards his other side. Still turning, she used his momentum to kick his legs aside as she swept his sword inward, impaling him with a mighty thrust before he hit the ground. Ruthus' death howl shuddered in her ears.

In the grip of fury, Alexa reached down, kicked over the body, and wrapped her fingers around the black hilt of his sword. Her fingers were sticky with blood and slipped as she hauled out the heavy blade. For a moment she was surprised at how heavy it was. It was like no other sword she'd ever held. After she gripped it with both hands, she spun around.

Swift as a shadow, Milo lunged for Anagar, and in one brutal movement, he slashed his saber across Anagar's throat. Blood sprayed Milo's face as Alexa watched the light fade from Anagar's gaze.

Milo stood staring down at the body, and a head that had the face of Anagar rolled to a stop next to his feet.

Two more bodies lay crumpled on the ground, pools of blood soaking into the carpet. She recognized Baruk. He lay on his back, staring blindly at the ceiling with a sword still in his mouth. Hadaz was a few feet away from his brother, half his throat missing with the rest torn to ribbons.

She saw Lance then, his golden eyes wide with a fierce wildness. His white fur was matted in blood, and fresh blood spotted his muzzle.

In a moment all was silent. Blood misted the air.

Milo's face was smeared in blood, and his body shook with rage. He felt her gaze on him and looked up, his eyes dancing with fire. And then the fury went out of his eyes, and she could see sadness and pain reflecting in them.

He had killed his own brothers.

She always knew Milo struggled with his personal demons, and now the death of his brothers at his own hands would haunt him for the rest of his angel days. Alexa felt the anger coiling inside her and pushed it away with pure willpower. She hated these Nephilim now, more than ever, because of what they were still doing to Milo. Even in death, they managed to screw with his head.

The three of them stood in silence. Wordlessly, Milo sheathed his spirit sabers, turned and strode off. He crossed the bar and disappeared through the lobby doors.

Alexa tossed the sword and made to move after him, but Lance's words brought her to a halt.

"Let him go, Alexa," said the dog. "Just give him some space. He won't go far."

Alexa and Lance shared a long look. After a few moments, they set off together following the angel warrior.

CHAPTER 8

THE SUN WAS WELL TO the west by the time Alexa, Milo and Lance reached the next town. A large red and green sign read *Henderson, Nevada,* and welcomed them to a vast, mountainous region with grasslands and rolls of sandy deserts.

The sky was lined in navy blue and pink. Sunset was coming on fast over the silhouette of the city in the distance. They moved fast in silence and made good time, meandering through the city. If it weren't for the Scout, Alexa would be completely lost.

Lance prided himself in knowing all the oracle safe houses on the North American continent. It was a hobby of his, and it was the only thing that actually cheered her up a little. But not enough to still the ache in her soul.

They trudged along Boulder Highway south as cars and humanity bustled around them. There were no bodies of the dead from what she could see, but it didn't stop the unease that crept into her soul. Only a few miles away, it had been a Nephilim apocalypse, yet here, it was as though nothing had happened.

A feeling of foreboding gripped Alexa's throat and choked her. Something wasn't right. But she didn't know what *it* was. Did Lucifer only pick designated spots to unleash his darkness? Why was Vegas hit and not this neighboring town?

She cut a covert glance at the tall angel. With his eyes on the street, he seemed far away, like his body was here but his spirit was elsewhere. Alexa felt a little hurt by his lack of enthusiasm at her being with him and the way he'd barely acknowledged her presence.

While in Tartarus, Alexa had played the scene over and over in her head, the day when she'd finally meet him again—the way-too-long-stare, the pause before the tackling embrace, and the passionate kiss that followed. Yes, she knew it was very immature, but those dreams had kept her company in Tartarus. The thought of Milo had kept her warm, inside and out. He had been her rock. Part of her, the crazy part, had wanted to crash into his arms and kiss him all over his face until he was covered in lip-bruises. The other part wanted to scream, "I'm right here!"

But she found herself unable to approach the gloomy angel. The way he walked—the tightness in his shoulders, the tight line of his mouth, his never-ending frown—said he didn't want to talk.

Milo had been silent the entire trip, which only made Alexa's unrest worse. It was clear from the look on his face that some kind of struggle was taking place inside him. Whenever she looked at him, her insides twisted and stretched as she struggled with her own war of emotions. More than once, Alexa had opened her mouth, ready to ask him what his problem was, only to shut it again, feeling abashed. Where would she start? What would she say? What would he answer?

She unclenched her sweating hands and wiped them on her pants. Her heart thumped painfully inside her chest, and she felt out of breath, like she'd just run a long distance. The sensation was too close to being mortal.

For the entire duration of her incarceration in Tartarus, Alexa had thought of nothing but Milo—his sacrifice, his kiss, the times he'd been a royal pain, and of the ache on his face when he'd let her go and stepped through the black mist behind Lucifer. She also remembered all too well her pain at watching him go.

Alexa had always known Milo was the silent type. He hid his emotions well and seemed to be guarding them all the time so they didn't interfere with his job. It had always been difficult to read him, unlike Erik who wore his emotions on his sleeves, plain for the world to see.

Why hadn't he spoken to her? Why wouldn't he even look at her? She didn't think he regretted the kiss. She knew Milo didn't do things without first carefully thinking them through. He did it because he had wanted to. So why wouldn't he look at her now?

But then she realized how selfish she was being. Milo had just killed his own family. No matter how evil they had been, they were still his brothers.

"What happened after you left? With your father?" Alexa questioned, sending her gaze to his face.

Milo answered without looking at her. "He took me to his home with Sabrielle. Of course he built himself a castle. It reminded

83

me of the Elder Guild's Icefall Castle, but without windows. I didn't find one window in that damned place, and I searched everywhere… except my father's quarters. It even had a dungeon. But this castle shifts and moves like a portal. It's never solid."

Alexa saw Lance's ears turn back towards them, though he kept his head straight, and she knew he was listening.

She turned her gaze and studied Milo's face. "Do you think you could find it again? If we knew where he was, it would make our lives so much easier." She knew if they could find Lucifer's lair, they would find him, and then all they had to do was open the vacuum rift.

At Milo's quizzical brow, she handed him the oracle's note and quickly told him about the tools they needed to open a vacuum rift and send Lucifer back to purgatory.

"No. It moves around." Milo gave her back the piece of paper. "It never stays long enough in one spot. It's not in Horizon or anywhere on Earth. It's another dimension, a portal within a portal. And it wasn't long after I got there that I discovered only *he* controls it. Think of it like a great vessel, docking at different ports around the world only for short periods of time. Whenever I felt a shift, I knew the castle had stopped somewhere. Sometimes demons would board, sometimes angels."

Alexa saw the tension on his face. "What happened to you in there? I mean, what was it like to be with your father again? It must have been tough to be with him, after all… you did distance yourself from him."

The frown on his face grew deeper. "Well, for one thing, I was guarded all the time, so I didn't get to have any real time with him alone. I was never allowed anywhere near my father's quarters where he discussed all matters of war with Sabrielle and other Greater demons I happened to see. He wanted me with him, but he didn't trust me enough to share his plans with me. Rightly so. I was planning to take all the information I gathered back to the Legion with me. Father never talked openly about his plans to me, but Sabrielle, well, she's proud and a fool. She told me that soon everything would change, that the mortal world would never be the same. She called it the *transformation*."

Alexa frowned as she walked. "You mean the destruction of the Veil? It's already happening. It's going to collapse soon if we don't stop Lucifer in time. All those demons… without the Legion to protect the mortals. I don't even want to think about it."

Milo looked fretful. "The collapse of the Veil was my first thought, but now I'm not so sure."

Alexa glanced up at the tall angel. "What do you mean? What other *transformation* could there be?"

"I don't know." Milo exhaled warily. "It was the way she said it, like she knew I had no idea what it was—this transformation—and I knew all about the Veil. She knew that I knew. I could be wrong, but I had the feeling she was talking about something else."

Sabrielle's smiling face flared up in Alexa's mind eye, and she felt a hot anger bubble inside her. "You don't think Lucifer wants to destroy the world and all the mortals in it? I thought that's what bad guys did, destroy worlds and everything in them."

"It's what we were taught to believe," answered Milo. "That Lucifer seeks the destruction of the mortal world and the Legion. To destroy what is good and infect it with his madness."

"And it's not?" Alexa studied his face. "What are you getting at?"

Milo's gaze traveled to the sky. "The natural disasters have stopped, right? Since I've been back, I haven't seen any hurricanes, tornadoes or forest fires. I think it stopped when Hades was destroyed." Milo hesitated for a moment. "I don't think my father wants to destroy the mortal world."

Alexa stared at him incredulously. "Then what? Kill all the mortals and let the animals roam free? It doesn't make any sense. He still infected the Veil with something. He's killing it. Whatever he's planning, it has something to do with the Veil—or at least, he needs it out of the way or something."

Milo glanced away from her as though searching for an answer but finding none. For a moment he looked even younger than his years, despite his spirit sabers and the stubble on his cheeks.

There was an intent look on Milo's face. "I don't know," he answered finally. "But whatever it is, it's worse than anything we can imagine."

"What could be worse than killing every last living soul?" Alexa studied his face, and when he didn't answer, she pressed. "And what about the Nephilim? We saw the devastation of what a few Nephilim could do. What would happen if a hundred of those creatures were loose in the world? Maybe that's what Sabrielle meant by the *transformation*. Maybe she meant your father was brewing an army of Nephilim. Those were only four. What about all the others?"

Milo was quiet, and then, "That's just it."

"What is?"

"There aren't any more Nephilim," Milo explained. "My father hasn't... spawned more. He hasn't resurrected the others, or maybe their souls were destroyed all those years ago. I can't be sure, but what I do know for sure," he looked at her. "Those Nephilim were the last."

Lance glanced over his shoulder. "If I wasn't still sore, I'd be doing my happy dance right about now. But I'm smiling, even if you can't tell. This is me smiling."

Alexa lifted her gaze to Milo. His face was expressionless—made of stone—and she couldn't tell how the death of his brothers affected him. But he had gone rigid all over, his stride stiff, as though his legs were bars of iron. Her eyes moved to his lips. Heat rushed to her face at the memory of them against hers, his hard chest pressed against her. She stifled the urge to pull his face to hers.

Milo turned his head, and their eyes met. Alexa quickly averted her eyes. "Was there an attack on the Legion?" he asked. "I heard Sabrielle boasting about how she would soon be reunited with the banished archangels Barakiel and Sorath."

"They attacked Tartarus." Alexa stared at the street as she walked, gathering her thoughts. "It's how I got out." She could still feel Milo's gaze on her, but it was her turn to avoid his eyes. "Before we left, the Legion evacuated everyone. Lance said they'd heard rumors that the order was going to attack Orientation, so they moved everyone from levels one and three and put them on levels two and five. They shut it down, Milo. The Legion of angels is on lockdown."

They walked in silence for a long while. The only sounds were Lance's nails scratching the pavement and the clanking of their boots.

"I'm sorry that happened to you." Milo's voice was soft. All of the hardness from before was gone. "You didn't deserve to be cast out to Tartarus. The Legion knew Sabrielle was acting on my father's orders. She tricked us." He was silent. "It was wrong of them to do so."

"It doesn't matter anymore." Alexa kicked a small pebble in the road, trying hard to quell the anger that was forming in her gut. "I got out, thanks to my friend Nathaniel and his buddies. I thought he was going to kill me. But he didn't. The idiot actually *thanked* me. Thanked me for rescuing Lucifer." Alexa felt sick as the words came out of her mouth. "According to Lance, the Legion says I'm a fugitive working with Nathaniel."

"They can't think that. Surely the archangel Ariel doesn't."

"Maybe not." Alexa gritted her teeth. "But I'm willing to bet Metatron and the others do. I made a mess of things. I just want my chance to fix it, that's all."

"We both did. We both made a mess of things."

When Alexa moved her gaze over to him, he looked at her for a while before a smile touched his lips.

Despite herself, Alexa found herself smiling back and had to pull her eyes away before they revealed too much. She couldn't help it. He had that effect on her. It didn't help that he was still watching her as they walked in silence. Alexa didn't trust herself to speak.

They were quiet for some time, and then Milo asked, "Is it true?"

"Is what true?"

"What my father said," inquired Milo, watching the street. "About your gift." He paused. "About not having the soul channeling ability anymore." His voice was hollow and urgent, like he didn't want to admit it and thought the loss of her gift lessened their chances of stopping Lucifer.

Heat rose to Alexa's face. "Yes." She averted her eyes as soon as she saw him turn back to her.

"How do you feel about that?" Milo asked. "I know how you were questioning it. You weren't sure if it was light or dark, good or evil. It frightened you, not knowing how to use it properly. I also remember a part of you was excited at the prospect of having something unique and powerful. What I'm trying to ask, very inarticulately, is how are you coping? It's a loss, in a way. A part of you is gone."

He was way too perceptive, and that was still as irritating as hell to Alexa. Her lips pressed tightly together.

When Alexa didn't reply, he continued. "I know I said I would help you train—"

"Guess you're free of that obligation." Alexa wasn't sure where the bitterness was coming from. She was ashamed as soon as she realized what she'd done. Milo was the last person she wanted to be spiteful to.

"I got my memories back" she said quickly. "At least, there's that to be thankful for. I remember all of it—the good and the bad. I remember my mother most of all, the life I had with her."

"Do you miss her?"

Alexa was surprised to feel her eyes burn. "I do. She's got no one to look after her now that I'm... you know... dead. I wish the Legion allowed us to check up on our family members once in a while. Not that it matters for me anymore. As soon as the Legion is up and running again, it's prison for me." She suppressed a shiver. "What will happen to my mother if the Veil disappears?" Her voice was low and harsh, and she swallowed to soothe the ache in her throat.

Milo didn't answer for a while. "Let's hope it doesn't come to that."

Alexa knew exactly what he meant—the destruction of mankind, the demon rule, the Lucifer rule. In her mind's eye, she saw the mortal world burning with death all around, like the devastation of what was purgatory, a world of ash and fire and monsters. The mortal world would eventually be empty of life. Only darkness would remain.

"How did you end up with your brothers anyway?" asked Alexa, as the last rays of the evening sun warmed her back. "If you say your daddy didn't trust you, why send you off with them? Why not keep you locked up in his moving castle?"

Milo's stride became stiffer. "It was another one of his tests. He wanted to see how I would react when my brothers decided to play 'how many mortals can you kill in under a minute.' He doubted my loyalty. I think he knew what my brothers would do if I'd tried to stop them. I tried to fake it for the sake of the Legion. I even had Sabrielle convinced. I endured their mockery of the Legion and the angels. But when the killing started…" Milo's jaw tightened. "It was like my childhood all over again. You got a glimpse of what it was like in purgatory. Once they tasted blood, they didn't stop. I tried to stop them, but when I stopped and tried to save a mortal girl of about ten, they overtook me."

"They beat you, didn't they?" came Lance's voice from ahead.

"They did worse than that," said Milo. "I slipped away when Hadaz was sewing his new kill to her chair. It sickened me. But I knew I needed to leave to let my body heal… as much as it could before I went back." The last of his words came out sounding forced, like he scarcely believed what he was saying.

"To kill them," said Alexa, and she knew it to be true as soon as the words escaped her lips.

Milo nodded. "To keep them from hurting anyone else ever again."

CHAPTER 9

THEY WALKED IN SILENCE FOR another mile until Lance led them to a small strip mall just off the highway lined with small, one-story gift shops, a gas station, local diners and a McDonald's. It was a far cry from the glittering and impressive buildings from the Vegas strip.

The Scout stopped abruptly before a small bookstore nestled between rows of shops. A sign above the door read JP's Curiosity Shop. The bookstore had a single red door snuggled between two large windows displaying teetering pillars of books and faerie figurines, dragons and very large mushrooms. A handwritten sign taped to the window read *Closed for Pixie and Gnome Removal.*

Alexa looked over her shoulder. Mortals were locking doors and turning over their open signs to closed. As far as she could tell, no one had noticed them. A bakery stood on the right of JP's Curiosity shop, and Alexa could still smell the scent of fresh baked breads and pastries.

"This is it," said Lance as he stood before the red door and scratched the threshold with his paw. "The oracle's safe house. They're pretty easy to spot once you know what you're looking for. The oracles seem to have a fondness for bookstores."

Milo moved past Lance and tried the door handle. "It's locked. You wouldn't happen to have a key, would you?"

"Do you see any pockets on me?" said Lance, a little irritated. He caught Milo's annoyed face and added, "I thought you could use your fancy swords to cut our way in." Lance looked at Alexa. "I heard they cut through metal."

Alexa moved her gaze over to Milo. "Everyone's closing up. No one's even looked at us since we arrived. You could use your sabers, and no one would even know."

Milo glanced down the street, and in one swift movement, he pulled one of his swords free. He moved towards the door, slipped the tip of his sword between the door and the frame, and pushed down. There was a soft *click* and the door swung open.

"Whatever you do," said Lance as he pushed in, "don't turn on the lights. We don't want the mortals to call the cops on us. I never want to have to look at the inside of the animal control cages again. I still have nightmares."

Alexa followed Milo in and then shut the door behind her. She found herself in a small shop of books and collectables, like a bookstore combined with an antique shop. It was gloomy inside, but with her angel sight, she could see well even without any lights. It was like her eyes were equipped with night vision. The air was stale and smelled of dust, mold, and secrets.

93

The shop had a feeling of neglect, as though it was not usually inhabited. The walls were completely covered in books, bound in old black, brown and green leather. A collection of creepy, antique-looking dolls, their clothes worn and faded like their faces, were spaced out evenly between the books as though their watchful eyes were guarding them against thieves. The room was strewn with various possessions: old rickety tables and chairs, vases, pots, paintings, lamp fixtures, tools, door knobs and pulls, and large wooden armoires topped with more disturbing dolls.

"So, what does Holy Fire look like?" asked Alexa. Her eyes scanned the room. Shadows stretched over every nook, crevice, and corner—the perfect spots to hide treasures and secrets. A mess of newspapers were scattered on a small desk at the back of the room.

"We're looking for the oil. Holy Fire comes from oil the oracles made," said Lance as he padded towards a shelf with a clown doll and began to sniff it. "Look for a container of sorts that'll hold the oil, like a bottle. It'll have a lid and I'm guessing it'll look old."

Alexa glanced about the room again. "It'll take hours to go through all this mess. You'd think oracles were more organized." But then as she thought of the haphazard piles of papers, documents, and filing cabinets at Orientation, the mess in the shop made complete sense.

"The oil is precious and very rare," said the dog as he trotted over to the next shelf and lifted the lid of a box with his nose to peer inside. Finding nothing, he moved to the next shelf. "They've probably hidden it well to keep it from ending up in the wrong hands. Places where you'd least expect it, I think. But it's here all right. And we need to find it."

"Hidden well *and* in a place where the oracles expected *us* to find it," said Alexa, her hand brushing the pocket where she'd kept Mr. Patterson's letter.

"Exactly. He has faith that you will," said Lance.

Milo sheathed his sword. "I'll start looking over here," he said as he began opening armoires and rummaging inside.

Alexa still had the feeling he was avoiding her. The fact that he had moved all the way to the opposite side of the shop didn't help. Milo was an angel of few words and Alexa had always thought of him as more of the silent type, but right now his silence cut her like a stab of his swords.

Focusing on the job at hand, Alexa made for the small desk. She moved around it and pulled open the first drawer. After digging through all three drawers, all she found were old bills, pens, a rabbit's foot and a dozen dice. No oil.

She moved over and squeezed herself between a stack of old vinyl records and a mahogany dresser to inspect the wall shelves behind the desk. Dust fell like snow as she brushed her hands between books, dolls, and old clocks.

After two hours of searching without any success, and the little shop looking a bit like it was hit by a hurricane from the inside, Alexa began to feel as though Lance had been wrong. Maybe the oil wasn't here. Maybe it never was.

Discouraged and anxious, Alexa fell into a small chair and watched Lance sniffing his way along the shelves like a customs detector dog.

"Can you smell the oil?"

"If I could, I would have found it by now." Lance sneezed and shook his head. "I'm trying to locate the oracle's scent. The last things they touched, for example. But I'm not getting anything. It's like this place has been vacant for quite some time."

"Maybe it's not here," said Milo, as though reading her earlier thoughts. "How many safe houses are there, anyway?" He stood in the center of the room, his face streaked in dust, but it did nothing to hide his handsome features.

"Too many to search before things go bad." Lance padded over to a rack of vintage clothes. "Keep looking."

Alexa glanced out the window and saw the street lights flicker on, illumining the streets and the front bay windows in a soft yellow.

"But what if it's not here," she said, looking at the dog. "If the oracles haven't been in this bookstore for a long while, maybe they took the oil someplace else to keep it safe, not wanting to take a chance by leaving it here for demons to take."

Lance turned around and his yellow eyes glinted in the soft light. "Demons can't touch the oil. They'll burn if they do. Only oracles, angels and archangels can handle the Holy Fire. Even if it was designed to trap a celestial being, it's fatal to demons. The stuff is rare and hasn't been used in such a long time… I doubt even demons remember it exists."

"And if we *don't* find it," said Alexa. "Then what? Can't we try another safe house? You said you knew where they all were."

"I know what I said," answered the dog. "Did either of you remember to pack mortal money for public transport? No? I didn't think so. It'll take about a month on foot to reach the next safe house—time we don't have. I know what you're thinking. I've made arrangements for only *one* covert trip jump back to Horizon. We have to use it wisely. The plan was once we've found the Holy Fire, we make the jump to Horizon for the Staff of Heaven. You see, *I* might be able to sneak back to Horizon without being detected. I am a Scout, after all, and sneaking around is part of my DNA. But the two of you might never make it out. And without an angel prison… You better hope we find it. I don't want to think about what they'd do to you."

Alexa leaned forward in her chair. "Surely not Milo. I understand why I'd get in trouble after the whole Lucifer incident. It was *my* idea to travel to purgatory. But Milo…" she moved her eyes over to the angel and found him staring at her. She swallowed and said, "He didn't do anything. He tried to stop me from going."

"The last thing we all saw was him agreeing to follow his father," said Lance. "And then he disappeared with him. These are troubling times for the Legion. They'll be on high alert. He'd have to go through vigorous questioning before they'd trust him again." His yellow eyes found Milo. "No offense, but your father *is* Lucifer."

Milo shrugged, but his voice was hard as he said, "None taken." He walked away, kicking over piles of magazines and

97

rubbish as he went. He still had that look on his face like he had the weight of the world on his shoulders. Her soul ached for him.

Alexa sighed loudly. "Why does everything always have to be so complicated?"

"Because it just is," said Lance. "It's here. Keep looking."

Alexa glowered at the dog, but she bit her tongue before she opened her mouth to lash out at him for giving orders. This wasn't Lance's fault. It was hers.

She leaned back in the chair and crossed her arms over her chest. Mr. Patterson intended for her to find it. She had to assume he thought she'd search the oracle safe houses. If the oil was hidden in a particular location, he would have mentioned it in the letter. Which meant the oil was here somewhere... but where?

Alexa scanned the ceiling, the floor, and the walls, her mind whirling with possibilities. If she were an oracle, what would be the perfect spot to hide such an important thing? Where would she keep it? There was no safe that she could find in the shop, and now Lance and Milo were going for another round of searching the same spots over again.

Lance said the oil would most likely be in a bottle of some kind, she thought. Bottles break. So, it had to be somewhere safe, somewhere out of reach, somewhere that a delicate bottle wouldn't accidently fall over, somewhere easily accessible and yet well hidden... the note had been left on the oracle's desk...

Alexa jumped to her feet.

Milo whirled around at the sound. "What? What is it?"

"I think I know where it is." Alexa leaped over chairs, antique side tables, and floor lamps as she rushed over to the desk. She pulled the first drawer open and felt inside with her hands.

"I thought you checked it already." Milo stood next to her, his face half hidden in shadow.

"I did," she said quickly as she dumped envelopes, pens, and pencils all over the surface of the desk. "But maybe... just maybe..."

"Maybe what?" Lance stood on his hind legs and rested his front paws on the desk. "You're killing us. Maybe *what*?"

"Maybe," she said, trying to keep her excitement out of her voice, "maybe I was too hasty—there's nothing." She pushed the right drawer back, feeling the beginnings of disappointment crawl into her mind.

Milo leaned forward. "You're looking for a hidden compartment." Their eyes met, and the grin on his face sent heat over her body until she felt like she stood before a fire.

Alexa pulled her eyes away, the corners of her mouth twitching, and moved on to the middle drawer. She yanked it open. After she emptied its contents of rabbit feet, dice, bills, and dried mushrooms folded in a handkerchief, she slid her fingers carefully along the sides, moving them over the bottom and then the top—and her fingertips felt a latch. She pressed it, there was a *pop*, and the false bottom popped loose.

"Holy Souls," gasped Lance.

"Clever fledgling," said Milo.

Excitement pounded through Alexa as she grabbed the false bottom and tossed it onto the desk.

A clay jug lay at the bottom of the drawer.

It was an unimpressive gray, like dried mud, with the archangel sigils carved on the sides and lid. Alexa reached into the drawer and took it out, holding it carefully between her hands. As she turned it over, she recognized all seven of the archangel houses. It was the size of a coffee mug and surprisingly warm, but it throbbed as though the contents were alive. As she held it, she threw out her angel senses and felt the familiar waves of energy that came with any supernatural power in the mortal world. It hummed with power—the power of oracles.

"Careful with that," said Lance, leaning for a closer look. "You don't want to drop it. Trust me."

"Why? What happens if I do?" Alexa hadn't thought about the effects the oil might have on them. Fear tightened into a ball in her stomach. Should she even be touching it?

"Well, for one thing," answered the Scout, "it traps *celestial* beings. We'd be trapped here, in this place, with all these human collectibles, *forever.*"

"I can think of worse things." Alexa gave a nervous giggle as she held the jug, her fingers sticky with sweat. And then the three of them laughed, Lance chuckling the hardest. She felt the day's tension leave her body in hot waves, the storm of emotions unwinding like the loosening of a tight knot.

When Alexa looked away from the jug, she met Milo's eyes. His smile transfixed her, and she found herself incapable of looking away.

"We have it," she said. She was afraid the moment she looked away, he'd never look at her again. "We did it. We have the first ingredient—"

"Are you making a cake? I love cakes."

The front door burst open and Alexa gasped. A girl with protruding black eyes twirled into the small shop like a ballerina.

CHAPTER 10

"IS IT CARROT CAKE? THAT'S MY *FAVORITE*," said Willow. Her smiling face was smeared in blood, human blood, as though she had rubbed it in a large open wound. Through the smears of blood, Alexa could see the rotten flesh underneath, blackened and gray and oozing. Her bald head gleamed in the soft light as she sucked on a lollypop.

A tear through her jacket at her left elbow revealed a mess of black stitches that went around her arm as though it had been stitched up in a hurry. Yellow and black liquid oozed from between the stitches.

Willow was quickly followed by four demons dressed in human clothes. Their faces were emaciated and scabbed, just like Willow's, only they were much worse. Their hands, stripped and skeletal, held long, slender death blades.

Alexa could see that there was nothing left of their mortal suits. Their human guises hung in ribbons where there was still some flesh left on their rotted bodies. She guessed it was only still there because their clothes kept it from falling off.

It was obvious they had reached their fill of mortal souls. Alexa cringed at the thought. How many mortal souls had they devoured? The air stank of sulfur and spoiled meat.

Alexa fixed her glare on Willow, who looked like she was an extra in a zombie movie. "What are you doing here, Willow?" Carefully, she moved her free hand to her belt—and froze. Her fingers brushed the smooth, familiar leather but no cold steel. Her soul blade was still in Vegas.

The girl's eyes widened along with her grin. "Looking for you, of course."

Alexa kept her eyes on the girl demon. "Well, you found me."

"I did."

A growl sounded in Lance's throat. He moved around Alexa so that he was facing Willow, his white fur standing up on his back. "So, this is the Willow I've heard so much about?" said Lance. "Funny, I expected her to be taller and more... mannish."

Willow stared at the Scout as though she'd just noticed him and then flashed him a smile. "Good doggy."

Lance snarled.

"You look terrible, by the way," said Alexa, sensing Milo's tension as he stood protectively next to her with his spirit sabers glistening. "Did you pull out *all* your hair?"

Willow rubbed her bald head, her black talons scraping her scalp, and black blood seeped from small cuts. "You like it?"

Alexa gave an unpleasant laugh. "Not really."

"It's much better this way. I never have to worry about styling it or *washing* it—not that I did in the past that often. anyway. Angels don't need to bathe, right? But what does it matter now? It doesn't." Her black eyes locked on to the jug in Alexa's hand. "What is that, anyway?"

Alexa slipped the jug inside her jacket pocket and pushed it down as carefully as she could under Willow's scrutiny, doing her best not to break it in the process. "Nothing that concerns you. I see you got your arm back. Did you stitch it up yourself?"

Willow flexed her arm and wiggled her fingers. "I did. See? As good as new."

"I beg to differ," mumbled Lance. "It smells like hell."

Willow stared at the spot where the jug lay hidden. "What's in the bottle?"

"Nothing."

Willow giggled, as though Alexa had said something hilarious. "Oh, but I think it's not nothing. I think it's *something*. Something important, right? Why else are you hiding it from me? And by that scared look on your face, I'd say whatever's in that bottle is important to you. Legion business, isn't it? Yes. Legion. Legion. Legion. The start of all the lies, and you fools believe in it. Have you ever stopped to think why you have to slave yourselves to the mortals? Why is it so important? Why does the Legion make you believe that their lives are more important than yours?"

"They don't." Alexa's voice was low. "Our lives are just as important."

Willow threw back her head and howled. The other demons joined in with wet hacks that sounded more like the screaming of pain than laughter. "You're *so* stupid. Do you even know what you're fighting for? No, I didn't think so. Stupid. Stupid. Stupid."

"Don't listen to her," came Milo's voice. "She's just trying to throw you off with her lies."

"Lies?" Willow's eyebrows rose up towards her bald head. She picked her way forward between a small wooden desk and typewriter, her black eyes on Alexa. She moved like water, thought Alexa.

"I'm really going to enjoy ripping out your souls," leered Willow. "I think I'll start with Thor's," she said and waved her fingers at Milo.

Alexa could feel the tension rise again, so thick she could cut it with one of Milo's swords. The other belphegors had moved in a semicircle around them, blocking the door. Again, Alexa was reminded that she had no weapons. Part of her wanted to kick herself for not keeping one of the Nephilim's swords.

Alexa looked at Milo and saw hatred, malice, and rage on his beautiful face.

"Where are the rest of your kind?" Alexa took in the four belphegors behind Willow. "I'd imagined there would be more of you by now. This doesn't seem like much of an army. It doesn't seem like much of anything."

Willow arched an eyebrow and smiled. "The angels are waiting for something better. Same as us. Soon everything will change. We will change."

Alexa had no idea what she was talking about. "Why are you here, Willow?" Alexa said again. "And how did you find us?"

"Actually," Willow's eyes settled on Milo, "we were sent to kill this one."

Milo gave a start, clearly surprised. "Who sent you?"

Willow pulled out her lollypop and waved it in the air like a baton. "Imagine my surprise when *you* showed up," she said, looking at Alexa. "I knew there was something more to it. Your being there wasn't a coincidence. So, I waited. And after you killed all the Nephilim, I followed you. I was curious. I wanted to know why you'd risk showing your face here. Maybe to live out the rest of your angel days in the quiet of this tiny store? I know you can't go back to Horizon. I heard all about your breakout from Tartarus."

"I had nothing to do with that." Alexa felt rage pounding through her.

"Face it," said the demon girl. "You're a fugitive. An outlaw. You're stuck in the mortal world until your angel body kills you. But I can help you with that. I can slice your throat right now and end your pain."

The belphegor demons laughed.

Primal anger sharpened in Alexa's gut. "Is Lucifer your new master? Who are you working for? Who wanted you to kill Milo?"

"I'm following orders, just like you." Willow thrust her lollypop back into her mouth. "This is what's going to happen. First, I'm going to kill you and the rest of the angels, and then I'm going to take that bottle from you."

"Try anything," growled Lance, the fur on his back standing on end, "and I'm going to rip you open like a bag of Cheetos."

Willow giggled and twirled around. "Bad doggy."

Alexa gripped her hands into fists. "I'm surprised you're following orders at all. What did Lucifer promise you? Power? A seat at his table? You're nothing to him but a tool in his plan to destroy all life. What will you do when there are no more souls for you to eat? You'll wither and die? Your bodies need to constantly feed, to replenish. Otherwise you rot. I know that for a fact. You're not like the other demons. I was told that belphegors can't enter the Netherworld either. You're a prisoner here. Just like me."

Willow pulled out her lollypop and then picked a scab from her arm. She smiled at Alexa, popped it into her mouth, and began chewing.

"Is that what you think?" Willow prowled closer. "That Lucifer wants to destroy all the humans and this world? To extinguish all life?"

Alexa held the girl demon's stare. "Well, doesn't he? They call him the Lord of Darkness because he wants to remove all the light, all the life, and replace it with death and darkness."

Willow shared a look with one of the belphegors. "They have no idea," she said as her eyes traveled from Alexa to Milo to Lance and then back to Alexa. "You have no idea what he plans. Do you? What he's been planning all along? What occupied his mind all those years in purgatory? Don't feel too bad. He's got the Legion confused too. They share the same delusions and confusion as you do, which makes it so much more... *exciting*."

107

Alexa could feel Milo's eyes on her. Was she right? Was Lucifer planning something else? Had Lucifer fooled them all?

Icy dread crawled up her spine. "I'll make a trade with you," said Alexa. "I'll give you this," she patted her jacket pocket where she hid the jug, "and you tell me what Lucifer's plan is."

Willow opened her mouth, and for a moment Alexa thought she was going to answer. "Ah-ha! You're trying to trick me into telling you," she spread her arms, "the *big* plan. The new strategy."

"What strategy?" asked Alexa. "Tell me. I'll give it to you. I swear it."

"Liar, liar, pants on fire!" sang Willow.

"I'm not lying," pressed Alexa. "Tell me his plan and it's yours."

Willow looked down at herself. "This body is only temporary. Soon, I'll have a new body, a *stronger* body, a *beautiful* body. It won't look like me, but it'll still be me."

Alexa frowned. "You're not making any sense. If you didn't want to end up looking like a rotting corpse, you should have thought about that *before* feasting on mortal souls. You knew what would happen. You did this to yourself."

Willow's smiled faded a little. "It doesn't matter what you think because soon you'll be dead."

"Fine, so why not tell me this big plan," said Alexa. She stepped away from the desk, again wishing she had a blade with her. No way was she going to let the decaying demon girl kill her. "If I'm going to be dead... who am I going to tell, right? You can tell me."

Willow pouted and shook her head from side to side. "No. I think I'll just kill you."

Willow shot forward. She moved like a midnight storm, faster than Alexa remembered, and in her eyes, Alexa saw she truly meant to kill her. She was barely aware of the other four belphegors' attacking blows on her friends as she focused on Willow.

Alexa sidestepped Willow's first blow, but strands of her jacket exploded all around her, falling like snow as Willow's sharp talons shredded through it as though it were paper. She twisted her body in the other direction to avoid a second strike. But the demon girl was so damn fast Alexa could barely register her movements. Even her angel instincts did nothing to block or anticipate the third blow. Willow attacked from the back, and Alexa went crashing into small tables and lamps. She twisted her body and kicked out, just as Willow leaped towards her. Alexa caught the demon girl in the chest, and with a shout, she went sailing backwards.

"Alexa! Catch!" shouted Milo.

Alexa reached out instinctively and caught one of Milo's spirit sabers just as Willow threw herself at her again, spitting and hissing like a wild cat.

With her both hands, Alexa swung the long sword in an explosive strike. She caught the demon girl across the chest, sending a shower of black blood spraying her face.

Willow cursed and jumped back. Alexa took that moment to look around.

Cries sounded all around her, followed by a dog's growl and the tearing of flesh. Then she heard the clash of metal on metal.

She saw Lance first. He was a flash of white fur and teeth as he attacked a belphegor demon viciously. Chunks of demon flesh and black blood showered his coat. Still the demon came at him, but Lance never stopped.

Milo swung his sword at three belphegors, holding his position in front of Alexa as the demons assaulted him. He kept them from her, protecting her again. The belphegors hacked with their death blades as they advanced. Milo parried a deadly blow from the side, but he wasn't fast enough to recover as a blade sliced him from the other side. Light streamed from a wound at his side, and his face twisted in pain.

Fury gripped Alexa. She leaped forward and cried out as she stumbled back. She felt a stinging slice along her back as she spun around.

"I want that bottle." Willow licked the end of her fingers, which were stained in blood. "Whatever's inside is important. I can tell, you know, just by how you're protecting it with your body. I'm going to take it from you."

"Not going to happen," hissed Alexa. She pulled her hand from her side and it was slick with her angel essence.

"Have it your way then."

Willow's face warped into something feral and grotesque as she shot forward in a blur of limbs and talons.

Whatever training she'd had in Horizon, now was the time to put it into practice.

Alexa swung the sword in a blind rage as Willow charged at her. The smell of carrion filled the air, and she was sprayed by the demon girl's blood as she slashed off the front half of a thigh. The bone splintered into white shards under her blade.

But Willow never stopped advancing. She attacked with more energy and skill, laughing fiercely. She was enjoying the hell out of this.

"You're dead. Dead. Dead," she cheered, spinning like a top.

Alexa looked over her shoulder and saw a belphegor's head burst apart in a black spray as Milo caught it with his saber. Then he faltered a little. He was tiring, and the other two were getting too close. He brought the blade up, ripping open the belly of another.

Alexa felt the air shift and swung her saber with both hands.

"You missed," laughed Willow as she easily dodged Alexa's strike. "Missed. Missed. Missed."

Alexa cursed. Then all at once, Willow came for her. She didn't have a chance to swing the sword again. She tripped on something hard, falling backward and sprawling into a stack of books.

Willow was on top of her in seconds.

Instinctively, she brought the sword up to impale her, expecting the girl demon to fall on her. But Willow smacked the sword aside, and sharp talons reached for the inside of Alexa's jacket.

Alexa twisted. The demon girl's longer arm came up, and she slammed her talons against Alexa's throat like a knife, holding her back.

"Give it to me!" Willow pressed her talons into the soft flesh of Alexa's throat, and she felt warm liquid pour down her neck and into her shirt.

Alexa attempted to answer, but she only coughed blood. She desperately tried not to surrender to the fear that the crazy girl demon would slash her throat, but her hands were pinned by Willow's weight. So she did the only thing she could—spat blood into the demon's eyes.

Willow flinched in surprise, and her talons slipped from Alexa's throat momentarily. Alexa reacted.

She head-butted the girl demon as hard as she could.

Willow fell back screaming, black blood pouring like an open tap from her nose. She reached up and touched her nose. "You tricky little bitch. You broke my nose."

A smile reached Alexa's lips. "Good. That's not the only thing I'm going to—"

Something dark and small zipped past Alexa, making her breath catch in her throat.

Pain exploded in her side just as she spun and saw the edge of a death blade. The male belphegor lunged for her again, but she swung her saber in fury between his clavicle and his skull, severing his head.

Black blood sprayed her in the face, blinding her. She reached up to wipe her eyes, but it was too late.

One sweep of Willow's foot and she was falling, twisting to catch herself, but not fast enough. Alexa pitched forward, and the saber slipped from her hand as she stopped her fall to protect the Holy Oil. Turning again, she landed on her side and screamed as she felt the wound from the death blade rip. She reached up and touched the hard clay of the jug—it was still intact.

Something grabbed ahold of Alexa's jacket and she was yanked to her feet. She threw her hands in front of her to ward off her attacker.

With one swing of Willow's talons, she sliced through Alexa's jacket, cutting it in half like a slice of cheese, and caught the clay jug.

Alexa's eyes widened as she threw herself at the girl demon. "No! Give it back!"

Willow barely noticed as she backhanded Alexa across the face with such force that it sent her to her knees, black spots dancing before her eyes.

Alexa coughed up more blood and felt the first burning sensation of the death blade's poison mixing into her bloodstream. Her ears whistled, and she shook her head, trying to focus on only one Willow. Her cheek throbbed where Willow had hit her.

When her vision corrected itself, Alexa saw the girl demon holding up the ancient jug. And then she shook it.

"Willow, stop," croaked Alexa, struggling to control the rising panic. She tried to get to her feet but stumbled and fell. "You don't understand what it is. It's dangerous." She was barely aware of the fight that continued around them. Her focus was purely on the girl demon and the precious jug she held in her hand.

"I *know* it's dangerous," said Willow. "What do you take me for? I'm not a fool. You want to use this against Lucifer, don't you?" She pressed her ear against it and shook it again. "What's in it? Poison? Unless it's a new oracle concoction that I've never heard of before, you do know poison can't kill Lucifer, right?"

Alexa stared at the girl's black eyes as though in a trance. Sounds of battle still rang through the little shop as she started gasping in panic, feeling as if a rock were pressing against her chest. Hopeless. This was hopeless.

With a grunt of desperate effort, she crawled ahead a few inches. That only made it worse, tighter. She felt the rock crushing her.

Alexa heard Milo's voice shouting her name over the pounding within her. But she couldn't take her eyes off the girl demon or the Holy Oil. She couldn't let Willow take the first ingredient. If she did, all would be lost. They were running out of time and options. Too many of her failures had already plagued the mortal and celestial worlds. This was their only chance to vanquish Lucifer— *her* only chance.

She had to try something.

"You're right," said Alexa, blinking the sweat and blood from her eyes and keeping her face as void of emotion as she could. "It's worthless to Lucifer." She felt Milo's attention sharpen on her as she struggled to her feet. "It's got nothing to do with him."

"Really?" Willow sounded dubious. "Then why did you hang on to it like your life depended on it?"

"Because it does." Alexa kept her eyes on Willow. "The oracles told me where to find the memory oil," she lied, talking fast. "I lost my memories when Hades—"

Willow dismissed her with a wave of her hand. "Spare me the dramatics. I know all about your memory loss." She peered intently at the jug, her brows low, and Alexa felt her insides turn watery. "And you thought *this* would bring them back?"

"They promised it would work," said Alexa. "It's useless to anyone else, well, anyone who hasn't suffered some kind of amnesia." She swallowed and took a careful step forward, keeping her eyes locked on to Willow's. "I want to *remember*. I want to know who I am. I can't function like this. It's like I'm only half of myself. I want to know all of me."

Willow watched her for a moment and then shook her head. "Why am I not surprised you'd risk the lives of these angels only to serve some selfish need to remember your mortal past. Like we care. You suck. You suck as an angel. You know that? You're even more selfish than I am. What does that say about you?" Willow flashed her pointy teeth. "Plenty, I imagine."

Just as Alexa sensed movement near her, she realized how quiet the shop had become. She glanced around at the startling amount of foul-smelling gore spilled across the floor and walls. The last standing belphegor charged wildly at Milo and Lance, and Alexa saw Lance hit the ground. The belphegor laughed, easily blocking Milo's attacks.

"Stop!" shrieked the girl demon.

The belphegor demon froze, his death blade hovering in front of him.

"Come here," Willow ordered. "They won't do anything. *I've* got the bottle."

Milo's eyes were fixed on the demon as it moved quietly to stand next to his mistress. His eyes met Alexa's briefly before settling on Willow.

"Please, Willow," urged Alexa, as she saw the satisfied smile on the girl demon's face. "Please just give it back. It's no use to you. Give it back and I'll—"

"You'll what?" Willow licked her lips. "You're dead anyway. No. I think I'll keep it." Willow moved her thumb over the lid.

"Don't open it." Alexa realized her mistake as soon as the words were out of her mouth, but it was too late. The smile on the demon girl's face widened.

"Here." Willow tossed the jug to the belphegor demon. "You open it. My hands are wet with blood."

"Wait!" cried Alexa.

But the belphegor had already popped the lid open. He brought the jug closer and peered inside. "Smells like corn syrup. I hate corn syrup." Sneering, the demon spread his fingers, and the jug slipped out of his hand.

Fear and desperation gripped Alexa's throat.

"No!"

The jug hit the floor and exploded into hundreds of chunks of clay. A splash of toffee-colored liquid pooled at the demon's feet.

The demon shrugged. "Oops."

Alexa froze. Milo and Lance cursed.

"What did you do!" shouted Alexa. The fight in her was abruptly gone, and her insides throbbed with a dull ache.

Willow laughed at the horror on Alexa's face. "Ah, poor little Alexa. I guess you'll never get your memories now."

Afraid to move, Alexa stared at the golden liquid around the demon's feet. It spread slowly around his boots, and as the light hit it, she was surprised by how ordinary it looked. She tasted the rising fear and rage at the sight of the laughing girl demon. Perhaps they'd been wrong.

"Nothing's happening," came Lance's voice, as he moved to stand next to her. "Why isn't it working?"

Willow wrinkled her brow and leaned forward for a better look at the golden liquid. "Why? What's supposed to happen?"

The oil burst into white flames.

Willow squealed and jumped back, cowering under a desk.

"What is this?" Confusion rippled across the male demon's face as the flames spread and licked over his body, reaching past his waist. "What's going on? Wh—what's happening? I can't move. I can't move!"

His clothes flapped around him as if caught in a breeze, but the demon was as solid as a statue. And still the Holy Fire rose until it grew high above his head and he was completely surrounded by a wall of white flames.

The same flames reflected in Willow's wide, fearful black eyes as she watched from under the desk. For the first time, Alexa saw real fear flash in the girl demon's eyes as she watched her companion burn.

"Help! Help me, Willow!" The demon's voice carried over the flickering of the flames. The stench of sulfur and rot was quickly replaced by an overwhelming scent of something sweet like honey.

The demon opened his mouth again to speak, but instead he spurted white flames as if he breathed fire. Flames shot out of his eyes, his ears, his fingers and toes.

The belphegor demon didn't have a chance to scream as he burned into cinders.

Alexa watched in horror and could almost hear the demon's silent scream, his plea for help.

With a final flicker, the Holy Fire went out. All that remained of the demon was pile of gray ash.

And when Alexa looked back under the desk for Willow, she was gone.

CHAPTER 11

ALEXA DIDN'T KNOW HOW LONG she sat on the sidewalk outside JP's Curiosity Shop, staring at the pieces of the jug she'd picked up from the floor.

A middle-aged couple walked by, but they scarcely noticed the angel. She rubbed her fingertips against the smooth surface and felt only clay. It was curious that there was no trace of the oil on the shards. Not even a tiny drop of the golden liquid could be found on the ground where the jug had shattered. It was almost as though it had never been there, never existed.

But it *had* existed. Alexa had seen its power. She had seen how it had devoured a demon. It had taken less than twenty seconds for the belphegor to be completely consumed by the Holy Fire and then burned alive until there was nothing left of it but a mere pile of ash.

To keep the morale up, Lance had decided to give the shop one more going-over for more Holy Oil, but Alexa knew it was hopeless. Like the wound at her side that would never heal without the help of the Healing-Xpress.

They had lost the first ingredient.

She was barely aware of Milo taking a seat next to her until she felt his thigh brush up against hers, and he spoke.

"Stop blaming yourself." Milo's voice was soft, and it sent shivers through Alexa, caressing every muscle, bone, and nerve. "I know what you're thinking. But this wasn't your fault."

Alexa turned over the pieces in her hands.

"You couldn't have known he was going to drop it."

Alexa squeezed the shard hard into her hand until she felt the soft flesh of her palm break. "I shouldn't have let her take it from me in the first place. I should have fought harder. I should have stopped her... I should have done lots of things..."

"And I should have found a way to stop my father and brothers years ago." Milo's tone was sharp. "You can't blame yourself for things that are out of your control. All we can do is try to repair some of the damage. Sometimes it's necessary to fall, to be able to rise again. You did the best you could, Alexa."

Alexa looked at him. "Did I? I don't think so. It sure as hell doesn't feel like I did." The sound of her own failure sent striking pangs of anger into her chest.

Milo leaned forward and rested his elbows on his thighs. "Why do you always torture yourself this way? We weren't prepared. We didn't know Willow would show up with her gang of demons. My father's looking for me. To kill me, apparently. If anyone is to blame for this, it's me."

"Don't be stupid."

"I'm being honest." Milo's eyes traced her face. "Willow said she was sent to kill me. Who else would hire a band of angels-turned-demons to chase after me? My father. He won't let me go that easily. Not after what I did to my brothers. I know my father. He won't rest until I pay for what I did. Until I'm dead."

Alexa exhaled and shook her head. "He was counting on me to find them—all the tools we need to vanquish Lucifer. How can we continue if we don't have the first ingredient? We might as well give up now and come up with another plan. This one's shot." Alexa was acutely aware of how close Milo was to her. He smelled of leather and steel. It was the first time they'd touched since the embrace they'd shared when he kissed her. And she found herself wanting to lean into him, to feel his arms around her…

"We'll find a way. This fight's not over. It's just small setback." His easy tone washed over her like soothing water.

Alexa opened her fist when she realized she was still squeezing the shard. Droplets of her blood trickled down her wrist and onto the ground.

"It's just… I felt that we had a real chance, you know," said Alexa. She tossed the shard away. "I felt with this plan—I could make things right. Fix my mistakes. And if miracles do happen, maybe, just maybe, the Legion might take me back."

"Our mistakes, Alexa," he said softly. "We went to purgatory together. I'm just as much to blame as you."

"No, you're not." Alexa looked up and locked eyes with Milo. Heat rushed to her face and she forced her emotions down. "You only went with me because I made you go. You didn't *want* to go. You even tried to reason with me, but I wouldn't listen to you. I'm such an idiot. I should have listened to you. But I didn't. Instead, I thought only of me. There, I said it. I'm a selfish fool, just like Willow said." She swallowed, preparing herself for the truth of what she was about to say next. "I knew you'd come with me. I knew you'd never let me go to purgatory alone. So you see, I'm to blame for this. Not you."

"You're not all-powerful, Alexa." Milo's voice was hard. "You didn't mind-control me to come along. I *chose* to go with you, to keep an eye on you, but also to see if this bone sword was real."

"It wasn't."

Milo sighed. "I had plenty of opportunities to stop you. I could have gone and retrieved Ariel or even Metatron, but I didn't. I chose to go, for my own reasons as much as yours."

"Maybe," said Alexa as she pulled her eyes away from his face and stared at a spot on the ground. "But you would never have gone if I didn't insist on going. If I had said no to Sabrielle, we wouldn't be in this mess. I seriously want to strangle that archangel the next time I see her."

"I'll see to it you get your wish." Milo's voice rumbled through her core.

He lifted his hand, and for a moment Alexa thought he was about to take her hand. His hand lingered in the air for a second, and then he seemed to think better of it at the last moment and clasped his hands together.

"My father would have found a way to escape from purgatory eventually, with or without your help. You just helped him get out sooner, that's all."

Alexa smiled weakly. "You're just saying that to make me feel like not such a gigantic failure of epic proportions. Thanks, but it's not working." Her eyes burned, and she felt the start of tears threatening to spill over her face. She turned away, blinking her eyes dry.

Milo shifted his body until their knees knocked together, his body pressed towards hers. "No," he said. His face was so close she could see how long his eyelashes were and the flecks of silver in his eyes. Goose bumps rolled up and down Alexa's body.

Milo raked his fingers through his hair, which only made it look more like he'd just stepped out of the salon. "I believe he's been scheming his vast plans for years, perfecting them to the very last detail," said the angel. "It was only a matter of time before he escaped and put them into play."

"You think so?"

Milo nodded, his eyes never leaving hers. "He was just too prepared. It didn't make sense. He didn't act like he'd just escaped a perpetual prison. He was too calm and collected. He was in control, always in control. It's like everything was already in motion." When he finally looked away, tension rippled across his face, making him appear much older and tired. "It's what I wanted to discuss with the Legion. I want them to know that Lucifer was on the *brink* of something important—*before* we went there. We were just... unlucky."

"Unlucky? Feels more like we were framed."

"Exactly. You can't blame yourself for events that are beyond your control. We might have helped set his plans in motion sooner, but they were bound to happen."

Alexa rubbed her temples with her fingers. "Do you think it's what Willow meant when she talked about the big plan? Do you think it has something to do with what you were telling me before? About Sabrielle's *transformation*?"

Milo looked at her for a while before he spoke, his face darkening. "I'm positive."

"But you have no idea what it is?"

"None," answered the angel. "It's not the destruction of the mortal world, that I'm sure of. It's something else entirely. Something we haven't seen before... something we haven't thought of."

"Okay," said Alexa. "So, whatever we think we know, we *don't* know, and it's the complete opposite? Now that's confusing."

Milo let out a small laugh. And when Alexa tried to laugh, she winced. She cradled her left side as searing pain shot through where the death blade had cut her.

Milo's expert hands were there in seconds. "You're hurt." His eyes met hers and he seemed to be waiting for her permission to check her. She gave a small nod of her head, and he lifted her shirt. When his fingers brushed her skin, she flinched involuntarily as a wave of goose bumps riddled her body.

His fingers were warm, surprisingly warm, and his touch felt softer than a feather pillow. A wave of heat rose through her body, and it had nothing to do with the poison.

Alexa did nothing to remove his hand from her skin as a strange delicious warmth formed in her gut. "It's nothing," she said, her voice a little tight. "Just a scratch."

"It's *not* nothing." Milo pulled her shirt back down. "The cut's deep. The infection has already spread and mixed with your essence." He opened and closed his mouth, unable to say what gave him that deep scowl.

"I know what you're going to say." Alexa looked away from him. "I can still function. I'm stronger than I look, even without any special gifts. I still have a few good hours left in this body. It's still workable. I don't even feel feverish."

"Not yet."

"I'm fine. I promise. I... I don't want to stop."

"Alexa." The way Milo said her name made her turn to look at him.

Milo stared at her for a long moment, and Alexa hardly noticed the looks a few passersby gave them. But Milo said nothing, his face unusually grim. His beautiful eyes were haunted and heavy. He reached up and tucked a piece of brown hair behind Alexa's ear, fingers lingering on her cheek and his callused fingers gently scraping against her skin. When his eyes traveled from hers to her lips, a delicious heat kissed its way up her neck and down her spine.

Why does he have to be so damn beautiful, she wondered.

Alexa's body went still as Milo leaned forward, his face inches from hers. With tremendous effort, she resisted the urge to grab his face and pull his mouth on hers. But then Milo's nose rubbed against hers, and he tipped his head slowly, his warm lips brushing against hers—

"Nothing! Absolutely nothing!" Lance came bounding out of the shop. "I looked absolutely everywhere. That was the only Holy Oil in the shop."

Milo pulled back fast, his face flushed and his eyes wide.

"I thought perhaps they'd kept a spare." Lance froze, his yellow eyes on the two angels. If he saw or suspected anything between them, he didn't mention it. He walked over to them until he was next to Alexa. He lowered his head and sniffed her wound. "That smells terrible."

Alexa scowled. "Thanks." She pushed herself to her feet and away from the dog's nose. "Any ideas on how we defeat Lucifer if we don't have the Holy Fire to trap him?"

Lance sat on the sidewalk. "We'll have to think of something else. There's no time to look for some more, especially now with a bounty on Milo's head. We can assume we've got the attention of angels and demons. With Willow gone, we know she'll go straight to Lucifer with what happened. He'll know what we're after, if it's not already too late."

Subconsciously, Alexa moved her hand over her jean pocket to where the oracle's letter still lay hidden. She tried to hide the disappointment that thumped inside her mind. Losing the Holy Fire was a setback, and she cursed Willow silently. She should have killed her when she had the chance.

"So where do we go from here?"

Milo got to his feet. He took a moment to adjust the spirit sabers strapped to his back. "First, we need to take care of that cut. It won't heal on its own. Not with the death blade's poison."

Alexa felt the poison boiling her blood—a darkness, a virus. She looked at Lance, expecting him to object, but the Scout said nothing.

"If I use the Healing-Xpress, the Legion will *know* I'm there," said Alexa. "Our covert trip will be blown. I'll be captured as soon as I'm healed."

"We have to chance it."

"But—"

"Do you want to die?" Milo's soft expression from before was replaced by fury. Feral rage smoldered in his gaze, and she flinched as she took in his features. The way he looked at her reminded her of the first time they'd met, the same contempt and frustration. "Well, do you?" he pressed.

Alexa crossed her arms over her chest and ground her teeth. She didn't appreciate his tone. "No."

Milo rubbed at his neck and then met Alexa's stare. She saw an ancient heaviness in his eyes and the set of his jaw. "Then we go back. There's no other way. If you stay, you'll just get weaker until the poison devours your mortal body completely, leaving you exposed to demons."

"He's right, you know," said Lance and then looked away when Alexa glared at him.

"I can't stop the poison from spreading," said Milo. "You need to be healed."

"I think we all need a little healing," ventured Lance carefully. "We just have to figure out a way to get into the Healing-Xpress without alerting the Legion. Then we just might be able to sneak back out."

Alexa was quiet for a moment, her eyes resting on Milo. She thought of the kiss they'd almost shared. "And you think we can still defeat Lucifer without the Holy Fire?"

Milo let out a sharp breath. "We must." He gave her a grim smile.

Alexa's insides clenched. Something primal inside her went still and cold beneath that gaze.

"Then it's settled," said Alexa, trying to convince herself. "We go back. Back to Horizon."

Her stomach was anything but settled. The loss of the Holy Fire still weighed heavily on her. Their plan was falling apart.

Alexa swallowed the lump in her throat and hoped Metatron wasn't waiting for her on the other side.

CHAPTER 12

AFTER ALEXA, MILO, AND LANCE dove into the small artificial pond in a neighboring park, they found themselves back in Horizon.

It wasn't the first time Alexa found herself blinking through the orange goo that was the healing substance in the Healing-Xpress— the only place in Horizon equipped to heal injured guardians. It was a risk using the great metal contraption of interwoven pipes and wires. But seeing as Alexa had been infected with a death blade's poison, there was really no alternative.

Nevertheless, she always felt a sudden fear and claustrophobia of choking whenever she used the Healing-Xpress. But just as the fear worked its way in her, she emerged with a new, fresh body.

Alexa patted herself dry as quickly as her arms could move. She dressed in silence and kept glancing over her shoulder, expecting an army of angels to come arrest her at any minute. But they never came. A new soul blade was secured around her weapons belt, which was probably another favor from one of Lance's friends. The chamber was unnaturally quiet and still, except for the pops and squeaks that came from the Healing-Xpress.

The archangel Metatron never came for her.

Once Alexa had laced up her boots, she met up with Milo and Lance, who waited for her by the elevator. She caught Milo's worried expression. His eyes never left her face as she walked towards them, and she felt a warm tingling all over her, like the rays from the sun.

A black Standard Poodle stood next to Lance, eyeing Alexa warily as she approached.

Lance cocked his head in a way of greeting. "Alexa. Meet Cathy. Cathy, this is Alexa."

The poodle's light brown eyes narrowed as she took in Alexa's appearance. "She better be worth it." The poodle stepped into the elevator without another word.

Alexa looked at Lance. "What was that about?"

Lance gave a nervous laugh. "Nothing to worry about. Hurry up. Let's go."

Alexa followed Milo and Lance into the elevator, which she noticed was still without an operator. She moved towards the back next to Milo, aware of the poodle's eyes on her. The door closed, and Alexa felt Milo move away from her. He pressed his back against the wall. The elevator had enough space to fit the four of them comfortably, but Alexa suddenly felt confined, the space too tight, too personal. Milo was so close, yet so far away from her.

Alexa was barely aware of the elevator's sudden shift and ascension. The silent Milo was harder to read at the moment. He had never mentioned any girlfriends from his past, not that there was a right moment to do so. Still, maybe he was just as new and uncomfortable as she was about the kiss and what it had meant. It was infuriating to think that she'd finally felt a real connection with someone, only to be told, to know it was forbidden.

Angry tears threatened to surface, and she pushed them away.

"Where are we going?" she blurted, her eyes on Cathy the poodle. The poodle met her glare but turned away when Lance answered.

"Level six," said Lance as he motioned to Cathy, who was now staring into space. "From there we've arranged a sky-car for transport. The only one still operational."

"Only because of me," grumbled the poodle.

Lance glanced at Cathy. He opened his mouth but said nothing.

"And then where do we go? Any ideas where the staff is?" Alexa had only just been made aware of the different worlds within Horizon. She was still trying to wrap her mind around it.

Again, Lance glanced at Cathy, who continued to ignore him. "After some careful investigation and discussion, we've determined that the Staff of Heaven must be somewhere on the Angel Isle. We believe The Order of the First have hidden it carefully there over the years. It's their headquarters, has been since they formed this rebellion. It's only logical that they'd keep it where they can keep an eye on it."

"I think it's on Soul Summit, but no one ever listens to me," complained Cathy.

Lance looked angry for the first time. "We've already been through this, Cathy. Soul Summit is barely habitable. Only a few angels have ever been known to take refuge there. It's mostly eagles and other such celestial creatures."

Cathy shrugged and watched the door.

"Do you know what the staff looks like?" inquired Milo, who had been silent the entire time. "I can't say that I remember reading about it in any of the texts."

Lance perked up. "As a matter of fact, I do. It is said to have been forged with delor metal."

"The oracle metal?" Milo leaned forward, clearly curious. "The precious metal that only the oracles are capable of handling?"

"The very same," said Lance proudly. "The hardest substance in Horizon. We know the archangel Michael created the staff but not without the oracles' help—their precious metal. I would image it would glow faintly and maybe be warm to the touch. Michael was very adamant about creating a weapon that he could use against Lucifer. He poured his power into it, which you will no doubt recognize by his mark."

"His sigil," said Alexa as the shape of the sigil appeared in her mind's eye. It looked like the letter P with a tail.

"Exactly."

Alexa's head pounded with tension and anxiety. Her stress level mounted in huge pulsing beats. The tightness in her stomach turned to tingling, and the tingling turned to a sense of dread. She'd lost the Holy Fire. She couldn't lose the Staff of Heaven.

Before Alexa could ask more questions, she was tossed gently to the side as the elevator shifted to a stop and the doors slid open. Blinding white light came flooding in, and she had to shut her eyes momentarily until her eyes adjusted.

Everyone climbed out onto the small platform of white clouds that supported the elevator. She felt Milo's arm brush up against hers as they both stepped out at the same time. But he quickly moved away, and it was almost as though she'd imagined it.

Alexa stood next to Milo and looked down. She couldn't help it. She did it every time she made it to the sixth level.

A vast plane of greens and beiges spread out below them. Blue curves twisted through the landscape and out of sight. Across from her, in the distance, was a massive city, floating on individual clouds, as if kept up by some sort of magic. And on one of those floating cities was the High Council.

She'd been tried and convicted there. Something like bile rose up in the back of her throat at the memory of the contempt displayed on the faces of the archangels. She let out a loose breath. This time, she wasn't going to the city.

The soft *tat tat tat* sound of a motor getting louder and louder reached her even before she saw the flying contraption. The familiar, oval-shaped cloud, the size of a normal car, sped towards them.

The driver was a great white bird with a long beak and a large throat pouch, which Alexa immediately recognized as a pelican. He was perched on the steering gear with a blue cap resting on his head that had the numbers 9595 stitched across it in white letters.

The driver pulled the lever down and the sky-car came to rest next to the elevator.

"Sky-car 9595, at your service," the pelican said. It then hopped closer to Alexa and Milo, opening its large beak.

Milo flipped a silver coin into its mouth and the pelican wiggled it into its throat pouch.

"Thank you for your payment," said the pelican. "All aboard!"

Alexa made to move forward but stopped. Only then did she notice that Lance and Cathy had stayed in the elevator.

"Aren't you coming?"

"Yeah, about that," began Lance looking at the ground for a moment before looking up. "No. We're not coming with you."

"Lance, this isn't funny," said Alexa, raging and roaring inside. She kept her voice low enough that they couldn't hear the fury in it as she continued, "You know we need you—*I* need you." At that, Alexa noticed Cathy's upper lip lifting over her canines. "Don't do this."

Lance looked guilty. "I'm afraid I cannot follow you. Not unless you want Nathaniel to suspect what we're looking for."

Alexa reached out with a trembling hand and held on to the side of the elevator door. "What do you mean?"

"The only way you can safely make it to the Angel Isle," said Lance, his eyes traveling from Milo to Alexa, "is by convincing The Order of the First that you're there to join the rebellion. Most of the angels with the rebellion have already deserted. The fact that you two are only now willing to join is, let's face it, suspicious."

"I get that." Alexa watched the dog, her temper rising. "You're still not telling me why *you're* not coming. We can all pretend we want to join that stupid group."

Cathy shook her head. "They'll never believe us."

"Why not?" said Milo, raising his voice over the sky-car's motor.

"Because we have a history with The Order of the First. And not a very pleasant one." At Alexa's questioning brow, Lance added, "Who do you think's been spying on them for the Legion for years?" He gave Cathy a nod. "*Us.*"

"And Nathaniel knows," interjected Cathy. "We infiltrated their group, feeding the Legion with information as it came to us. But Nathaniel became suspicious in recent years and managed to *remove* those whom he suspected weren't in it wholeheartedly."

"Removed permanently, that is," said Lance. "Mike and Steve were never to be seen again. That was thirty years ago."

Cathy nodded. "Nathaniel knows of every Scout in the Legion. He'll never buy that we've suddenly changed sides. He's a fool, but he's not stupid."

"But you two, on the other hand," said Lance, "don't have a history with them. At least," he said, looking at Milo, "not one that involves spying. You'll have to find the Staff of Heaven without us."

Alexa shook her head. "So, then, what's *our* story?"

"Yes, Alexa's right," said Milo moving an inch closer to her. "You said it yourselves that Nathaniel will be really suspicious of anyone joining the rebellion so late in the game. What gives you the impression that he'll accept us? Granted, he knows who I am. But I don't think that will be enough to convince him." His light eyes found Alexa. "And what's Alexa's story? Why would they believe her now when she refused to go with Nathaniel after they destroyed Tartarus?"

Lance shifted uneasily on his feet. "Because of our master plan."

Alexa's grip tightened. "Which is?" Her every nerve screamed that she wasn't going to like it.

Lance looked carefully from Milo to Alexa. For a moment he said nothing, as though he were preparing himself or them for what he was about to say.

"That the two of you are involved," Lance raised his brows. "That you're *together*, together. The two of you are an item."

Alexa's grip slipped, and she caught herself before she fell forward. "*What?*" She turned and looked at Milo for support, but he was staring at Lance, his mouth slightly open with a strange expression on his face.

Lance bounded on the spot like his paws were on fire. "I know. I know what you're thinking, but trust me when I say it's the only way."

"He's right," said Cathy, a strange smile on her poodle face. "It's the only way."

Somehow Alexa suspected the poodle was enjoying herself.

Lance gave Alexa a sad puppy face. "It's why Cathy and I can't come with you."

136

Alexa righted herself. Her face burned like hot needles poking just under her skin. "But-but-but-that makes no sense," she blurted, her tongue suddenly too thick in her mouth. Her mouth was terribly dry.

"Just think about it for a minute," said Lance. "The two of you as an *item* is the perfect lie. And when you think about it, *really* think about it, you'll see how brilliant it is. They'll believe it. It's the perfect way to infiltrate the group."

An item. The more Alexa heard the words from Lance's lips, the more her head spun. This was insane. She and Milo had only ever shared a kiss, a very passionate one, but they were far from being involved. She didn't even know *what* they were. How could they pass off as being together if Milo didn't believe it? Nathaniel wouldn't believe it either. They were going to be killed.

Alexa kept her eyes on the Scouts. She couldn't dare a glance in Milo's direction. What was he thinking right now? Would he bolt?

"Nathaniel will never believe that," said Alexa, her face tingling with warmth. "The Legion forbids it. It's crazy. This is going to get us killed. There has to be another way. Nathaniel knows the Legion had me locked up. He'll accept that I've decided to switch sides. I'm a fugitive. He'll believe it."

"And what about Milo?" said Lance. "You need him with you to find the staff."

"He left the Legion to be with his father."

"Yes, but everyone knows Lucifer didn't give him a chance. He was forced to go."

Alexa shook her head. "It's not going to work."

Lance watched Alexa. "He'll believe it." The intensity in his voice made her shiver.

Alexa's face was on fire, and whatever else she was about to say got lost somewhere between her throat and her jaw.

"It's brilliant."

The spark of animation in Milo's voice took her by surprise, and she found herself staring at him in disbelief.

"You believe if we confess our—like you say—involvement openly to them," he said to Lance, "about of our *feelings* for one another... they'll believe us." Milo nodded his head, swallowing. Alexa saw the tension in the muscles of his face.

"That's ridiculous."

Milo's eyes rested on Alexa. "You know romance of any kind is strictly forbidden in the Legion. The punishment of angels caught in romantic affairs is Tartarus. I know of many angels that have deserted for this simple reason."

Alexa glowered at his use of the word *simple*. There was nothing simple about the complications of human—angel emotions.

"Angel relations are complicated," said Milo as though reading her mind. His voice was oddly constricted, as though he was out of practice using it. "It's been the cause of many heated discussions for centuries. I think it goes all the way back to the Legion's beginnings. It's always been an issue. If I were to guess, I'd say most of The Order of the First deserted the Legion solely for that reason, or something of that nature."

Alexa didn't know how long she stood there staring at the angel warrior. Had he shared those feelings before with someone else? She wouldn't have been surprised if many angel rookies or fledglings had fallen for the ruggedly handsome angel.

At that moment, there were so many things she wanted to say to him, but she felt as though everything was slipping away from her.

Milo leaned closer until she could smell the leather of his jacket. "I'm willing to do what it takes to put my father back where he belongs. We can pull this off. I know we can. But only if you're willing. I won't do anything you're not comfortable with. Are you with me, Alexa?"

The sound of his voice, gentle and warm, traveled down her spine in a sweet caress. Part of her hated that anyone could have that effect on her.

A flicker of the memory of their shared kiss flared up in Alexa's mind. But that was all that had ever happened. A romantic relationship? That was *way* past kissing. How the hell was she supposed to pull that off? Her mind whirled with questions, her body pounding with feeling.

She pulled her eyes away and gazed at the Scout. "And you're sure it's going to work? This plan you've concocted—without consulting me, by the way. Thanks."

Lance moved his shoulders in what Alexa took as a shrug. "Nothing in the world is certain, but if you can think of a better plan... now's the time to tell it. We don't have much time. The Legion will know soon that we used the Healing-Xpress."

"We've got about a minute before they send someone," said Cathy, not sounding stressed at all, but rather bored.

Alexa sighed. "I can't think of anything right now. Not on the spot like this. But if you're sure—*absolutely sure*—the order won't believe my idea for switching sides…"

"They won't," said Lance, his words registering like a blow. "Not when you refused him the first time. With this new development, your refusal can be interpreted as though you were waiting for someone." He looked at Milo. "For Milo. You're a pretty girl. He's a handsome fella. It makes sense."

Alexa felt Milo looking at her, but she refused to make eye contact. She kept thinking of how to act once they made it to the Angel Isle. And the more she thought about it, the worse the sense of panic filled her mind.

"Alexa?" came Milo's voice, and Alexa recognized a hint of anxiety in it. He thought she'd back out.

"Fine," she said resolutely. "If it's the only way. I can do this. Yes." The words felt more like she was trying to convince herself than them.

Without looking at Milo, Alexa climbed into the waiting sky-car. She heard Milo say something to the driver, but she couldn't make it out over the hammering in her head. She shoved her shaking hands between her thighs, rocking slightly. She felt the sky-car sway as Milo took the seat next to her.

"May the souls protect you," she heard Lance say as the sky-car shot forward into the bright blue sky.

CHAPTER 13

THE SKY-CAR FLEW ACROSS the sky, picking its way through and over clouds. The wind whistled in Alexa's ears as she tried to calm her mind. Finding the Staff of Heaven was more important to her than her feelings. She focused on the beautiful landscape below them. Squinting through the wind, she could see miles and miles of aqua oceans gleaming below. She couldn't make out land or even islands—only sparkling blue water that seemed to go on forever.

They rode in silence. Alexa's hands couldn't stop shaking and her throat was tight. She wanted to talk to Milo, but she didn't trust herself to speak. She was extremely relieved when Milo decided to break the silence.

He turned around in his seat and faced her. "We need to work on our story." His voice rose over the roaring wind. "Come up with a plan. We only have one shot to make this work. We need them to believe that we're... you know..."

"Boyfriend and girlfriend?" Alexa's voice came out hard before she could control the emotions in it. She looked into the angel's eyes, but there was none of the softness she'd witnessed before on the night he walked away with Lucifer. He was all business with only icy determination in those remarkable eyes. It was the same hard resolve he'd greeted her with the first time they'd met, like she was meeting Milo again for the very first time.

Milo's lips were a tight line. "I know this is a little—"

"Intense." *Confusing*, she wanted to say. Although every nerve in her body was on fire, she wouldn't look away from him. Straining, she fought to keep her emotions at bay and her face from showing the roller coaster of emotions that spun inside her.

Alexa looked to the driver. "Does he know where to take us?" she asked, changing the subject.

"Yes, I told him."

"And will he wait for us to take us back?" Alexa knew that once they had their hands on the staff, they needed a quick getaway. What better way than a sky-car?

Milo mustered a small smile. "I'm afraid not. The sky-car to the Angel Isle is a one-way ticket only. We can't risk having a waiting sky-car discovered. If they see that a car is waiting after *we've* arrived in it... they'll know we don't plan on staying long. They'll know we've deceived them. We'll have to find another way to leave the island."

"It's an island right," inquired Alexa, stating the obvious. "Can't we just jump in the water that surrounds it?"

"I would think so, yes."

"With the staff?"

"With the staff." Milo's stare was intense. His eyes, honest and transparent, caused the familiar reaction on her skin.

Alexa stared at Milo without blinking. "Let's pray to the souls that the staff is actually there. That this trip—all of... this... whatever *this* is... all of what we're about to do, won't be for nothing." *Because it'll be as embarrassing as hell*, she thought.

Milo's brows rose, seemingly reading her mind. "Alexa, I know what you're thinking—

"No, you don't." Alexa debated whether to bring up the whole kiss thing, but she had the feeling it would just make matters worse. "Don't worry, I can do the girlfriend thing if that's what's got you worried."

"I'm not worried about that." His voice was calm and sure.

"Good. Then we understand each other. We're here for the staff," said Alexa. Then she lowered her voice as much as she could without worrying about the driver overhearing their conversation. She didn't know if she could trust the bird, but the pelican stared ahead and gave no indication that he was listening.

"Let's focus on that. The staff. Everything else doesn't matter—won't matter—if we mess up our chances again. We go in, play our parts, find the Staff of Heaven and get out."

A shadow flitted across Milo's face. He turned back around in his seat without another word.

Alexa wasn't sure what to make of the warrior's sudden silence. She knew he'd wanted to talk about *something*, perhaps maybe even *the* thing, but she was frustrated with him and didn't want to give him the satisfaction of showing her true feelings—that he'd been right. Her eyes traced along his jaw and saw the familiar tightness there whenever he was stressed.

The muscles in his shoulders stood out, sharp and tight. Their outlines were visible under his jacket. Something was definitely bothering him, and she suspected it had nothing to do with the Staff of Heaven.

She needed to be clearheaded and unyielding in order to endure the next few hours. Her thoughts drifted at the first sight of land.

It stood out like a lonely ship lost at sea. It was a large, mountainous island of lush tropical rainforest covered in greenery that stretched up into the surrounding hilltops. The closer they got, Alexa could see white-colored sand around the edges and clumps of wild native flowers in warm shades of pinks and reds and orangey provided jolts of color in a world of turquoise waters.

The largest mountain stood out right in the middle of the island like a skyscraper, taking up much of the island's range. Alexa gripped the side of the sky-car and leaned forward for a better look. The mountain was covered in lush greenery and rock. She could see a road from the bottom spiraling around it and reaching the very top.

But she saw no movement, no angels.

Alexa was thrown back suddenly as the sky-car plunged, making a dive for the island. Her clothes and hair flapped around her as the sky-car shot downward at an incredible speed. She could barely see anything through the squint of her eyes. But then the wind stopped and when she could open her eyes wide again, the sky-car was hovering over a sparkling white beach. It swayed and then dropped onto the sand.

Alexa sat still. She hadn't realized how nervous she was until the sky-car stopped moving. She stood up on shaking legs, hoping that Milo didn't see any of it. He was already out of the sky-car. He offered his hand, but Alexa ignored it and climbed out. A dizzy spell came and went as she felt the strength in her legs returning. Alexa looked around.

Although the island looked like any tropical island, as soon as Alexa stepped onto the white sand, which was more like tiny crystals than fragments of coral or rock, she knew this was an ethereal place. She could feel it, sense it in all of her being to the very pores of her skin. It hummed with a supernatural pulse that couldn't exist anywhere but in Horizon.

The air wasn't humid. It was dry. The sun gave off no heat. A familiar scent of salt water from the ocean filled the air around them, just like the pools in Orientation, and Alexa wondered if this was where the Legion gathered the water to fill the pools.

There was no sound of waves crashing against the beach. The water was unnaturally still, as though a thin layer of ice rested above it.

"Thank you for using a sky-car!" piped the pelican. And with a pull on the vehicle's gear, the sky-car soared into the air and sailed across the sky.

"Are you okay?"

Alexa tore her eyes from the sky to find Milo staring at her. He was clenching and unclenching his fists, as though his hands didn't work without his sabers in them.

"I'm fine," she replied with a shaking voice, which only made her angrier with herself. With Milo's worried expression, she knew he could tell how nervous she was.

"It'll be all right." Milo moved next to her, his voice gentle. "I won't let anything happen to you."

Alexa brushed past him. "I'm not some damsel in distress. I don't need your protection." The white sand pulled at her boots as she stomped across the beach.

Milo was next to her in a second. "Maybe not. But we need each other. This isn't the Legion, Alexa. The Order of the First won't follow the Legion's rules. There's nothing to stop them from killing us if they feel like it. This island is crawling with *bad* angels—the worst. Some worse than my brothers."

"I never expected a welcoming committee," said Alexa, staring at the line of trees that wrapped around the beach like a protective wall. "I knew the risks. And they are risks I'm willing to take."

"Even your life?"

Alexa laughed softly. "What life? I died. Became an angel. And the angel life I had... I threw it all away because I was stupid. There's nothing left for me. The Legion thinks I'm a criminal, and now, a deserter. I'm as good as dead in their eyes anyway. So, what does it matter."

"It matters to me."

Alexa's skin prickled, but she kept her eyes on the strange crystalized sand. "Without the Holy Fire, we really need this staff to do what the oracle said."

Milo's shoulder brushed against hers as he walked. "The easy part will be to be accepted. The hard part will be to *find* the staff."

Alexa knew Milo was right. The island was huge. They could have stashed the Staff of Heaven anywhere.

"I just wish…" sighed Alexa, kicking up some sand with her boot. "I wish we could have had some extra help with the Legion. Did you hear anything? Any news?"

Milo kept a respectful distance between them. "While you were in the Healing-Xpress, Cathy told us about the Legion's plan."

Alexa looked at him curiously. "What plan?"

"The Order of the First intends to conquer all angels and destroy humanity," said Milo. "They want to purge the mortal world of humans—to cleanse it, as they put it."

Alexa's mouth went dry at the tone in his voice, and she clenched her hands into fists. "That *can't* happen."

"I agree," said Milo. "And the only way to stop them is—"

"To remove them."

Milo gave a slight nod of his head. "If the Legion doesn't stop them, sooner or later they will be ruled by the order. Which is why the Legion's not taking any chances. They've separated into three different groups. The first group is made up of archangels and highly experienced angels and oracles. Their job is to stay in Horizon and guard all newly appointed angels. The second unit's job is to hunt and kill *all* the members of The Order of the First."

Milo's expression darkened. "And a third unit will go after Lucifer themselves." He looked at Alexa. "The Legion's been training and preparing the angels for *war*."

"War." Alexa's skin prickled at the word.

The promise in it pulled her stomach tight, and fear washed through her. War equaled death, and Alexa felt sick in the pit of her stomach at the thought of all the angels who would lose their lives in this war. But she knew the Legion couldn't let Lucifer and The Order of the First destroy humanity. Innocent lives. Children's lives. She would have fought alongside them if she could. If the Legion had let her, she would have given them all she had.

Perhaps this was her only way to truly show her loyalty to the Legion once and for all.

"What about us?" inquired Alexa, her voice a little weaker than she'd wanted. "Did she mention anything about you or me? Does the Legion still think I'm part of the order? Are they looking for me?"

"I don't know," answered Milo, and Alexa could have sworn she heard something like sympathy in his voice, which made her cringe inwardly. "That's all Cathy said. It's lucky that she told me any of this. As a Scout, she probably got most of her information through her own informants. She's not privy to the information above her station."

"So, she spied on her own Legion."

"She's a Scout. That's what they do," agreed Milo. "If she had heard something about either of us, she would have told me."

Alexa felt a little pang in her chest at his words. It was stupid. She knew the Legion had discarded her like an old shoe, but there was still the hope that Ariel believed her, that the archangel had managed to convince the others of her loyalty to the Legion, that this whole thing had been a terrible mistake.

"You told me that your father is moving around in some sort of enchanted castle," said Alexa, changing the subject. "How do they know where to find him?"

"With the Veil." Milo's face tightened. "It's a way to locate him. The most extensive tears have the strongest pull. So, they're searching the largest rifts, the greatest holes in the Earth's magnetic fields, where the most dangerous demons are pouring through from the Netherworld."

"We can use that as well," said Alexa, her hope rising in her chest. "Once we have the staff, we can look for rifts in the Veil too. At least it's a way to track him unless you have a better idea."

Milo was silent for a moment. "Maybe. And then there's the blood of the willing demon. We need that before we track him down. Did the oracle say how we were to obtain the demon's blood?"

Alexa felt her small bubble of hope burst. "No. I guess any demon will do. It doesn't say what kind of demon. Just demon."

"But a *willing* one," said Milo. "I don't want to sound too cynical, but our chances of finding a demon who's willing to give us its blood are… slim."

"I know." Alexa knew the third ingredient would be the hardest to find, maybe even impossible. "Who knows. Maybe we'll get lucky." She tried to smile, but her lips just gave a nervous twitch that probably made her look like she was going mad.

Alexa didn't like the way Milo was staring at her, so she pulled her eyes away and gazed at the miles of white beach that surrounded the island. For a moment, she could almost make herself believe that she and Milo were here on vacation. Almost.

"Did we make a mistake coming here? Where are the angels?"

Milo freed one of his spirit sabers. His grip was tight. "There's only one way to find out. Come on. I remember seeing a path through those trees over there."

Alexa wove her way across the beach following Milo. The white sand crystals crunched under her boots, and the sound of their tread echoed around them. It was the only sound. It was unnatural, another reminder that she was far from the security of the Legion.

Alexa couldn't stop a shiver from tracking down her spine as her fingers grazed the hilt of her soul blade. Their plan wasn't much of a plan. Would Nathaniel believe them? Was he even here?

Her mind drifted to the piece of paper that lay hidden in her pocket. Perhaps the oracle had put too much faith in her. Perhaps this mission should have been someone else's.

The note.

If she was searched and the angels found the note... the note that described how to destroy their Lord of Darkness...

Alexa halted. The sudden realization of her mistake sent a cold pounding through her.

"Milo. Hang on." Alexa reached into her pocket—

And then the forest screamed as a horde of angels came crashing through the tree line towards them.

CHAPTER 14

MILO SWORE, LOW AND VICIOUS, and if Alexa wasn't so terrified at the mass of angels galloping towards them, she might have laughed. But she barely had time to blink as she stared at the tip of a blade pointing in her face.

Twenty angels surrounded them. The scent of lemons and something sweet that Alexa couldn't identify stuffed itself up her nose, and the forest went still again.

The angry frowns and grimaces of strangers flared everywhere. There was nothing she or Milo could do—nowhere to run, even if they wanted to. She would feel the sting of blades before she could stop them. Even if they'd wanted to change their minds and go back—there were too many. Dear souls, there were just too many.

Alexa willed the strength of her body and her mind. She did not allow herself to flinch when she beheld the twenty angels standing around them, tall and lean and bearing their soul blades. *Run*, her body screamed, but she held her ground.

"Don't even think about drawing that blade, lesser angel," said a female angel with heavy brows. Her dark eyes moved to Alexa's hand that had been reaching for the note. "Move your hand away or I'll gut you."

Alexa dropped her hand. She moved her gaze around her, taking in the scene. Their ages, body shapes, and genders all varied as much as their skin colors. But their eyes all held the same open hatred and fury.

All these angels wanted to destroy humanity—kill innocent children, the elderly, the sick, everyone. They didn't discriminate. Instead of a chill, the heat of anger surged through her body. When Alexa realized she was about to do something she might regret, she immediately took control of her temper. Still, she could feel the rage powering in her bones, her core.

A male angel stepped forward. Light shivered on the jagged metal of his blade. The dark sword in his hand was angry looking, making it look more like the swords Alexa had seen the Nephilim use rather than an angel blade. But where the Nephilim were all dark, this angel was all light and fair. His light hair complemented his light-colored eyes. He was thick and broad shouldered, every bit an angel warrior, but Milo was a few inches taller.

The male angel's eyes flickered to Alexa and lingered there. And then in the next second, Milo stepped closer to her with his powerful, predatory ease. He regarded the male angel's cold scowl with unruffled authority, and his fingers tightened around his saber.

"If you move your sword hand," he said to Milo, "you'll be dead before you can even finish raising it."

The other angels all crept closer, their blades glimmering in the sun, anxious to use them. Milo's jaw twitched, his eyes darting around at every angel, but he remained silent.

The male angel watched them with a dubious expression. "Names."

To Alexa's surprise, by the time her lips had parted, Milo spoke up.

"Milo, and this is Alexa."

Alexa moved her eyes along the angels for any flicker of recognition at the mention of their names but found none. The band of angels had the demeanor of officers; their eyes shined with confidence and indignation. The female angel with the blade in her face lowered her brows in a frown, but Alexa only saw a deep loathing, nothing more.

"We're here to join the order," said Milo, his voice strong and true and filled with confidence. "We seek protection from the Legion."

"I don't trust them," spat the female angel with the blade in Alexa's face, her breath sour and hot. "They smell like Legion spies to me." She pushed the blade against the skin of Alexa's neck. "Give the order, Brent, and I'll cut her down."

Alexa glared at the female angel, her anger resurfacing. She looked to be in her early thirties. She was thick and strong, and no doubt had years of training over Alexa. Still, there was nothing more she wanted at that exact moment than to punch her across the face. But she knew the moment she moved, the angel would slice open her neck with a flick of her wrist.

"It's not up to you, Naja," answered Brent. "Don't spoil the angel meat just yet." At that, Naja moved the blade from Alexa's neck, but to her dismay, she stayed right in her face. Too close. It only angered her more.

Brent's eyes moved to Milo's neck. "I know who you are. Only one angel has a mark on his neck like that." He cocked his head to the side. "Lucifer's infamous estranged son."

"It doesn't matter who I am or what you think you know about me." Milo lowered his sword until the tip rested in the sand, his posture casual. "We seek refuge. We came here to join your cause. Everything's changed. What I used to believe... what I thought it meant to be a guardian. Nothing's the same. Nothing's what I thought it was. They lied to me. To us. We've been banished when we've only ever wanted to help the Legion. And now the Legion wants us both dead. We have nowhere else to go."

A distant smile touched Brent's lips. "The Legion wants us all dead. Why should we care about two strangers? How do we know you're not spies? Why come to us now and not before? You must admit showing up here now is a little unusual. Don't you think?" He hesitated for a moment. "Why did you come here. The truth now."

Milo kept his calm demeanor. "Because," he said, and he looked at Alexa, his eyes sparkling, "because she and I are..."

Alexa's stomach tightened. Her horror achieved new depths as she realized he couldn't say it. Those two words. Not even as a lie. He couldn't say the words. Heat rushed up her neck to her face and she felt the angry tears behind her eyes before she could control them.

Don't let them see me cry, she thought. *Not now.*

Alexa pulled her eyes away from Milo and, with surprising control, mastered her tears before they got them both killed. She could feel Brent's eyes on her, but she stared at the white sand, afraid that if she met his eyes he would see the lies in them.

"You've been banished because of your affection for one another?" Brent's voice was suddenly filled with understanding. Alexa looked up at him. He was watching her, and whatever he saw in her face seemed to convince him. She couldn't help but wonder if Brent had been a victim of forbidden love. Somehow, she felt as though he had.

"We have," said Milo. His voice was so sincere, his face so convincing, that Alexa found her anger shedding from her like the casting off of old clothes. She met his gaze—those light gray eyes so bright in the sun. But she also saw a shadow of grief and something else she didn't understand.

"They're lying," argued Naja, jolting Alexa's attention back to her. "They'll say just about anything to keep us from slaughtering the Legion's filth. I say we feed them to the eagles. I'm sure lesser angel flesh will taste the same to them," she scorned, her face transforming into something more feral than angel. She reminded Alexa of Willow.

A few angels sneered in agreement.

Brent watched them both with great interest. "It's not up to us to determine their fate. Nathaniel will know what to do. Take them."

Brent turned on his heel and made for the line of trees.

Alexa found it strange that they weren't disarmed. Maybe they knew there was no hope of defeat. They had passed the first test, more or less. At least they were still alive.

Alexa felt a small surge of relief wash through her, and the tension in her body loosened a little. Before Alexa could look at Milo, Naja was in her face again.

The angel female lifted her chin and smiled at Alexa. "Don't look so smug. You're not out of the woods yet. If you think you're safe now, you're in for a major surprise. Others have come here *uninvited*, and it didn't end well for them. But I'm sure you know that already. Don't you?" Her smile widened. "Now move." She shoved Alexa forward brusquely.

It was difficult walking in the sand, but Alexa was grateful that she didn't fall once. Although she did come close a few times, she always managed to steady herself. At least her pride was still intact.

Brent led them and the band of angels up the sand dunes and to the trees. Milo and Alexa walked behind a group while the remaining angels came up from behind, seemingly to keep them from changing their minds and running away. She thought of the water, the oceans of water that surrounded the Angel Isles, and wondered again if their means of escape was a mere dip in the ocean.

She threw a few covert glances at Milo, but the angel was staring ahead as they climbed out of the sand and entered the forest. His eyes were distant, and he had a slight frown, as though something in his head was troubling him.

Brent and his band of angels ushered Alexa and Milo through a jungle of trees and onto a narrow trail. The eerie silence was getting to her. No one spoke. The only sounds were their echoing tread crunching the pebbled path. There were no animals. No bugs. Even the leaves of the trees lay still. Even in this ethereal place, Alexa thought she would have seen at least a few living creatures. Naja had said there were eagles, probably the giant white ones that the angel escapees used to flee from Tartarus. So why not other types of birds?

No one spoke as Milo and Alexa were led through the forest. Up ahead, Alexa could see that Brent had his head bent and was conversing with another male angel with striking red hair. The two angels appeared to be in some sort of heated discussion, seemingly forgetting about their prisoners.

They began the long, spiral climb that led up and around the tallest mountain. The narrow path was flanked by towering trees and some kind of bush that looked like bougainvillea shrubs. They were all bursting in reds, oranges, and pinks—stunning in the sun.

When they reached the topmost part of the mountain, a pyramid-like structure made of limestone greeted them. It looked like something the Mayans would have built with intricately carved stone constructed in a stair-stepped design. As they neared, Alexa could see that the pyramid had a flat top platform. Four giant white eagles were perched at the top, their eyes on Alexa and the others as they approached.

Naja caught her staring at the eagles and she winked at Alexa, a wicked gleam in her black eyes.

Brent directed them to the stone pyramid. He glanced over his shoulder once, but his expression was lost to Alexa, hidden by another angel's head. Then they began the climb up the steps. Alexa picked her way carefully around the large, white-washed stones of bird droppings, the foul stench burning her nose. Bird droppings littered everywhere. She wrinkled her face as she stepped over a large, fresh-looking dropping. As she climbed, she spotted a pale stick that looked a lot like a human femur.

Once at the top, they were led through a large opening and down a hallway. Apart from Naja, the angels didn't push them, didn't touch them, but rather allowed them a wide berth. Alexa trailed down the hallway next to Milo, each footstep alternating between iron-willed control and growing fear. What would happen when they faced Nathaniel?

Ahead of her, Milo's own steps were silent on the dark stones of the hallway. Lit torches hung on the walls, casting long shadows in the murky interior.

They strode through two ancient, enormous stone doors and into a vast chamber carved from the same limestone. The room was held by countless square pillars, carved with designs that depicted angels and mortals in various battles and positions of movement. Countless stories of the Legion and Horizon were etched on them. Iron chandeliers hung from the high ceiling, staining the stone floor with hints of gold.

The chamber was packed with angels. Leering faces, cruel and harsh, watched Alexa and Milo as they passed. None looked mildly concerned that there were two strangers in their midst, within their order.

But most of the angels ignored them completely, and when she took the time to really look, her breath caught in her throat.

An assembled crowd took up most of the space, some of them lounging on sofas or chairs, even tucked away in shadowed corners. Some were milling about chatting, almost like a party. Alexa had never seen so many angels so restful and leisurely. She'd only seen the angels at the Legion, busy with orders, saving lives, doing their jobs. This was different.

Alexa eased her way next to Milo until their shoulders touched. She matched his walk. She caught his slight eye movement towards her, and she knew he was listening.

"Something's not right," she whispered, staring at the angels sprawled leisurely on couches and chairs.

"What do you mean?" Milo's lips barely moved.

"Don't they seem a little too relaxed? If there's a war coming," began Alexa, "if The Order of the First is planning some sort of attack on the mortal world, shouldn't they be gathering up weapons or making combat plans or something?"

Milo watched the scene, his features slowly lowering into a deep frown. "You're right. They seem too calm and even a little lazy. The complete opposite of those on the brink of war."

"And why does that make it worse?"

"Because it means that whatever they're planning, they believe they've *already* won."

Alexa's stomach turned. Milo was right. These angels, The Order of the First, believed whatever they were planning, they had already won. Her mind wrestled with the possibilities, the notions and designs of what the order was after. What had them so cocky? What was it?

"Well, now, this is a surprise," came a familiar voice that stopped Alexa in her tracks.

She looked up to find an angel with skin as dark as oil making his way towards them. He looked just as she remembered—dressed in loose white clothes, leather bracers sheathing his arms from wrist to elbow, and the same wicked-looking sword hanging from his waist.

"We found them on the beach," said Brent, moving to stand next to his leader. "They say they want to *join* us."

Nathaniel laughed without humor. "Do they now?" He stepped away from Brent with a casual grace and stood before Milo and Alexa. She never realized how big he was until he stood next to Milo. Nathaniel was bigger, taller, and there was an acute intelligence in his eyes that Alexa had only ever seen in the eyes of the archangels. He just stared at Alexa—unfeeling, unmoving. Unimpressed.

Then Nathaniel's smile turned wicked. "Never thought I'd see you here, Milo."

Milo's jaw clenched. His face was stripped of all emotions until he looked like a sculpture, similar to those carved on the pillars.

"Things change."

Nathaniel watched him for a moment and then turned his dark eyes on Alexa. "I'm surprised they brought you in as a prisoner and not as a special guest."

Brent moved forward, his brow furrowed. "What do you mean? You know her?"

Nathaniel raised his voice. "Do you *not* know who she is?" he called to the angels in the chamber. "Do you not recognize her? Some of you have probably crossed paths in the Legion." He looked around at the confused angel faces. "No?" He turned and smiled at Alexa. "This here, my friends, is the very angel who made all of this possible. The one and only—Alexa Dawson—the one who freed Lucifer from purgatory."

Brent's face went slack as the chamber became as still as the forest. But it only lasted for a second as gasps rippled through the assembled chamber.

Alexa could feel the energy of the chamber home in on her, and she hated it. She hated all the attention, but hated what she was now infamous for most of all. She would forever be known as "the angel who freed Lucifer." She pulled her eyes away from the curious looks and met Nathaniel's quizzical brow.

Nathaniel waited for the angels to absorb the new information. He eyed Alexa skeptically, as though he already had misgivings about the reasons for their arrival.

"Why are you here, Alexa?" he asked finally.

Alexa thought it strange that he didn't asked Milo that question. "To join your cause, to join the order." A tremor reflected in her voice, and she prayed to the souls that Nathaniel and the others didn't hear it.

Nathaniel's face was wrinkled in doubt. "But why now? Why now when I had offered it to you when we first me in Tartarus?"

Alexa's nerves ricocheted inside her as though her stomach was lit with firecrackers. She knew what came out of her mouth now would determine their fate. If she made a mistake, made the wrong decision and said the wrong thing, she and Milo were dead.

A part of her began to doubt her skills at lying, and she couldn't fathom being responsible for Milo's true death. There were still so many feelings, so many conversations they still needed to have...

Without even thinking, Alexa turned and looked at Milo. She traced her eyes over his face as he turned and looked at her, seeing the familiar stress along his forehead and the tightness of his jaw that only those close to him would know. Only she could recognize the fear in his eyes, the fear of what would happen should she fail.

"I couldn't join you before," she began, her throat a little tighter than before. Although Lance's words flowed in her mind, she didn't need them. "I couldn't leave. Not without Milo." She saw softness flicker across his face before it vanished and was replaced by the familiar tight expression, his face impassive.

"Interesting." Nathaniel rubbed his chin. "You left the Legion for love."

When Alexa turned her attention back to Nathaniel, she didn't like the grin on his face nor the way he was considering her, like she

164

was about to be tested. It was the same grin Metatron gave her right before the High Council sealed her fate.

Nathaniel's eyes gleamed as he said, "Prove it."

Alexa's head raced. Warning bells went off in her head, making her stomach clench. He was testing her. This was it. The test that would either set them free or be their end. She wasn't ready to die.

To her own surprise she turned around and faced Milo. He blinked, probably not expecting her to move so quickly. Their thighs touching, she leaned forward until their hips rubbed. The truth was, she had wanted to kiss him again since the time she'd had but a taste. This time it would be on her terms.

Milo's eyes were large. His skin gleamed with a golden sheen. Her fingers trailed along his cheek as she gazed at him, needing no words. For a moment, the world stopped.

Licking her lips, Alexa leaned forward, so close the tip of her nose ran over the skin of his cheek. And then she grabbed fistfuls of his shirt, pulled his face down to hers, and kissed him fiercely.

His lips brushed hers, soft and warm. And then he met her kiss right back, harder, but nothing like the way he'd kissed her before. It had none of the desperation of the kiss he'd given her in Hyde Park before he left with his father. This was different. It spoke of dreams and evenings together. It spoke of a future.

She kissed him, soft and lingering, and her body melted into his. Then Milo pulled back, leaving her standing with her face on fire. Milo watched her, long and deep, his eyes wide and filled with longing. She could still feel the softness of his tongue, the pressure of his lips on hers.

A loud clap shook Alexa back to reality.

"Good," said Nathaniel, apparently pleased. "Very good." He spread his arms wide and said, "Welcome to The Order of the First."

CHAPTER 15

ALEXA AND MILO HAD BEEN on the Angel Isle for about a week, and there was still no sign of the Staff of Heaven.

They were even given a private chamber to share. At first, Alexa had been pleasantly surprised that they'd been treated so well. She'd never had a room or even a locker to herself in the Legion. But her enthusiasm soon vanished when her eyes found the large king-size bed shoved against the stone wall. The fluffy pillows and comforter only made Alexa's face redder when she considered that angels didn't sleep.

It had never even occurred to Alexa that angels could have real, meaningful relationships. Coming to this place was an eye-opening experience for Alexa. It showed her a complete opposite way of life for angels.

It wasn't long before the island felt familiar and even comfortable to Alexa. She found herself getting used to seeing angels holding hands and even kissing until she barely noticed it anymore. It was like being back in the mortal world.

She found herself questioning the Legion. Why were angels forbidden from falling in love? Angels weren't robots. And these feelings—feelings she shared with these rebel angels—came naturally. If angels weren't supposed to feel, why did they?

A few hours on the island was all it took for Alexa to realize how different it was from the Legion. She knew the first time she felt and saw the fiery sky and deep blue colors of dusk.

Nighttime existed on the Angel Isle.

Alexa had only ever seen the bright sun on levels two and six, no matter what hour of the day it was in Horizon. It was *always* daytime.

"But how is this possible? I thought there was no time difference in Horizon?" she had asked Milo their first night as she goggled at the dazzling stars. The moon was a bright sphere in the black sky, which made Alexa think of a giant soul.

"I'm not sure," Milo had said, looking just as puzzled as she felt. "Probably some kind of enchantment to make it feel like night. An illusion of some kind."

"It's beautiful," Alexa had said with a little ache of pain in her chest at the sight.

Then to add to Alexa's surprise was the sound of beating drums just as the sun disappeared over the horizon. With the continual drumming, dozens of bonfires popped up along the beach. Angels chanted and sang in a language Alexa didn't understand. They danced around the fires in wild, feral-like dances, swinging their arms and legs with the beats of the drums.

Every night was the same. The Order of the First threw a party.

During the day Alexa and Milo did most of their sneaking around, looking for the staff. The order was predictable but also methodical in their daily activities. There were parties at night, and then there were meetings during the day. Always in the same large chamber on the west side of their pyramid, and always Alexa and Milo were not invited.

"You need to earn our trust before we can allow you in on our meetings," Nathaniel had said to them on their second day on the island. "Then you'll be invited to join us."

Alexa wasn't sure how they were supposed to earn their trust. But it was clear they were not sharing everything with them. Brent, Nathaniel's watch dog, was always there watching them. They took turns giving Brent the slip, so that either Alexa or Milo would go in search of the staff whenever he was following them.

She didn't blame Nathaniel. She would have done the same. Still, it didn't stop them from searching everywhere they could. They worked fast, knowing that every minute they spent on the island was a minute wasted on the fate of the mortal world and the Legion.

Even with the strange nighttime parties, there was still a calmness about the rebels that unnerved Alexa. Not once did she see signs of preparation for war or attack. It didn't make sense. It seemed the angels were more interested in drinking or just hanging out and doing nothing.

"We should try Nathaniel's chambers," said Alexa as she walked next to Milo on one of the many stone paths in the manicured garden. She brushed her fingers over the yellow and pink hibiscus hedges. "Tonight, while he's at the party with everyone."

"You're sure he'll be there? It's a big risk if we get caught."

"He hasn't missed a party yet." Alexa looked over at two teenage male angels walking in the garden and lowered her voice. "It's the only place we haven't searched. It's there. I *know* it is. Besides," she added, eyeing the angels as they neared, "I overhead some angels talking earlier about today's meeting. I couldn't catch what the meeting was about, but I heard enough to know that whatever they're planning, it's going to happen soon. I just wish we knew what that something *was*. Maybe even warn the Legion somehow."

Milo reached over and grabbed her hand, making her skin tingle. His calluses scraped her skin gently as he entwined their fingers. She knew it was just for show, but it always took her by surprise whenever he did it.

"Without the staff, it won't matter what their plans are," said Milo. "We've already been here too long. We don't know what's happening out there." His eyes traveled to the angels as they made their way towards a large circular sand pit. "We can't stay here."

Alexa looked up at him surprised. "Of course not. Why would you even say that?"

"Because," he murmured, his thumb rubbing against her hand, "I can see how you like it here. I've never seen you smile back in the Legion. But here… here you're smiling. You seem happy—and that's dangerous."

Alexa tried to pull her hand away, but Milo doubled his grip. "What are you trying to say? That I really *want* to join them? That I want to be part of the destruction of mankind? How can you even say that?"

"I'm just saying I know how attractive this all seems to you," said Milo, "the freedom to do whatever you want, whenever you want." The intensity in his eyes almost made Alexa look away. "But it's not all parties and fun. Don't forget who they are and what they want."

"I know that," grumbled Alexa.

"They don't trust us, but at least they don't know what we're after." Milo traced his thumb along her hand again. "They think we're here to spy on them, not to go after the staff. Let's keep it that way for as long as we can. It's our only advantage at this point. We need to get out of here, soon."

With a grim glare, Alexa nodded. "I know."

Alexa looked away from Milo as she noticed more angels piling out of the pyramid's front entrance. "It's not just me," said Alexa after a while. "You're different here too."

"How do you mean?" Milo sounded mildly surprised.

Alexa swallowed as she fell into step with Milo's pace. "You seem more relaxed, more open. You're back to the Milo I remember, the self-assured and annoying one. Just the way you are with me… our *pretending*," she added carefully, "seems to come to you naturally. It feels as though it's …"

A smile curled its way on Milo's lips. "It's what?"

Alexa glowered. She had the distinct feeling he knew exactly what she meant. "You're going to make me say it, aren't you?"

"You brought it up." Milo was walking with a sudden added spring in his step.

Fine," said Alexa. "It feels *genuine*. There I said it. Happy now? The times you take my hand, the way you smile at me, like the way you're smiling now—feels real."

"And you want to know if it *is* real."

Yes, you moron, Alexa wanted to say. She'd been struggling with her feelings—his feelings towards her—ever since they'd shared that first kiss.

Milo never lessened his grip as he leaned closer and whispered, "Alexa, I—"

Shouts erupted. Alexa and Milo both turned as a large group of angels marched out of the stone pyramid and trooped down the steps. If she had to guess, she'd say the entire order was spilling out of the temple, including Nathaniel. Two very large angels flanked either side of him, and Alexa shuddered at her sudden recognition of them—the archangels Barakiel and Sorath, who had escaped Tartarus with all the other convicts. They were both twice as thick and a head taller than any of the largest angels in the order. Thick and muscled, their ancient armor glinted in the light, marking them as true warriors, as killers.

It was the first time she'd seen the archangels since her arrival on the island, and she wondered where and how they could hide being so large and imposing. Or better yet, why hadn't they appeared at any of the nightly parties?

The dead expression on Milo's face chilled her, but she knew he recognized them.

"I was wondering when they'd show up." Milo's eyes darkened like tiny storms.

"Really? I was hoping to never see them again."

"Horizon isn't big enough to harbor these monsters." Milo's eyes never left the two tall archangels. Alexa opened her mouth to ask more about them just as the beasts turned their heads in unison, as though they'd heard Alexa and Milo talking about them. The archangels watched him for only a moment before glancing away, and they were too far away for Alexa to make out any of it.

"Makes you wonder why they decided to let their presence be known now and not before?" Alexa noticed how Nathaniel walked a little faster between the two archangels, making sure to keep a foot ahead, as though he didn't want the rest of the angels to think the archangels were in charge.

The last of the crowd emptied out from the temple and spilled onto the circular sand pit. The angels stood at the edges of the sand and waited.

Alexa followed Milo as he made for the sand pit, and together they stood with the other angels. Alexa's curiosity rose to higher heights as Brent marched to the center of the pit, a large sword dangling in his hand. His face was lined in anger, his teeth bared like a wild animal about to slaughter its prey.

Alexa leaned forward. "What do you think this is? He looks like he's about to kill someone."

"This is a fighting ring," said Milo. "My—my brothers had a few. Never thought I'd see one in Horizon. We're about to meet his challenger."

Alexa's brows rose. "You're kidding? Huh. Now this is—" the rest of her sentence died in her throat as one of the archangels stepped into the fighting ring.

"Brent's going to fight *him*?" asked Alexa, disbelieving. "Can't be. Can it?"

Milo's jaw was tight. "This isn't right."

"Ya think?" Alexa's voice was loud, and she caught the few neighboring angels glare at her. She glared back before thinking better of it, remembering that she had to keep her true feelings to herself if she wanted to pull the whole Order-of-the-First-GO-campaign off. But she couldn't help but feel a hot anger building inside.

To her dismay, the larger of the archangels had stepped into the fighting pit. Worse, he discarded his armor, tossed it aside as a show of strength, like he didn't need it. He pulled a long, ragged-edged blade from his belt and stood facing Brent. His raven hair draped loosely over his shoulders, and rows of golden loops daggled from his ears. His small eyes were lost under heavy brows. And when he looked down at the smaller angel, who was by no means wimpy by Alexa's standards, he sneered. It chilled Alexa because at that moment he reminded her of Michael, the Head of house Michael. But where Michael was molded to manly perfection, this archangel was on the side of a brute. He was just too big, too muscled to be handsome.

Brent didn't move. He seemed unfazed by the archangel's much larger body, but then his eyes darted over the archangel's shoulder and his frown lessened. Alexa saw his cool slip for just a second. It wasn't fear that registered in his eyes, but pain. She followed his gaze. A tall female angel with a pretty face and curvy body stood apart from the crowd. She was looking down, her hands clenched into fists. The perfect oval of her face looked pale in the light of the sun. She would not look at Brent.

Nathaniel walked along the pit like a master of ceremonies. "As promised, I told you there would be entertainment."

The sudden hush following Nathaniel's speech felt barbaric. Soon, Alexa could smell the excitement and sweat from the crowd. Alexa felt nauseated, her insides jumping at every shift of Milo's feet.

"We have a situation, dear friends." Nathaniel's voice echoed in the silence, his lips pulled back in a wicked smile. "An angel's honor is at risk." A gasp rippled through the assembled crowd. He paused, giving ample time for the effect of his words to settle amongst the crowd.

Alexa's gaze traveled back to Brent. Shadows traveled along his face making him look older, shaken out of its handsome lines as he wrestled with something. He gave a withering glare at the archangel that would curdle milk. But the archangel had never stopped smiling.

Nathaniel's eyes sparked. "A disagreement that can only be resolved by a challenge. Both opponents have accepted to settle this dispute by duel and have agreed to fight with equal weapons."

"How's that equal?" expressed Alexa. "The archangel is twice Brent's size. I don't care how big his sword is. There's no way this is a fair fight."

Milo's mouth tightened. "This isn't a fight."

Alexa frowned. "Then what is it?"

"You all know the rules, *our* code of honor," Nathaniel called, his voice deeper and businesslike. "Once a duel is accepted, there is no turning back. There is no forfeit. You fight to the death. As is our law."

Alexa's intake of breath was echoed by Milo's low curse. She realized he had expected it. He had known all along what the sand pit was.

Although Brent was on the wrong side of the Legion, she felt sorry for him. He was going to risk his life for that female angel. She was sure of it. The pretty female angel still wouldn't look up, but she teetered slightly as though she was about to faint.

Looking smug, Nathaniel turned his attention to the two opponents. "Do you accept?"

Brent was the first to speak. "I accept."

Nathaniel's smile widened as he turned to the large archangel. "And you, Barakiel. Do you accept his challenge?"

"I accept." Barakiel's voice was nothing like Alexa was expecting. It wasn't rough and hard like his exterior, but rather deep and smooth like the purr of a tiger. He stole a look over his shoulder to the female angel, and Alexa felt a tremor along her skin at the look in his eyes.

Nathaniel stepped back into the crowd and shouted, "To the death!"

"To the death!" repeated the angels.

"I think I'm going to be sick," muttered Alexa.

Much to her surprise, Brent delivered the first attack.

With motion almost too quick to be seen, Brent dashed forward like a piston. He leaped in the air, his sword arm high. He brought it down fast, a killing blow, and Alexa was reminded of Milo's fighting agility. But Brent's next strike went wide, and his sword's tip buried itself in the sand.

There was a blur of sand. Barakiel slashed Brent on his back before Alexa saw him move. It was like nothing she had ever seen before. The archangel moved like a specter, like a shadow of himself. Brent hissed loudly, lost his balance and pitched forward, landing in the sand with his arms bent awkwardly. White light spilled from a large opening on his back.

Alexa's stomach dropped. *Brent's dead,* she thought. But in the next moment, the angel twisted around, and he was back on his feet. His face wore a look of awe and fear, but he was still alive. Alexa was impressed.

Barakiel also looked impressed. "You surprise me, angel. But your show of strength is useless. You're no match for an archangel." He lifted his sword and pointed. "I'll take good care of Sarah."

A sound similar to Lance's growl erupted from Brent's throat, and he leaped forward again. He'd lost his composure to his anger. By the smug smile on his Barakiel's face, it was exactly the response he had anticipated.

"We have to stop this, Milo. Brent's going to get killed."

Milo sighed. "We can't, Alexa. If we do anything, it'll be like we don't agree with the order. They'd see it as a reason to kill us next."

Despite the anger bubble that threatened to explode through her chest, Alexa knew Milo was right.

Brent moved with the fast elegance of a dance—a dance with death. And Barakiel was there, whirling with cold grace. With an almost bored expression, Barakiel blocked every strike without an effort. It was an onslaught of flashing blades. Pivoting, Brent came up and around the big archangel, going for his thigh with the point of his blade. But Barakiel knocked it away, using his momentum to run him through the chest with his sword. Alexa saw the archangel lean forward and whisper something in Brent's ear before he pulled back his sword.

Brent fell to his knees. His angel essence ran from the corners of his mouth and down his neck. He touched his stomach, looking at his angel blood as if it meant something.

Barakiel moved to stand in front of Brent and raised his sword. "You fought bravely, but you were foolish to lose your life over a female."

Alexa's soul cracked at the pain in Brent's face. The agony in his eyes wasn't from Barakiel's blows, from any physical pain, but from the emotional pain of losing a loved one.

Alexa felt Milo's fingers tighten around hers, and her eyes burned.

Brent moved his lips and closed his eyes. Barakiel's sword came down in a frightening sweep, taking Brent's head right off his shoulders. It landed with a thump and stopped moving.

Alexa jerked forward, ready to shout, but Milo squeezed her hand so hard it hurt.

"Don't."

Brent's body shimmered and then broke apart into tiny brilliant particles, until they dissipated into the air and nothing was left of Brent but his sword in the sand.

Alexa was horrified at seeing an angel's true death for the first time. There was no coming back from this, but she was even more upset that no one said anything.

The crowd of angels was silent, their faces void of expression, almost robot-like. They stared at the evaporating particles that had once been Brent with an acceptance that made Alexa nauseated. She hated this group of cowards more than anything.

The sound of shuffling reached Alexa's ears as the crowd parted. Her eyes moved to Sarah, but the angel was gone.

CHAPTER 16

BRENT'S DEATH HAUNTED ALEXA. It left her feeling sick and disturbed. No matter how much she tried, she couldn't get over the last look on his face before he died—sadness with an acceptance of defeat, but with a broken heart.

It pained her to think of the way he died, with everyone watching like he was the entertainment of the day. His death was just a show for the members of the order. There was no way back from an angel's true death. Knowing now that a mortal soul was reborn when the mortal died, it left her feeling empty that Brent's soul would never be reborn. His death was final.

Alexa tipped her glass to her lips. She rolled the wine over with her tongue, tasting grape with a hint of chocolate. She could taste the alcohol. There wasn't much, but she could taste it. Her eyes moved around the assembled angels, drinking red and golden liquid from their glasses. Lance had told her once that an angel needed to drink a lot to feel the effects from alcohol. She suspected that each angel had drunk at least twenty or so glasses, their laughter and level of voices increasing with each glass.

She had sipped the same glass for the past three hours. Milo hadn't drunk anything, or even pretended to. His refusal did grant him a few suspicious looks, but then when they saw Alexa sipping from her glass, it seemed to calm everyone down.

The drums beat faster and faster, making her on edge as she sat next to Milo on the beach before one of the four giant bonfires with the bright stars twinkling above them.

Alexa stared across the fire to where Nathaniel lounged on a bed of pillows. His black eyes seemed to burn in the firelight. A boy angel who looked about twelve, in a linen robe-like garment, poured golden liquid into Nathaniel's cup from a crystal decanter. His hands trembled, and the liquid spilled over Nathaniel's outstretched hand.

"You idiot!" Nathaniel hissed and smacked the boy across the face. The boy dropped the decanter as he cowered to his knees. "You spilled it all over me." He whipped the cup at the boy's head. "Get me a new cup."

With trembling hands, the boy gathered up the cup and decanter and, still bent in submission, managed to walk away.

There was a loud snort followed by laughter.

Alexa's eyes rested on the other archangel Sorath, lounging on top of pillows and a Persian carpet. He laughed alongside Nathaniel as the boy struggled to keep his bent position up the steps to the pyramid.

Alexa dug the fingers of her free hand in the sand. Next to Sorath sat Barakiel. He dragged a finger, seductively over the angel Sarah's neck. Even in the darkness and distance, Alexa could see the broken female trembling. Her pretty face was pinched tightly, her eyes a mixture of fear and resentment.

Alexa pulled her eyes away and began to swirl the contents of her cup. It wasn't hatred she felt for Nathaniel, the order, and the archangels, she decided. Hatred was too small a word and emotion to equal what she felt inside.

"The order doesn't seem to be bothered that they've just lost one of their own in a stupid duel," murmured Alexa. "They're acting like it never happened. Like Brent's life meant nothing."

Yellow flames reflected in Milo's eyes. "Makes you realize how little they think of mortal lives if they can murder one of their own without shedding a single tear."

A group of female angels in shapeless linen robes arrived with decanters and began to serve the angels assembled around the fire.

Alexa leaned closer to Milo, doing her best to ignore the prickling of her skin at his proximity. "These servant angels," she whispered, "did you know about that?"

Milo's lips were a tight line. "Nathaniel's not happy unless he exploits some of the angels. He has his favorites while he has groups of lesser angels to do as he commands. Treats them like slaves."

Alexa raised her brows. "Lesser angels? That's what the angel Naja had called me when we first arrived here. I thought you said all angels are equal in Horizon."

182

"I did. Lesser angel is a highly derogatory term. It's used to imply those angels created from a human soul, angels who were once human."

"Like me," whispered Alexa, feeling a little sick again.

"It's really offensive. We don't use the term anymore," said Milo. "But there are those who are prejudiced against angels who they consider to be of lower worth and undeserving to be equal. Nathaniel and a group of the first created angels decided to put themselves above the others because they felt more powerful, more deserving. Many older angels place great emphasis on the first created and reject association with newborn angels who've had a mortal past, whom they consider greatly inferior to themselves. The notion is foremost in the minds of The Order of the First and other followers of Nathaniel."

Alexa gripped her cup. "Well, I think it's disgusting."

"They are the deluded ones!" came a voice to her far right. Alexa turned and saw the angel known as Chris standing around another fire. His voice was loud over the beating drums, and a drink was in his hand. "Slaves to the inferior mortal creation. Chained to do their bidding! Us! Angels! It's absurd. The Legion has misled us all for thousands of years. Sacrificing ourselves for them! Them! The lesser creation."

A growl escaped Alexa's throat, low enough for only Milo to hear. Her face twitched as she tried to keep it from showing any emotion.

"It's sacrilege," said another female angel, who was built like a wrestler with neck muscles bulging and her face framed in an angry frown. "We should have never agreed to it."

"Blasphemy!" cried a tall dark angel as he threw his drink into the fire. "We should have destroyed the Legion years ago!"

"Calm yourselves, brothers and sisters." Nathaniel's voice rose above the others. He waited for the angels to quiet themselves before he continued. "Soon you will get what was promised. These mortal dogs can make our kind so lust-blind that we lose all common sense. Better for us to see their true nature. Our slaves," he laughed. "We will rejoice in all the fine wines of the world and all its pleasures."

There was an answering cheer from the crowd of angels. Nathaniel's eyes traveled over the angels and settled on Alexa for a moment before moving on.

"Time's nearly up," said Nathaniel. "The Legion had their hour. Our time has come, the time for the first creation to rule both worlds—mortal and celestial. The time is now."

The large female angel spoke up. "I'm tired of waiting. Why not strike now? Why do *we* have to wait in hiding when it is our right to take what we want? We have the numbers—the strength to do it now."

"Because, dear Samantha." Nathaniel's smile was sinister, and Alexa heard more danger in the silkiness of his voice than in the powerful blow from the archangel Barakiel. "You forget who we serve… the only and one true lord. We wait for our lord's orders."

Tension surfaced on Samantha's face at the challenge in Nathaniel's voice. "Of course," she said. "Of course we wait."

Satisfied, Nathaniel's gaze rolled over the beach at the gathered angels. "Anyone who continues to resist—archangel, angel or even lesser angel—will be slaughtered. We are the *true* angels, born of noble stock, and we will take what is ours. Rejoice, brothers and sisters, for our hour is near. Rejoice in the new world we shall build together!"

Another cheer welled from the gathered angels along with a fresh outbreak of laughter. Chris cheered the loudest as he stumbled around and nearly fell into the fire.

Movement caught her attention and she saw Barakiel leading Sarah away from the fire. Alexa kept staring at the tension in the woman's shoulders and the way her legs dragged like she didn't want to go anywhere but was forced and had no choice. She kept watching until Sarah's delicate shape disappeared through the brush and there was only darkness.

Alexa turned away, clenching her jaw. Nathaniel leaned back into his plush cushions. His eyes met Alexa and she thought she saw them narrow for a second. His gratified smile looked more like a snarl as she forced herself to look away before her face betrayed her.

She felt Milo tense next to her. Soon, their façade would fail, and she knew eventually their emotions would give them away. Even Milo couldn't pretend for much longer. He was losing his cool.

"The battle is won," said Nathaniel in a voice that burst with triumph. "The Legion is finished. We shall not be here for long."

A murmur of agreement from those assembled echoed around her, stabbing her like tiny knives.

Alexa looked over to Milo, his face echoing the fear she felt inside.

"Well, as it happens," said Nathaniel. "I'm bored to tears of this sullen silence. More wine!" Nathaniel grabbed the wrist of one of the servant females with long, raven-black hair and pulled her onto his lap.

Alexa looked away, her insides twisted. It took a concentrated effort not to empty the contents of her cup. Instead, she buried her cup in the sand.

"It's time." She leaned forward and turned her head so that her back was to Nathaniel. "He'll be busy for a while. Let's do this now. I don't know when we'll get another chance."

Milo's expression was grim, but he nodded. He stood up, pulling Alexa with him. His chest crushed against hers, and his arms wrapped around her tightly. Alexa's head swam as he leaned forward. His lips brushed against her ear as he said, "Relax. This is just for show."

Alexa couldn't relax. She didn't think she could talk. Her body trembled slightly at Milo's touch, his strong arms around her. Her body temperature went up a few degrees as he released her, and when he grabbed her hand it was exceedingly gentle despite the hard calluses. Smiling, Milo led Alexa away from the fire, and she couldn't help but think that he was enjoying the pretend relationship status a little too much.

Alexa and Milo moved away in silence. A fire burned in the middle of the beach, and its flickering light fell over a crowd of angels as they danced to the beat of the drums. She felt the watchful eyes of the other angels as they walked past. Some of them were still dancing while others lounged in the sand huddled together.

The image of Nathaniel's triumphant smile haunted her. It fueled her with both anger and fear—anger at the thought of the devastation of the mortal world at the hands of the order and fear that he felt as though he'd already won the war.

Alexa's mind whirled with questions and uncertainties. What if he *had* won? What if Alexa and Milo were on a fool's errand? What if they were risking their lives searching for the Staff of Heaven for nothing? What if it was already too late?

Alexa kept her fears to herself as she let Milo pull her along, up the steps, and past the pyramid's main entrance. Lit torches lined the walls, illuminating the hallway in shades of gold, and cast long, quirky, dark shadows on the stone floors.

"Where do you suppose his quarters are?" inquired Milo as they passed the main hall and made their way towards a large staircase made of the same stone as the walls. His callused fingers stayed wrapped around Alexa's hand as they walked.

"Well," she said as she slipped her hand free, seeing as there was no one around. "Since Nathaniel has such a high opinion of himself... I'm thinking the top floor. We've never had the chance to look up there."

Milo's smile was radiant. "After you, darling."

Alexa wanted to punch him, but she didn't want to mess up his pretty face. "Thanks, hot stuff. We better hurry. Nathaniel gets bored really quickly. Let's hope he hasn't noticed we're gone."

Together, they dashed up the stairs two at a time, climbing past the first and second landings without seeing anyone. Just when Alexa felt it was way too easy, a servant angel female bobbed into view, carrying a load of pillows and blankets.

Milo grabbed Alexa and pinned her to the wall, her shoulders smacking against the cold stone, and kissed her.

His warm lips crushed against hers and Alexa's head swam. She heard the other angel giggle as she moved past them, her footsteps echoing loudly against the stone stairs.

Just when Alexa had relaxed into the kiss, when she couldn't hear the angel's footsteps anymore, Milo pulled away.

"She's gone. Come on."

Alexa forced the smile away from her face as she raced to catch up to Milo's supernatural speed. They continued up the stairs until they reached the topmost and final landing where there were only two doors. Milo crept towards the first door. While his right hand was wrapped around the handle of one of his spirit sabers, he lifted the iron latch and pushed the door open. It swung open with a loud screech, making Alexa flinch.

Both Alexa and Milo waited to hear the servant's footsteps coming their way, but after a few moments Milo gave Alexa a nod of his head as he crept in first. He waited until Alexa had moved past him and then he shut the door quietly.

Alexa followed and glanced around. Two things hit her immediately—the musty smell of sweat and perfume and how dark it was. The room was covered in darkness. There were no windows that she could see, and she immediately wished Milo hadn't shut the door. They could have used the light from the hallway.

"Don't worry. Your eyes will adjust in a moment," came Milo's voice from somewhere behind her, making her jump.

Just as Milo had said, Alexa's eyes adjusted to the darkness, and shapes came into view. The chamber was set up as a bedroom. It was spacious with a large four-post bed sporting an intricately carved wooden headboard and multiple layers of colorful throws and blankets. The blankets were heaved in messy piles over the bed as though someone had jumped out of bed quickly or had had a fight. The bed was obscured by long velvet curtains. A chandelier thickly coated in dust hung from the tall ceiling, its candle scrubs still resting in its sockets.

She could make out two iron mounted torch holders fastened to the back wall, one on each side of the bed.

"I guess lighting the torches would be a bad idea, huh? I don't know how we'll find anything in the dark like this. Even with our *special* eyesight. We're not cats."

Milo's boots padded near her and she blinked as his face came into focus. "If someone sees the light beneath the door," he said, his voice low, "we're done for it. We can't risk it. We'll have to work in the dark. No choice. Besides, the dark won't matter. The staff is made of delor metal. It'll glow. So, it's probably better that it's dark in here. Trust me, if it's here, you won't miss it."

189

The wardrobe doors stood open and clothes lay in piles on the floor while other still hung neatly inside. There was a giant mirror that went from floor to ceiling.

"This is Nathaniel's bedroom," said Alexa.

Milo whirled around, his voice curious. "How do you know? It could be for one of the archangels."

"Only he would have such a giant mirror to fit his *giant* head."

Milo snorted. "You check the wardrobe—and I'll check the bed and small tables."

Slightly irritated, Alexa began to search the contents of the wardrobe. She was even more certain that this was Nathaniel's dressing chamber as she picked through white linens that matched his style. Her nose wiggled at a faint citrus scent. All angels had the same lemony scent. It was how they could sense each other. But Nathaniel's scent was different, not as lemon-flavored and more like curdled milk.

Alexa gagged. Making a face, she moved the clothes out of her way and slid her hands inside the wardrobe, looking for a secret door. But after a few minutes of searching it was clear the staff wasn't here.

"It's not here," said Milo as he pulled himself from under the bed and crossed the room towards the door.

Alexa gladly heaved herself out of the smelly wardrobe and followed him. "If it's not in here, it has to be in the next room."

Alexa's stress rose to a higher level as Milo tried the second door.

"It's locked." Milo looked strained and anxious. "Move back."

"Yes, master." Alexa gave him a sarcastic smile and he stood there with a strange expression on his face.

"What?" Alexa's face warmed.

Voices flowed up from the first landing.

"Hurry!" hissed Alexa, but Milo had already pulled out one of his swords and with a quick slice of his saber, cut the iron lock. There was a clunk as the severed part hit the stone floor.

Milo pushed the door open with his shoulder. Alexa followed him in. The second room wasn't as dark as the first one. Filaments of silver light spilled from a window across from them, and the same velvet drapes from the previous chamber hung from a thick wooden rod and framed the window. Instead of a bed, there was a large wooden desk, its legs carved in the shape of eagles. Papers and maps littered the top. Books and scrolls lined the back walls in floor-to-ceiling bookcases.

Alexa's gaze wandered to a portrait that showed Nathaniel sitting in a throne-like chair. At his feet was a giant white eagle. Alexa was strangely reminded of Metatron.

"This is his study," exclaimed Alexa, her nerves pounding through her.

Milo followed her gaze to the portrait. "Now that's interesting."

"More like creepy."

As Alexa moved deeper into the room, she heard a scurrying of feet and the murmur of voices.

"Someone's coming! Hurry!" she whispered.

Alexa and Milo went into action. They raced around the chamber without speaking. Milo sheathed his sword and went straight to work on the bookcases while Alexa attacked the desk. She yanked open the drawers, and it was only as she searched the last one that she realized her mistake.

"How big do you think the staff is?" her voice was loud with desperation, and she hated herself for it.

Milo dropped a handful of scrolls. "No idea. But if it was made for the archangel Michael, I'm guessing it's probably big."

Alexa stared back at the desk and its small drawers, shaking her head. Angry tears threatened to spill as she looked about the room. It wasn't here.

"The drawers are too small," she whispered to herself. Desperation and fear filled her, suffocating her until she felt as though she was drowning in water.

She strained her ears and heard the footsteps and voices getting louder and louder. Panic sliced through her like the stab of a death blade. She couldn't fail. She had to find the staff. She'd already lost the Holy Fire. If they couldn't find the staff...

A small frustrated cry escaped Alexa as she pushed the thoughts from her head and cleared Nathaniel's desk in one sweep. Books fell with a loud thump on the ground. She didn't care. If they didn't find the staff now, it wouldn't matter if they got caught.

The voices grew louder until Alexa felt as though they were in the next chamber.

Alexa's pulsed raced. "It's not here. I was so certain. I—I was wrong."

Milo's face was wrinkled in worry. "It has to be here. It's the only place he'd hide it."

"Maybe not," said Alexa, her voice trembling. "Maybe he buried it somewhere on the island. Maybe we'll never find it…"

Fear lapped at her as she looked over the chamber, at the piles of books and papers that littered the floor, the desk and the walls. The room looked burglarized.

She had failed again. The oracle should have entrusted someone else with the task.

Dread and guilt gripped Alexa at the sight of Milo's anxious expression. If they were to die now, if they were caught, it was her fault, all her fault. She had consented to the plan, given Milo the idea… She had been so sure Nathaniel would have hidden it here…

"Maybe we're looking at it wrong," she whispered to herself, "maybe it doesn't glow… yes, it doesn't glow… and it's long and tubular…"

Alexa's eyes moved past Milo to the window. The curtain rod was made of wood, and Alexa felt it was way too thick to hang drapes. It was long, tubular, the perfect size for a staff…

"Son of a—"

"What? What is it?" Milo turned on the spot.

"The curtain rod," she said and rushed to the window. "How could we have missed it?"

Even now as she stood before it, she felt it. It was faint, enough to have missed it, but when she pulled her angels senses towards it, there was no mistaking that this stick—this curtain rod—was a celestial creation.

"I thought you said it was made of delor metal? This is wood."

"I thought it *was*," said Milo as he shrugged next to her, his eyes on the curtain rod. "I was wrong."

"It's a stick—a wooden stick—a wooden staff."

Alexa reached out and pulled her hand back. "Maybe you should take it." The power of the staff reminded her of the Helm of Darkness, and for a second she feared she would lose herself to its power.

Milo shook his head and gave her a warm smile when he saw the fear in Alexa's face. "No. You should take it. The oracle left you the instructions, not me. Besides, I don't think I should touch it. It's giving me a strange feeling... like some kind of warning that I shouldn't touch it."

Alexa observed the shadows that danced across Milo's face. "Because you're Lucifer's son."

"Because I'm Lucifer's son," he repeated. "The staff was created to destroy Lucifer. It might recognize the part of my father that's in me. I think it already has. It might even kill me."

Alexa felt her chest cave in on her. "But you're an angel now. You can't be blamed for who your father is and what he's done."

"Even then," said Milo. "I wouldn't underestimate the power of that staff. Let's play it safe. You take it. Go on. Take it."

Alexa stared at the staff. And when she reached out again, she noticed that her fingers were shaking.

"It can't hurt you," said Milo, seeing her distress. "Take it."

"I hope you're right."

Alexa swallowed hard, hauled up on her toes, reached out and grabbed the staff. The drapes fell to the floor as she lifted it off its hinges. With her fingers wrapped around the wood, she gave a start at the warmth of it, as though it had been sitting in the sun for hours. It pulsed slightly, like the soft murmur of bees. She pulled it closer and inspected it, rubbing her thumb with the grain in the wood.

"There're no markings," she said as she flipped it over. "I can't see any sigils. It looks just like an ordinary wooden stick—"

"I can assure you that it is nothing of the sort," came a familiar voice.

The chamber door crashed open.

Alexa's hand froze around the staff.

Nathaniel stood in the doorway, his dark skin contrasting against the white of his clothes. Barakiel grinned next to him, and a dark sword hung in his beefy hands.

Nathaniel's eyes narrowed at the sight of the staff in Alexa's hand. "I knew the two of you were up to something. It's why I had you followed. I never believed your story. Not for a second. You might be in love or you might not—I really don't care—but I knew whatever feelings you might have for each other weren't reason enough for Lucifer's son to want to partake in his father's plans. We know you've been distancing yourself from him since you were born."

Milo shifted his body protectively in front of Alexa. "What can I say? You're right. I would never be involved with my father's insane plans. And I'll do everything in my power to stop him from spreading his evil."

"Is that what you think?" Nathaniel laughed softly and Barakiel joined in. "Spreading his evil?" he repeated as he stared at the staff. "Your father was right in not sharing his plans with you. You can't be trusted. And you—" said Nathaniel as he looked at Alexa. "The only reason I wanted you here was to keep an eye on you. You're still very much a mystery. Things seem to fall into your hands. Don't they? A wonder at your inferiority. But you never belonged here. The Order of the First is exactly that—made up of the *first* angels. You on the other hand are a newborn, a lesser angel that doesn't deserve to be a part of our order."

"Who says I'd want to belong in your psychotic cult?" spat Alexa.

"I thought you were spying for the Legion," jeered Nathaniel, his body taut as his dark eyes stared, like a snake that was about to strike. "I thought you were sent to discover our plans. But seeing you now with *that* in your hands… I'm not so sure." He cocked his head to the side. "It seems to me that you're here on your own. It's just the two of you, isn't it? Tell me, has the Legion abandoned you?" He laughed.

"You're nothing but a thug." Alexa's anger rose at the truth in his words, devouring any common sense. "You're a psychopath. Just like Lucifer and Hades."

Nathaniel clicked his tongue. "Yes, yes, yes. Give me back what's mine."

Alexa stood her ground. "It doesn't belong to you. It belongs to the Legion."

Nathaniel stepped into the room. "You have no idea what you're holding."

Alexa watched as Barakiel broke away from the doorway, tossing his sword from hand to hand in anticipation, as though he couldn't wait to get the fighting started.

"I think I do." Alexa wiggled the staff and grinned. "It's a walking stick, right? Or is it a wizard's wand? No, wait—I know— it's a hockey stick."

Nathaniel spat something at her in a language that sounded like Latin. "You're going to wish you'd stayed in Tartarus after I'm finished with you." Nathaniel's smile would have frightened an ordinary young angel, but Alexa didn't feel ordinary anymore, so she smiled back at him.

"You think you're something special. Don't you?" expressed Nathaniel. "Because of the soul channeling power you once possessed? *Once* being the operative word here. You've been stripped of your powers because you're not worthy."

Alexa flinched, and her grip on the staff slipped as she struggled for something to say but couldn't find the words. She was surprised at how much losing the soul channeling ability still affected her. Was he right? Would another angel, a more valued angel, have kept the special gift?

"Don't listen to him, Alexa," said Milo. "You're worth a thousand of him."

Alexa strained to keep it together. This wasn't the time to let her emotions take control of her. There was too much at stake. She was strong. Stronger than Nathaniel thought.

"You're nothing but a filthy lesser angel," sneered Nathaniel. "A mistake that I'm about to rectify. Kill them!"

With a powerful throw, Barakiel threw his sword like a lance. Its tip winked as it came straight for Alexa—

But Milo was there. With surprising speed, he was already pulling Alexa with him towards the window. The window from the third floor. Before she even knew what was happening, Milo jumped out the window and pulled Alexa down with him.

CHAPTER 17

ALEXA SCREAMED LIKE A BANSHEE all the way down, a mortal reaction to plummeting to death. Blurs of taupe and beige rose up on either side. Three thoughts came into her mind. One, she knew she wouldn't die from the fall. Two, her ankles would snap as soon as her feet touched the ground. And three, she would kill Milo if he wasn't badly damaged.

Alexa tightened her muscles and braced for impact. It was going to hurt.

Yet she rebounded on something soft, bouncing like she was on a large trampoline. Alexa lay on her back on a bed of white feathers, the staff still secured in her hand. A nervous giggle escaped her. That's when she heard the loud screech before she was thrown in the air and landed on the ground next to a giant white eagle. The bird screeched angrily again, and with a great beat of its wings, it lifted off the ground, hovering for a moment, and then soared in the air and flew away.

Alexa squinted through the dust and looked up. Nathaniel's angry face stared down at her from the window. His lips moved and then he disappeared back into the chamber.

A hand wiggled in her line of sight.

"Come on," said Milo as he grabbed Alexa's hand and pulled her to her feet. "We've only got a few seconds before the entire order is after us."

"Please tell me you knew there was an eagle outside that window," exclaimed Alexa as she ran alongside Milo.

"I didn't." Milo's voice held a trace of mischief. "Lucky for us there was."

Alexa snorted. "I don't believe in luck."

They crossed the front gardens and headed towards the beach. Alexa cursed as she fell behind in a matter of seconds. She wasn't running fast enough with the staff. It was long, and holding it kept her from using her right arm to push her run. Soon Milo had disappeared through the first line of trees.

He came bounding back into view. "Alexa, what are you doing? You need to run faster!"

"What does it look like I'm doing? Picking flowers? I'm running as fast as I can!" she yelled, slightly irritated as she nearly tripped. "You try and run with this thing! It's almost as tall as I am."

Milo reached out as if to take the staff from Alexa, but he hesitated at the last moment. "I can't. I can't take it. I'm sorry but it has to be you."

"Fine." Alexa could feel the strain in her arm from holding the staff too tightly. "Just don't run so fast. My legs aren't as long as yours."

"There they are!" roared a voice from behind them.

Alexa turned to see a group of at least twenty angels barreling towards them, their faces wrinkled in anger and fury, all heavily armed with soul blades and swords.

The sound of angry shouts echoed in the air as another voice bellowed, "Don't let them reach the water!"

"Quick! We need to reach the shore before they do!" Milo shot forward, branches snapping around him as he made his way through the trees, leaving a clear path for Alexa.

Alexa cursed as she galloped behind Milo, her legs straining with the effort to keep up with his supernatural speed. But it was no use. No matter how hard she tried, her legs didn't move fast enough. Milo slowed his speed so that she could catch up. He turned his head over his shoulder, his face pulled tight, and his handsome features sliding in and out of sight as the branches of overhanging trees broke the moonlight. Stress pumped through her body like warm blood through veins, pushing her like a shot of adrenaline, but still she wasn't fast enough.

She was slowing them down. The staff was slowing them down. They weren't going to make it.

Fear licked up her spine as she heard what sounded like hundreds of angels coming after her, uttering loud war cries. Darkness surrounded her, the thickness of the trees blanketed the light of the moon and the stars. It was pitch black. Even with her angel night vision, she could barely see. Led by her hearing, Alexa followed the snapping of branches and the heavy tread that came from Milo.

More cries sounded behind her. Louder. Closer.

Blinking around in the darkness she suddenly realized that she'd lost Milo. She stopped, panic pulsing in the pit of her stomach as she searched the forest for her companion. Her spirits plummeted. He was gone—

Light spilled from her right. Through the thicket of trees, she could make out a clearing and the top of a blond head.

Alexa bounded forward towards the clearing, putting all her energy, all her strength into her legs as she crashed through the trees. Branches slapped at her face, cutting her skin like hot knives. But she never stopped. She could almost feel the hands of the angels behind her, wrapping around her neck, squeezing. She pushed harder.

Alexa sensed, by a freshening of the air and the smell of salt water, that she had reached the edge of the forest. Branches and shrubbery crackled beneath her feet as she sped toward the clearing. She belted past the last of the trees, her boots dragging and heavy in the sand. Then she crashed into a hard body.

"Milo?" she looked up, stumbling. "Why did you stop? We need to keep moving."

But Milo just looked straight ahead.

Alexa followed his gaze.

An army the size of the one that was coming up from behind them formed a line on the beach, blocking their way to the water.

Alexa recognized most of them as the angels who had been partying by the bonfires.

"Stay close." Milo pulled his spirit sabers free. He stood shoulder to shoulder with Alexa. "Whatever you do, don't let go of the staff."

Alexa drew her soul blade with her other hand, clasping it tightly and wishing she was ambidextrous.

There was a shuffling of branches and the other army of angels that had been pursuing them spilled out of the forest, forming a tight circle around them. The angels parted, and Nathaniel strode towards Alexa and Milo, Barakiel and Sorath following closely behind him like brute bodyguards. They stood shoulder to shoulder, swords pointing at Alexa and Milo.

"Did you think you would steal from me and I'd let you leave?" asked Nathaniel in a soft voice like a snake's hiss.

Alexa shrugged. "Maybe." She smiled at the frown on Nathaniel's face.

The crowd stirred as they drew in a collective breath. Alexa brought the staff closer to her chest. Her arm started to strain from the weight. It was heavier than it looked for a mere piece of wood.

"You'll never leave with it. Hand it over." Nathaniel's face was lost in the darkness.

"We're not giving it back." Milo's voice was strong as though he was confident he was going to win their fight, and it filled Alexa with a new sense of courage.

"That is unfortunate," said Nathaniel. "You don't even know how to use it."

Alexa swung the staff in her hands. "We'll take our chances."

Sorath gave a delighted laugh. "It'll be a pleasure to kill that one."

Alexa made a rude gesture with her finger.

"You have two choices," said Nathaniel, the white of his clothes glowing in the light of the moon and making him look like a great big light bulb.

"Only two?" mocked Alexa. "Lucky us."

"Give me the staff and I'll be merciful and kill you swiftly," said Nathaniel, his voice controlled as if he was discussing a business proposal. "One clean cut across the neck. No suffering. No mess."

"That doesn't sound very clean to me," muttered Alexa and her chest swelled at the smile on Milo's face.

"Or two," continued Nathaniel as though Alexa hadn't spoken, "we'll gut you like the mortal-loving pigs that you are."

"Better that than being in love with Lucifer," spat Alexa. She saw shock flit across Nathaniel's face, but it was instantly dispelled as he began to laugh. The sound was more frightening—a cold, humorless and insane laugh that echoed around the silent gathering of angels.

"Most of you lesser angels have chosen to side with the mortals and forget why we angels were created."

"Really?" asked Alexa sarcastically. "And why's that?"

"To rule," he said. "To rule over the lesser creations. Mortals. Angels. It doesn't matter. Anyway," Nathaniel went on, "the first-born angels have specific powers the lesser angels don't. We don't have a natural-born affinity. We just exist…to rule."

"I seriously doubt that." Alexa trembled in anger and gripped her soul blade in her sweaty hand.

Nathaniel huffed a vicious laugh. "For having the nerve to request where I slaughter you, I'll let you in on a secret, lesser angel. The order will claim your miserable life and all the lives of the lesser angels for they are not the true form. They don't even deserve to live."

Alexa glanced around at the gathered angels, looking for any of the angel servants, and was thankful she didn't see any. But she noticed how close they were. The angels had closed in on them while she and Nathaniel had been chatting.

There were angels of every shape, age, and sex, different in all ways except for one—the hateful glare they all shared for her and Milo.

Forty plus angels against two was a massacre. Nathaniel's winning smile said it all. There was no hope. There were just too many. Even if they had the staff, she didn't know how to use it, and she doubted she had the time to swing at one while five more angels sliced her head off.

But Alexa wouldn't go down without a fight. She had to try. It was the least she could do, and she promised herself she'd take down as many as she could.

"We duel," said Milo. His voice was low and rough, and his eyes were full of hate. "I challenge two of your best warriors against the two of us. As angels, we have a right to fight for what we believe is true. The code applies to all angels, even those not in the order."

A wave of agreement wafted through the angels, and Nathaniel's eyes narrowed.

"If we lose, we die, and you get your staff back," said Milo. "But if we win, you let us go. Agreed?"

Nathaniel's face was void of emotion, but Alexa could tell he was struggling with something.

"Let them fight," said a male angel with glasses resting on his plump face.

"Yeah, let them," agreed another.

"Honor the code," said another.

"Do you decline the challenge?" pressed Milo, taking a confident step forward.

"Agreed," Nathaniel said finally. He hesitated for a moment and then added with a callous smile, "I accept your challenge."

Immediately the angels moved back, leaving a large circle—a fighting circle.

Alexa leaned forward and whispered, "Milo, what are you doing?"

"Trust me," he said, as though that was enough to calm her nerves. It wasn't.

Alexa's knees quaked, and she tried to keep her shaking to a minimum. She wouldn't let Nathaniel see how nervous she was.

Nathaniel laughed. "Are you willing to accept your fate so easily?" When Alexa and Milo just stared at him, he said, "It makes killing you far more enjoyable. As you wish." Nathaniel snapped his fingers, and the two archangels came forward, long, angry swords dangling between them. The light of the moon cast shadows on their faces making them even more brutish and ogre looking than before.

Alexa felt herself go weak in the knees. "I hope you know what you're doing," she hissed. "You do remember that I'm barely out of fledging status. Your words, not mine. Although I hate to admit it, I do feel you might be right at the moment."

Milo shrugged and said, "I figured our odds were better two against two than two against forty."

Alexa raised her brows. "Ya think?"

Milo's smile lit up his face. He looked like a school boy who'd just stolen the principal's keys to his office. "I do."

"Kill them," barked Nathaniel, "and bring me my staff!"

At once the archangels charged before Alexa could express how unfair she felt it was fighting an archangel. Without her soul channeling powers, she was as good as dead. Worse, the bigger archangel came straight for her.

The archangel Barakiel swept before her like a gust of wind. She threw her blade arm up and saw light from one of the fires bounce off his armor as he spun past. She heard the ring of steel and realized she was on her knees. Her blade hand tingled and stung. How could he move that fast? She'd seen Milo in action, and with his archangel blood, he was faster than most. But Barakiel's speed was surreal, and fear formed in the pit of her gut.

Something moved in her peripheral vision, and Alexa pitched forward, rolling on the ground. Feeling something move over her head, she jumped to her feet with her soul blade brandished before her and the staff secured in her other hand.

"Don't let go of the staff!" she heard Milo shout just as Barakiel charged at her again.

Sand sprayed around them. Alexa burst into action, diving forward with her blade. But she tripped when her foot tangled with the staff.

She went down, driving the tip of her weapon into the archangel's cold face, only to be hurled off with a twist so swift that she could hardly follow the movement. Alexa hit the sand hard but heaved herself to her feet and faced her opponent. She knew a second wasted on the ground was all the archangel needed to drive his sword into her chest.

Across the pit, she spotted Milo, wide-eyed with his spirit sabers in his hands. Sorath was grinning like a starving man before a feast. Angels whispered amongst each other, their eyes locked on the pit as hungrily as Sorath.

"Say nighty night, little lesser angel." Barakiel attacked once more, sending blows of such wild wrath and wicked delight.

Then they were again a blur of limbs and blows and sand. Alexa didn't know how long her luck would stand. She blocked and parried with her soul blade, using it as an extension of her hand. But she faltered as she tried to keep the staff close to her body. It was hindering her more than anything. The staff was going to get her killed.

"Shame you're not even pretty enough to tempt me to keep you as one of my consorts," said Barakiel as he pointed his long sword at Alexa.

"Glad to hear it," said Alexa although her pride was a *tiny* bit hurt. "That's probably a good thing for you. I wouldn't be a very good lady friend. See, I'd kill you in your sleep."

Barakiel smiled. It made his features soften and he was almost handsome. Almost.

He moved like the wind again. Alexa made to move her arm, but it was too late. Laughter reached her ears as Barakiel's hand came up, and the air moved as Alexa felt a blow to her face, hard as a hammer. Pain exploded on her cheek and jaw as she went hurtling in the air. She blinked the black spots from her eyes, seeing the archangel smiling and his fingers curling.

The crowd of angels cheered, and Barakiel took a bow. He straightened, his arms resting on the hilt of his sword.

"On your feet, lesser angel."

Alexa blinked and saw Milo and Sorath in a blur of limbs and swords. At least he was still alive.

She spat the sand from her mouth and pushed herself to her feet. Her ears rang, and then there was pain. She felt as though her bones were broken from the inside, and she couldn't stop her body from shaking. She clenched her jaw to keep herself from crying out. Her head felt as if a tree had fallen on it. The crowd's answering roar made her stomach bubble in anger.

"I can't kill you right away," said Barakiel to Alexa's questioning frown. "Need to provide some entertainment for my fellow angels."

Alexa winced at the stinging pain from her cheek. "And I'm the entertainment."

"That's right. You can blame your death on your friend's foolish challenge. But I have to give the angels what they want."

"Fantastic." Alexa caught Nathaniel's eye and he flashed her a triumphant smile that said it all. He knew she was going to die.

Barakiel lifted his sword. "I'm going to give you a chance to fight me."

Alexa wiped the blood from her mouth. "I doubt that." She heard a cry of pain and turned to see Milo backing away from Sorath, his chest bleeding out with his essence.

"I'm giving you a head start," said Barakiel.

Alexa's head throbbed as she turned her attention back to her opponent. "How much of a head start—"

Something hard caught her in the stomach and sent her slamming into the sand. She slumped, choking on her angel blood. Her soul blade flew from her grip. Tears filled her eyes and she managed to turn on her back.

The archangel hurtled for her, and his sword flew at her neck with incredible speed.

There was nothing she could do to stop it.

Instinctively, she hurled the staff before her, wielding it like a lance against the archangel's mighty body. It hit his armor—and exploded.

Wood splinters showered her face and body, and she felt something warm against her skin like the rays of sunlight.

Terror surged through her as she feared she had broken the staff. But then she realized she hadn't broken it.

She was still holding on to the staff, but instead of a wooden staff, she now held a glowing silver metal staff. It was beautiful—carved with the archangel Michael's sigils and other markings she couldn't decipher. Its power pulsed, making her arm shake. In the calm center of her being, Alexa felt the staff's power. It rippled through the staff and made its way up her arm until she felt it rip through every fiber of her being, screaming onward. In that timeless place of her mind, Alexa knew what to do.

She heard a grunt just as she remembered she was still fighting the archangel.

Barakiel's sword came crashing down on her again, and again Alexa held out the staff.

It hit him square in the chest, on his armor, directly on the spot where, if he had one, his heart would have been.

A rumble of thunder without sound jolted the night. A blast slammed through the air, and even the stars above seemed to stagger. The shock shuddered the trees and rippled the water. Sand lifted around Barakiel, billowing outward in a ring. The impact of the staff had sent her deeper into the sand, and the violence of it made every joint in her body cry out in sharp pain.

Barakiel's gloating smile froze, and his eyes seemed to bulge. The large archangel fell back, stumbling to his knees. His fingers splayed, and the sword slipped from his hand.

She expected to feel the cold metal slice into her skin, but there was nothing. She heard the shouts before she realized what had happened. Blinking, Alexa pulled herself up and gave a little gasp.

Barakiel's skin started to crack. Light leaked from the rivulets over his face, neck, and fingers—everywhere his skin showed—until Alexa had to squint in the light just to look at him.

The archangel's eyes widened. He opened his mouth in a silent scream and then exploded into silver dust.

Everything slowed in Alexa's mind. Angels screamed, Nathaniel's angry roar the loudest of all, but she barely heard them over the tiny voice inside her head telling her what to do next.

Wincing in pain, she hobbled over to Milo and Sorath who were still in combat. They hadn't seen what had happened. Sorath's back was to her, but she caught Milo's wide eyes at the sight of her. Sorath turned at the look on Milo's face.

"What's this?" he laughed. "Coming to rescue your prince? Lucifer's son isn't man enough to fight his own battles? He needs a little girl to rescue him?"

"Something like that."

Sorath lowered his eyes to the glowing staff in Alexa's hand. He didn't have time to move as she gave it a whack, hitting him on the thigh.

The effect was instantaneous.

There was a mighty wallop. The invisible blast of celestial power came down hard, throwing Alexa back again.

Sorath dropped his sword, his eyes widening in fear, and stumbled like a drunk in a circle. His skin cracked like crumpled plaster, and in the next moment, he exploded into a shimmering cloud of silver dust.

The yell of shock and the shouts of fury were stifled at once.

Milo hurried over to Alexa and helped her up, careful not to accidentally touch the staff.

He turned around and addressed Nathaniel. "We won. We fought and won our duel. You promised we could leave if we won." Although Milo stood tall and straight without any visible fear, Alexa could detect the smallest amount of fear in his voice.

Alexa's gaze rolled over the assembled angels. They looked like they were about to charge at them, but she could see the fear in their eyes at the sight of the staff she held. They wouldn't come near them, she realized.

Alexa waved the staff before her, just for show. The crowd was afraid, and silence fell abruptly and completely as Nathaniel and Alexa looked at each other.

Nathaniel's voice was cold with controlled fury. "You've just killed two of my oldest friends." He broke away from the circle and came forward, his features cast in shadow making the whites of his eyes stand out. He looked more like a demon than an angel. "They were Lucifer's best lieutenants."

"Will you let us go?" inquired Milo, his body taut. He looked like he was about to bolt or strike.

Nathaniel's eyes rested on the staff, his fingers clenching and unclenching. He looked at Alexa, and in his eyes she saw a promise of death there. "Our laws forbid me to kill you now, but don't think I won't hunt you down and kill you for what you've done."

"I wouldn't put it past you," said Alexa loudly, and in the total silence her voice carried like a trumpet call.

Milo pointed with the tip of his sword over the line of angels' heads that blocked them from the ocean. "Then tell your angels to move and let us pass."

For a moment Alexa felt that Nathaniel had lied, and they were about to meet their fate.

"Let them pass," came Nathaniel's voice in a growl that sounded anything but angel and more like animal.

At once the angels parted, leaving a large enough gap for a dozen angels to pass easily between them. Alexa could see the stars reflecting on the black waters in the distance. Water. Home.

"Come on," said Milo and urged Alexa to follow him.

Her legs were sore and heavy as she shambled in the sand next to Milo. He turned around and walked backwards, watching their backs as they walked past the angels. He held his swords up, waiting for them to attack.

But the angels didn't attack.

Relief washed through Alexa as her boots splashed around at the water's edge and she nearly fell over. She had to strain to keep from letting herself fall face first. She didn't want Milo to see how exhausted she was.

Still, a smile crawled to her face. They had the staff.

The Staff of Heaven hummed gently against her palm, as though it recognized that it was going home. Alexa didn't want to think about what waited for them on the other side, once they reached the Legion. She just wanted to get away from the freaky angel cult and its leader.

Milo walked into the water until only his shoulders and head were visible. He turned, his body already lit in brilliant light as he gave Alexa the signal to submerge together.

She made her way next to him, letting the cool water soothe her broken body. It felt glorious.

"I'll be seeing you very soon, lesser angel," came Nathaniel's voice.

And then Alexa submerged her head and let the darkness of the waters take her.

CHAPTER 18

"YOU WANT TO COVER THE STAFF OF HEAVEN IN DUCT TAPE?" Alexa stared at Lance in disbelief. "The Staff of *H-e-a-v-e-n?*"

"Not *just* duct tape." Lance pulled something black out from behind him with his mouth and dropped it at her feet. "And a black garbage bag. Stop looking at me like that. It was the best I could do in such short notice," answered the dog. "It's the middle of the night here in the mortal world and we're in a freaking alley that smells like last month's garbage. There are puddles here, which I'm not even willing to discuss. I'm not about to go knocking on doors to find glittering wrapping paper to make you feel better. Besides, no one will know what it is. It's better to keep it in disguise until we speak to Ariel."

"He's right." Milo stared at the glowing staff. "Better hurry up. We can't go around town looking for Ariel with the staff glowing like that. Celestial weapons are demon magnets here in the mortal world. The demons will track it down. We don't want that."

"And you don't want to be touching angels with it by accident," said Lance. "Nathaniel probably had the wood case made to cover the staff so he wouldn't accidentally touch it and combust into fairy dust."

"Fine." Alexa puffed out a sigh as she set the staff down on the ground. She stole a look over her shoulder to the busy street at the end of the alley. Mortals hustled past the alley, quite unaware of the little trio and the staff. Mismatched concrete buildings rose up on either side of the tight alley, blocking out the moon or any other light. The street lamp was too far away to give them any illumination, so Alexa had to work in the dark.

She grabbed the tape and garbage bag and began to wrap it around the staff.

Lance nudged closer and rested his head on her shoulder. "So, how did it feel?"

Alexa secured the bag around the tip of the staff. "How did *what* feel?"

"You know... using one of the most powerful celestial weapons in Horizon?"

Alexa didn't have to turn and look at him to know that his eyes were bugging out of his head. "It was... interesting."

Lance sat back on his haunches. "Interesting? That's all you're going to give me? Come on. I'm dying over here. You've got to give me something more to go on. I did get you out of Horizon safely—*again*." He tapped his back leg impatiently, and Alexa felt that if he could cross his arms over his chest, he'd be doing it now.

"Okay, okay," she said and tore a piece of duct tape off between her teeth. "As soon as the wood came off and I touched Barakiel with it—"

"One of the archangels disintegrated," interrupted Lance.

"Right," said Alexa. "It was like the staff sent a blast of invisible power. And it only affected what it touched. I was blasted back, and it did hurt—just a little—but not enough to let go. It was awesome. I wish I had used it on Nathaniel."

"And you weren't injured by any of it?" inquired the dog. "Now that's freaking fantastic. You think it'll work on Metatron?"

Alexa smiled. "Don't tempt me." She sighed. "We know it works on archangels. Let's hope it'll do the same with Lucifer." Alexa didn't want to show her fears to the others, but Barakiel and Sorath were like tiny cubs compared to the lion Lucifer.

And there was still the issue with the demon blood…

"Think Ariel will believe us?" Alexa said as she tore another piece of tape off with her teeth and pushed her negative thoughts away. "You know what happened the last time I saw her. She didn't exactly back me up when they tossed me in Tartarus."

"Once she sees the staff she'll believe us," said Lance. "She has to. She'll come around. You'll see."

"I hope you're right." Alexa wrapped a last piece of tape around the middle of the staff. She stood up and felt the familiar pulsing of the staff's power through the plastic. "Where do we go from here?"

Lance bounded on the spot, his tail wagging. "Not far. Ariel and a large team of angels are assembling in an abandoned meat packing plant on Ring of Kerry Street. Their intel says Lucifer's castle will appear here in Cahersiveen, Ireland. It's where they think he's going to strike first."

"Then let's get going," said Milo. He looked at Lance. "Lead the way, Scout."

Alexa and Milo followed the white dog out of the alley and turned right on Ring of Kerry. They moved through the street, their boots thumping on the crooked, cobbled street. Lance's nails scraped the stone, echoing loudly around them.

The night air was cool as it spilled over her sweaty skin. They passed small cafes and shops with whitewashed brick exteriors and red or orange roofs. A few mortals wandered past them wearing bleak expressions, but mostly Alexa and the others were the only ones out in the early morning.

"Don't you find it strange that the streets are nearly deserted for a Friday night?" she said, glancing around. "It's a perfect night for mortals to be hanging out in the local bars and pubs. But there are hardly any around."

Lance's ears turned to the sides. "Yeah. It is weird. Should be packed with young mortal teens with fake IDs."

Alexa fell into step with the others as they headed along the crooked, cobbled street. Her unease for the lack of mortals quickly disappeared and was replaced by dread.

A stonewashed, red brick mammoth-size building stood towering over the little shops. Yellow light leaked from rows of windows. Only the faded black letters M E A F Y remained on a worn sign, which was barely visible over the third-floor windows.

Alexa fought back a chill. "You'd think the Legion could have picked a more cheerful place."

"It fits the bill, doesn't it?" said Lance. "Demons and angels are about to be slaughtered. What better place to start than a slaughter house?"

All too soon they arrived at the foot of the concrete steps leading up to the metal doors. Two very large men stood on either side of the door like bouncers. Both were formidable and over six feet tall with wide chests and hard, thick arms corded with ropy muscles. Their faces were different. One was clean shaven with a mess of blond hair, and the other sported a long black beard. The hilts of swords were visible just over their left shoulders, and Alexa could make out daggers strapped around their thighs. Six more hung from their weapons belts. They were armed for war.

Alexa felt a supernatural aura emitting from them as a citrus scent fanned towards her. These were angel doormen.

"Do you think they know who we are?" whispered Alexa. She felt her angel heart thumping in her throat.

"It's too late for that," said Lance and held his head high with confidence. "Pray to the souls that they let us in to speak to Ariel. I don't want to have to fight these two."

Alexa felt the eyes of the angel guards sharpen in on them. She saw their lips move as they neared them and the unmistakable twin frowns they sported at the sight of the trio.

"They don't look very happy to see us," she mumbled.

Lance glanced over his shoulder. "I got this." He padded up the steps while Alexa and Milo waited.

"Evening, gentlemen," said the dog, his tail wagging. "We're here on official business and we require an audience with the archangel Ariel."

The angel with the beard glared down at Lance. "Get lost, mutt," he almost growled.

Lance's tail fell and he lowered his ears. "Mutt? Really? Have you seen the hair on *your* face? What do you call that? The lumberjack special—"

"Lance," warned Alexa.

"I've got moves that don't even have names yet," said Lance, as he swung out his legs in rapid motion.

"Lancelot!"

Lance froze, let out a long sigh, and forced a smile. "We simply want to speak to the archangel Ariel."

"She's not here," said the other angel through gritted teeth. "Turn around and leave before we make you leave." His hand reached up and clasped around the hilt of his sword. But by the time his hand had reached it, Milo had his two spirit sabers out before him.

Surprise and a bit of envy flashed across the angel guards, and Alexa could see the recognition on their faces. Now they knew who they were.

Lance's fur rose on his back, and when he spoke, he did it with a little more teeth. "I know she's here. Trust me, she'll want to hear what we've got to say. Tell her that Lance, Alexa and Milo need a word. The survival of the mortal world depends on it."

Alexa shot a covert glance at Milo. His sabers were still drawn, and she could swear there was a strange smile on his face and a glint in his eyes.

"Wait here." The blond angel disappeared through the front doors leaving Alexa and the others staring after him. He came back a moment later. "Follow me."

Lance glanced back with a nod before he disappeared through the doors after the guard. Milo sheathed his spirit sabers, and Alexa followed behind him as they climbed up the steps and walked through the main entrance.

Alexa blinked at the brightness of the light and gave a start. The inside of the factory was a great echoing chamber of thousands of voices bouncing off the concrete floors and metal walls. Thousands of angels were cramped into the factory's first floor, and Alexa was immediately reminded of her first experience in Orientation. But here, the angels weren't newly born, these were trained warriors, demon killers.

Alexa wasn't fooled by the elderly angel, who could have been anyone's granny, piling soul blades, three firestones, two moonstones and a bag of salt into her purse.

Milo moved next to Alexa and dropped into step with her. "Angels are divided into groups, no doubt by seniority or by job description."

"I see what you mean," Alexa noted as she squeezed between a short bald male angel and a tall teenage angel with toffee-colored skin. Both were armed to the teeth.

Lance moved easily through the crowed space, closely following the guard angel. Other angels moved out of his way, barely taking notice of the three outcasts. Alexa spotted an angel that reminded her of Rachel, but this angel didn't emanate Rachel's toughness. This angel's pretty face was tight with worry, her bottom lip trembled, and she was staring at a soul blade in her hand like she didn't know what to do with it.

That's when Alexa noticed that not all angels looked ready to go to war. A few seemed scared and out of place, with expressions like they wished they were somewhere else.

The angel guard was leading them towards the center of the factory, Alexa realized. And there, standing gracefully like an Amazon princess amongst the angels, just as stunningly beautiful and fierce, was the archangel Ariel.

She wore the usual black cargo pants tucked into a pair of tall black boots and black jacket. The hilt of a sword peeked behind her shoulders, tucked behind her curly hair. She was surrounded by a dozen angels dressed in the familiar Counter Demon Division gear. Alexa recognized Tina, Stuart, Prisha, Marie, Pierre and Marco, but the others were strangers to her.

As they approached, Ariel's toffee-colored eyes settled on Alexa before moving over to Milo and finally Lance. The glare she was giving them nearly made Alexa stop in her tracks. A year ago she would have.

But Alexa soldiered on despite the growing fear she felt, with the hammering in her ears that had nothing to do with the thousands of voices. She threw her gaze across the factory, but there was no sign of Metatron. Her chest welled with courage. Ariel would be easier to convince without Metatron, she hoped.

Alexa and the others moved toward the imposing archangel, her eyes taking in the various details around her. Would Ariel believe her? Would she strike her down with the large sword she carried? What would happen to Milo? All these thoughts went through her head in a split second, the single split second before the archangel in the middle of the factory pulled her sword free and spoke.

"I'm not sure whether I should kill you now or later," said Ariel, her voice dripping in anger unlike anything Alexa had ever heard from her. The angels closest to her went silent.

Alexa halted. "Just hear us out. That's all we ask."

Ariel pointed her sword at Alexa. "You're in no position to make demands."

The angel guard stood next to Ariel and crossed his arms.

"When James told me who was at the door," continued the archangel as she circled around the trio, "I almost had an army sent to execute you on the spot."

"Glad you changed your mind," muttered Lance. He lowered his ears and tucked his tail behind him.

Ariel stopped circling them. She stood with her sword resting before her. "You must be mad coming here after what you've done."

"Ariel," began Alexa, her voice trembling, "I can explain—"

"It's *archangel* Ariel," said the big woman, her voice like the bite of a snake, "and don't you forget that. Or have you abandoned our ways and replaced them with those of the order? Yes. I know about your excursion on the Angel Isle. Forming new allies?"

Heat rushed up Alexa's face. "They're not my allies."

"Weren't you with The Order of the First?"

"Yes, but—"

"My informants tell me that a sky-car dropped you and Milo off to the Angel Isle. Is that true?"

Alexa felt Milo shift next to her, but she kept her eyes on the archangel. "Yes, we were there, but only because—"

"Treason is punishable by death."

Alexa's eyes burned. "I didn't commit treason. Just give me a second to explain—"

"I spoke up for you, Alexa." Ariel's eyes narrowed. "I was working on the High Council to lessen your conviction. They had agreed to let you go in my custody on a trial basis. Pity my efforts were for nothing. Imagine my surprise when I was told of your assisting the traitor Nathaniel with the breakout and destruction of Tartarus."

Alexa recoiled. "No. That's not what happened," she said, feeling a tremor begin in her hands. "I didn't help anyone escape. In fact, I was the only one left. I was left there alone."

"You used an eagle to escape," said Ariel. It wasn't a question.

Alexa closed her free hand into a fist so Ariel wouldn't see it shaking. "I did, but it was one of the prison guards. It offered to help me. Listen, please, we have the—"

"And you, Milo." Ariel came closer to Milo, close enough to touch him if she had chosen to extend her hand. "After sacrificing

225

yourself for the Legion, you choose to side with the order? With the deserters and traitors? Was I wrong about you? Were you in allegiance with them this entire time? Have you fooled us all? Have you always been loyal to your father?"

Milo sucked in a breath. "No. I've only ever been loyal to the Legion."

But Ariel continued as though he hadn't spoken. "We feared the worst for your sake, and now here you are. Why are you here? Are you turning yourselves in?"

"This is really not going like I envisioned in my head," said Lance, and Ariel stared at him as though she'd just noticed he was there.

"Lance," she warned, "why am I not surprised at your involvement. If I hear that you had anything to do with the missing sky-car…"

Lance sat back on his haunches and raised his front paws in submission. "I've pledged my soul to serve the Legion. Scout's honor."

Ariel sighed, and for the first time Alexa thought she looked drained. "I don't have time for this." Her gaze went around the factory. "We're in the middle of a war—a war of worlds. You couldn't have come at a worse time… to… to do whatever it is you're doing."

"That's precisely why we came here," said Lance, his eyes pleading. "We brought something that will help us win this war. But you must listen to us. You must give us a chance to explain."

Ariel rubbed her eyes with a free hand. Her eyes found Alexa. "What are you talking about? Helen!" Ariel bellowed, looking over their heads, "get your team ready. We leave in two minutes."

An angel with a tight chignon and a neck nearly as thick as her shoulders, gave a nod of her head and then bent in conversation with another angel male.

"As I was saying," said Lance and cast a worried glance at Alexa and Milo, "we have with us the tool to bring down—"

"Wayne!" called Ariel to some angel on her far left, "don't forget to tell Nijan about the changes."

"This is going to take all night," grumbled Lance. "Archangel Ariel," he said, his voice loud, and waited until Ariel looked at him before he continued. "We have something that will make a difference. Something real, something tangible, something that truly works. Alexa?" Lance motioned for her. "Show her."

"Right." Alexa fumbled with the staff with trembling hands, regretting using so much duct tape. "Just a sec." Alexa smiled nervously, feeling like a fool as she struggled with the duct tape.

"Now, Alexa," said Lance from the corner of his mouth, "everyone is watching… do it now…"

"I know," she hissed, "it's this damn duct tape. It's sticking to my fingers. I just—crap—I just need a minute. I've got part of it off—"

"Here, let me help." Milo reached out his hands, fingers barely grazing the tightly wrapped garbage bag and then pulling away. He met Alexa's eyes and shook his head. "I'm sorry. I can't."

A dark-skinned male angel slipped through the surrounding crowd and stepped forward. "We're ready, archangel Ariel," he said, towering easily over Milo. He gave Alexa and the others an empty stare. "The archangel Metatron is at the front line. His troops are ready and waiting."

"Good," answered Ariel. "Thank you, Gabriel. You may tell the archangel Metatron that we are on our way." Ariel raised her voice and it echoed above all other voices and sounds. "TEAM LEADERS!" she called, and the silence was immediate. "The time has come. Get your troops ready. We march now."

There was a heartbeat of absolute silence, and then the faint noise of angels shouting orders filled the factory. The ground trembled like a small earthquake as every angel moved at once. The factory was a confusing mess of shouts and milling angels. Cool night air leaked in through the open front doors. Black CDD uniforms were everywhere along with the wink of silver metal blades and swords. The stench of fear and sweat caught Alexa's nose, and her insides twisted.

She turned to Ariel. "Archangel Ariel... if you could just let me explain—"

The archangel's sword rested before Alexa's eyes. And in one quick flick of her arm, she sheathed her sword behind her back.

Her eyes rested on the three of them. "Tie them up!"

"What?" shouted Alexa. Her head felt as if it were full of swirling smoke. "NO! Wait! We have the Staff of Heaven!" But Ariel had already turned away and was halfway across the factory floor, thousands of angels running in her wake.

Rough hands grabbed her, and before she could fight back, she was pushed down hard against the ground. The staff slipped from her hand as she tried to break her fall. Her shoulders screamed in pain as James yanked her arms back and tied them around a metal post beam. She felt a body fall next to her as two thick angels forced Milo down and tied his hands. Her heart broke at the sight of an angel female securing Lance with a metal chain around his collar. She secured the end to a bracket in the concrete floor, and the four of them walked away without a glance or a word.

"You can't tie me up! I'm a Scout! This is a disgrace! I—I can't do chains!" Lance grabbed the chain in his mouth and began pulling franticly, whimpering between growls.

Hot, angry tears fell around Alexa's face as she pulled on her restraints, but even her supernatural strength made no difference. It was like trying to pry open a rock with her bare hands. It was hopeless.

"We're too late," said Milo. His head was bowed, but Alexa could see his eyes welling up in what looked like grief and frustration. "It's over."

CHAPTER 19

SHOOTING PAIN SHOT ALONG ALEXA'S ARM, and agony blanketed her senses. The more she pulled at her restraints, the deeper they cut into her skin. It was as though they were designed that way to keep their prisoner from trying to escape.

Alexa didn't know how long they were tied up. Minutes? Hours? The Legion had left them behind while the rest of them risked their lives to save the mortal world from Lucifer's darkness. She should be there, fighting with them. They all should, not left tied to a post like discarded animals.

What if no one ever came back for them? What if Ariel was killed in battle?

Frustration more than pain overwhelmed Alexa to the point of screaming whenever the wire cut into the soft flesh of her wrist. The wetness around her fingers told her the cut was deep, and if she continued, she would saw off her wrist bone.

She had no other option but to sit there, letting the wound gnaw on her strength, trying her best not to feel like a failure. But worse than that was the growing panic—panic that all their efforts had been in vain.

Her gaze moved to the garbage-bag-wrapped staff on ground next to her. She had ripped off a significant piece when she'd been pushed down to the ground. Light leaked from a large tear in the makeshift disguise, illuminating the ground around it like a flashlight. *If only Ariel had seen it,* she thought. If only she had given her a moment to explain.

Her only comfort was Milo's hard shoulder that pressed against hers and his own grunts of effort as he tried to break free from his restraints. But then her comfort evaporated as the guilt settled in.

No one spoke after the last of the angels had disappeared through the front doors. They all wallowed in their own misery and thoughts. Alexa could feel the tension between them, thick and dangerous. Lance lay on his stomach, his head between his paws and his eyes wet, looking like he was about to be sick.

And when she threw out her angel senses and hearing, she could no longer hear the distant murmurs of cars and humanity drifting in from the open doors. It was as though the world had stopped.

Alexa tried her best not to think about the constant throbbing from her wrists or the shot of pain like tiny sparks of lightning through her arms and shoulders from the constant pulling and yanking. Somehow they needed to escape.

"You'd think with our angel superpowers we could break free from these simple bonds," said Alexa. "What are they made of anyway? Kryptonite?"

She felt Milo's shrug brush up against her shoulder. "Really hard plastic?"

"Ariel could have had us executed, but she didn't," expressed Alexa, her voice loud in the echoing silence and her mouth dry.

"Your point being?" Milo cocked his head so that his hair brushed against Alexa's temple.

"That part of her still wants to believe in us." Alexa pushed forward and yanked at her restraints with all her might. "If—only—we—could—get—away—" she said between her teeth and then gave up pulling. "We can show her the staff. I should never have used so much stupid duct tape." Alexa kicked the staff with her foot. It rolled a foot away, opening the tear more through the bag, and stopped.

Lance lifted his head up from his paws. "I thought I was helping."

"You were," said Alexa, feeling guilty. "This isn't on you. None of this is your fault. It's mine. I'm the idiot who set him free."

Milo nudged her with his boot. "Don't go there again. There's still a chance to fight Lucifer. They think he's here somewhere close by, right? If they did manage to figure out where his castle would reappear, we've still got time. We can still do this."

"That's really great, Milo," said Alexa, trying to keep the cynicism from her voice but doing a poor job, "but you forgot one major problem."

"What?"

"Blood of a willing demon," answered Lance.

"Right, how can I forget," Milo said, too quietly.

Alexa leaned back and her head bumped on the cold metal post. She had left Horizon somewhat gratified and collected, having just stolen the Staff of Heaven, but every passing second wound her tighter. Her mind kept going over her plan, finding giant holes in it. Everything was falling apart. She had been so sure—so convinced Ariel would have listened to her—that now just thinking make her cringe at her own stupidity. Of course Ariel wouldn't listen to her. She was a convict. Worse, a convict that the entire Legion believed had aided and abetted Nathaniel and his order to escape from Tartarus.

Alexa looked through the open doors to the street that lay beyond, silent and ominous. She kept expecting to see Ariel bounding through the doorway. Surely a part of the archangel believed her? But Ariel never came through the doors. No one did.

The staff was useless to them if they couldn't use it. The bonds around her wrists were angel proof. There was no way they could rip them off.

She felt that nothing but action would lessen her feelings of guilt and grief. She ought to set out on her plan to find and destroy Lucifer as soon as possible. But Alexa had failed—failed to retrieve all of the three ingredients required to destroy Lucifer and send him back to purgatory.

She hoped, prayed, the Legion would figure out another way to send The Lord of Darkness back where he belonged.

Alexa hit her head on the metal post, wishing she'd never found that note the oracle left her. Milo and Lance wouldn't be in this mess if she hadn't. Why had the oracle left it for her? Why her and not another more competent angel?

But then another part of her, a voice of belief in herself, told her she'd been chosen for this.

It wasn't faith that had made the oracle write that letter. Perhaps he had seen it in one of his visions of the future. Perhaps he knew Alexa was the one. Perhaps he saw her beat Lucifer...

Excitement surged through Alexa like an adrenaline kick. She didn't know how she knew. She just did. She was certain they were going to get out of here. They were going to destroy Lucifer. The oracle had seen it!

Suddenly everything became clear, as though she was looking at life with a different pair of eyes. Her confidence bloomed inside her, brimful of the conviction in the oracle's premonition.

"Ha!" laughed Alexa in delight, realizing only afterward how loud and crazy she sounded, but she didn't care.

Lance looked from Alexa to Milo. "What's wrong with her?" he said with the corner of his mouth.

Milo shrugged, looking puzzled. "I'm not sure." He leaned forward and turned his head so that he was facing her. "Alexa? Are you feeling okay?"

Beaming, Alexa looked around the factory. "It's gotta be here. I know it is. I know it. I can almost *feel* it."

"What is? What are you talking about?" asked Milo, his voice full of concern.

"The tool for our escape," she said. "It's here. It's here! In here with us! We just haven't discovered it yet. But it is here. Has to be."

Lance and Milo shared a look, and then Lance said very carefully, "Alexa... did you hit your head or something? There's nothing here but us. And unless you can melt your metal bonds with your mind, we're royally screwed. We're even more screwed if demons find us first. Imagine? We can't even defend ourselves if the Legion doesn't send someone to retrieve us. It's almost as though they left us here to die—on purpose."

Alexa ignored the concern in his voice. Her confidence grew like a giant bubble in her gut, squishing out all previous fear and doubt. There was no more second guessing, only certainty, piles of it.

With her angel heart hammering in her ears, her eyes rolled around the floor and the ceiling, stretching her neck as far as it could go. She searched frantically for that special something—the device that would help them escape.

"I never thought it'd end this way," lamented Lance, and he sniffed. "I've still got so many good years in me... my dream of becoming The Scout of the Millennium—gone—instead, I'll be devoured by demons. They're going to ruin my perfect fur. I mean... have you ever seen fur this thick and glossy? I know a few demon females who'd kill to get their hands on it. Now it looks like they're going to get their chance."

Alexa's gaze moved to the white dog. "Lance, will you shut—" her eyes widened. "Oh. My. God. Lance!" Alexa shot forward, and winced at the pain in her shoulder, forgetting about her restraints.

The dog flipped his ears up. "What? Why are you smiling? Do I have something in my fur? This isn't funny, Alexa. We're in really deep, in case you've forgotten. Milo… does she look delusional to you? Please tell me she's not going crazy on us. That's all we need now, a demented angel who sees the fun at being devoured by demons."

"Shut up, Lance! Your collar!" shouted Alexa.

Lance narrowed his eyes. "What about it? It's new. You like it? I thought the yellow would bring out my eyes. You think it's not manly enough? Great. I knew I should have gone with blue—"

"It's loose, you dummy!" laughed Alexa. "When she attached the chain to your collar, she mustn't have paid attention to all that fur of yours. She thought it was tight around your neck when in fact it was just an illusion. She never checked it. Your collar's loose!"

"She's right," said Milo, a smile materializing on his face as he leaned forward, staring at the yellow collar. "You have a two-inch gap. Try slipping it off."

Lance was still staring at them like they were nuts. "O-o-k-a-a-ay." He mumbled something too low for Alexa to hear as he stood up. He lowered his head and started walking backwards until the chain went taut. He pulled his head back, and with a final yank, his collar slipped over his head and plopped to the ground with a thump.

Lance stared at the collar on the ground, sniffing it once. "Well, would you look at that? It's more yellow than I thought. I think I can see a little orange too, right there in the stitching—"

"Lance!" growled Milo and Alexa together.

The dog gave a start. "No need to shout. You nearly gave me heart failure. Okay, I'm coming." Lance bounded over to Milo, and with his teeth pulled out one of Milo's sabers. With precision that impressed Alexa, Lance held the sword's blade with his teeth and sawed off Milo's bonds.

"Thanks." Milo grabbed his saber, and Alexa felt a slight tug on her wrists while he went to work on her bonds followed by a glorious release.

Alexa pulled her arms forward, rubbing her wrists. "Thanks. A little longer tied with those things and I think I would have sawed through my bones." She pushed herself to her feet, already feeling the tingling of her skin stitching itself back around her wrist. She felt eyes on her and turned. "What?"

Milo sheathed his saber. "How did you know about Lance's collar. Anyone could have missed it. I did. Hell even *he* did."

"Hey, I heard that," grumbled Lance as he scratched behind his ear and then shook his head. "I happen to like them a little loose. That way it's like I'm wearing a necklace and not a choker."

"But you knew somehow," continued Milo, his eyes dancing with something Alexa didn't understand.

Alexa flushed under Milo's intense stare. "I just did. I realized that the oracle who wrote me that note," she pulled it out to show them again, but also just to feel it in her fingers because it made her declaration more real, "had seen me destroy Lucifer, or some version of it. The oracle gave me the note because he saw me in one of his visions. If he saw me, I knew we wouldn't die here. I knew we were supposed to free ourselves."

Her eyes moved over the handwritten note, excitement pounding in her body. She could barely stand still.

"I knew it," said Lance. "I knew we'd get out. Never doubted it."

Milo's face looked like he was torn between annoyance and a desire to laugh as Lance stretched and then shook his body, sending waves rippling over his white fur.

Alexa stifled a laugh as she folded the note and pushed it in her jean pocket. She reached down and grabbed the staff. She squeezed it with her hand, feeling its power pulsing against her palm, warm and inviting, as though it wanted her to use it.

She looked up from the staff. "We'll have to run. But if we leave now, we might still catch them."

"What about the blood of a demon?" asked Milo. "We still don't have that."

"I don't know," said Alexa. "We'll figure it out. Trust me. We have the oracle's vision on our side. It'll work. Just have faith."

"I hate to be the one to kill the happy party we have going on here," said Lance, looking guilty, "but everyone knows the oracles' prophecies don't always come true. I'd say they're wrong, like fifty percent of the time. It's why you can never get a straight answer from them. They can't even tell the right prophecies from the false ones." Lance rolled his eyes. "Glad I don't have their job."

A hum of excitement went through her. Still smiling, Alexa shook her head. "No. I know this is going to work. I can feel it. Just... just trust me on this. It'll work. We need to find Ariel! Come on!"

And the three of them dashed out the front doors into the night.

CHAPTER 20

IT DIDN'T TAKE LONG FOR ALEXA and the others to find Ariel and her band of angels. All they had to do was follow the sounds of battle—metal clashing against metal along with the unmistakable grunts and the wailings of the dying.

They ran, slipping around the corner of a pub called Tasty Brew and into an alley. It was narrow, choked with empty beer bottles, shredded plastic, moldy boxes and dirty rags with dark maroon spots she didn't want to think about. They passed rows of townhouses, their lights on. The mortal world was waking. They broke through the end of the ally and found themselves running through rows of townhouses with manicured lawns.

Alexa felt the change in the air along with the smell of salt and moisture, but there was also the overwhelming stench of sulfur and the rotten smell of demon and blood. Even then, she felt something different. An unnatural pulsing, like the beating of a giant heart.

Stones kicked up as she ran, and Alexa could make out the point where the townhouses ended and the lane turned into open country with a sparkling harbor. Nestled between picturesque, deep green mountains was a large flowing river, cool in the blue light of dawn. Private yachts, sailboats and smaller ships were docked in the harbor, bobbing in the restless dark waters. The landscape seemed to grow larger and more detailed as Alexa squinted over the side of the river and mountains.

At the end of the lane, a sign written in bold green letters read *CAHERSIVEEN MARINA.*

Chaos reigned at the marina. Angels and demons swarmed the harbor grounds, screaming and waving their weapons. Demons charged, scattering the angels. Alexa could feel the stamping feet as more demons approached from the nearby town.

The battle was still raging along the marina, which was good because it meant the angels hadn't all died yet. It meant whatever plans Lucifer had unleashed, the Legion was still standing.

Near the edge of the harbor, swathed in mist, was the shadow of a castle. Made of black stone, it was carved in the shape of a skull complete with eyes, nose, and a portcullis with large metal teeth that looked like an open mouth ready to devour anyone foolish enough to attempt to pass. And what looked like a crown made of swords sat above its head. Its enormous shadow slid over the harbor like a giant dark cloud. The air pulsed around it, coming from somewhere inside.

Lucifer's castle. The Legion had been right. He was here.

Alexa cursed silently as she saw a major problem. To get to the castle they would have to cross through the angel Legion, who were fighting what looked to be thousands of demons. A sudden wail sounded, a terrible, drawn-out cry of misery, pain, and dying. But she was too far away to determine if the cries were from angels or from demons.

"Wait!" Milo held up his hand. Both Alexa and Lance skidded to a stop. Lance's hair stood on end like he'd just stepped out of a dryer.

Milo narrowed his eyes as he took in the battle. "Something's not right. These demons... they feel like... they feel *strange...*"

"Demons have always *felt* strange," offered Lance. "It's the first sign that tells us they don't belong here."

Milo shook his head. He drew both sabers and said, "No. That's not it. We should be coughing at their stench with a crowd that size. It should be burning our throats like acid. But I'm not getting that feeling. I'm barely getting anything as it is. I can't explain it, but I know something's just not right."

"Milo's right." Alexa had barely spoken when an unnatural chill descended on her like a cold mist, and sudden cries made her shudder where she stood.

A swarm of Higher demons was gliding along the port. Their white skin was a sharp contrast against their dark suits. They stopped just outside the battle, watching. Alexa could feel their chill, smell the poison from their death blades, even though she couldn't see their weapons.

"Why aren't the Higher demons attacking?" she asked, her eyes never leaving their eerie, identical faces, which always freaked her out.

"They're like hyenas." Lance made a face. "Cowards and scavengers, waiting for the other demons to do the hard work for them."

Milo's grip was tight on his sabers. "No. Higher demons aren't cowards. They relish in killing. It's what they were made for—to kill angels."

"Why are they just standing there? It's almost as if they're waiting for something." Alexa couldn't suppress the feeling of dread that was slowly trying to burst her confidence bubble. She'd never seen Higher demons stand back and watch a battle. In her experience, they were always the instigators, but none of the Higher demons moved. They were waiting.

A growl rippled in Lance's throat. "Waiting for what?"

"I don't know." Alexa tightened her grip on the staff. "Do you think they know about the staff? Nathaniel might have told them."

"Could be," said Milo as he wiped the sweat from his forehead with his right arm. "They do look like they're waiting for something."

"Or someone," said Lance.

"They can never get their hands on the staff," said Milo, his face pale and deadly serious.

"Can they even touch it?" asked Lance, his eyes roving over the staff in Alexa's hand. "You told me it vaporized those two archangels. Maybe it would do the same to them?"

"I don't know." Milo was silent for a moment, his eyes traveling over the Higher demons to his father's castle and then back. "If Nathaniel is here, my father's already aware of the staff and our plans."

Alexa stared at the battle, her nerves jumping inside her like a swarm of bees. "How do we get past that," she asked, pointing with the staff to the battle ahead.

"We'll need Ariel's help to reach my father's castle," answered Milo. "We need to persuade her to lend us a team."

"And you're sure he's in there? What if he's out there fighting?"

"He sees battles like these as being below him," answered Milo. "He's the true coward."

Alexa watched Milo's face go through a few different emotions in a few seconds—frustration, disgust, contempt, even pain. She felt sorry for him. What kind of person would you grow up to be if you knew your father was Lucifer?

"There!" shouted Lance. "I see her. Quick before I lose her scent." The dog bounded ahead of them, leaving Alexa and Milo having to double their efforts to catch up to him.

Alexa kicked into action. She ran as fast as her legs would take her, but the staff was still a hindrance in her movements. She galloped, commanding the muscles in her legs to push harder, faster, forward. Alexa gritted her teeth. Wind pushed at her face, her hair ripping out of her braid and waving like a brown banner behind her.

The cries of battle were all around them until she couldn't even hear her own footsteps crunching the stones beneath her boots. She had no idea where Ariel was. All she saw was a blur of faces, clothes, limbs and swords. She knew without Lance's keen sense of smell they would have never found the archangel in all the chaos.

Alexa's mind went over the oracle's note, and she willed her legs to move faster. She *would* bring Lucifer down. She was almost smiling.

Faces around her began to take shape the closer they got to the fighting. Alexa's confidence faltered, and her legs lost their spurt of intensity. Her stomach shot right into her throat as they approached the first line of fighters.

What she had first thought were demons fighting against the angels were not demons at all, but humans.

The angels were fighting *mortals.*

Milo halted suddenly, sending Alexa crashing into him. It was like hitting a tree at forty miles per hour, but she barely noticed. His eyes, the shock Alexa saw there, explained everything she felt.

"What in the souls?" Lance stopped short next to Alexa.

What she saw next tore at every nerve in Alexa's body. The mortals were *attacking* the angels.

It was total anarchy, a commotion of screams and movement. The landscape was covered in a mass of mud and blood, turning into a pink paste. Alexa had never witnessed a battlefield of this magnitude, and there was hardly any way to distinguish angel from mortal because they all looked human. Alexa winced as she stared, unable to turn her eyes from the battle.

Suddenly there were crowds surging around her, hands grabbing her and pulling at her clothes. Alexa pushed them away and saw the angels scattering, trying to save themselves by jumping into the river. But the mortals dove into the battle, crazed and fighting as though the angels were an army of zombies and their mortal lives depended on their success. Some angels never made it to the water.

Alexa didn't know how many mortals were out here fighting. They were everywhere. She never imagined the kind of sounds the mortals could make, never thought she'd hear such things from a human mouth—the wailing, the grunting, the sick laughter and the sounds of stabbing and cutting flesh with hungry satisfaction.

Suddenly, she felt a ripple of darkness, the presence of death and of something not from this world. Alexa felt the eerie feeling of being watched. Following the feeling, she moved her gaze to the Higher demons. They were watching her. They hadn't moved.

A split second before she turned her head, Alexa caught another scent on the air—the familiar stench of rotting flesh and garbage. Behind her, on the lane next to a row of townhouses, was a nightmarishly jumbled wall of lesser demons—scaled skin, winged beasts, worm-like masses and reaching claws. The scent of carrion and the vile, burnt smell of death and rot wafted through the air making Alexa choke. She even saw a handful of belphegor demons. She looked for Willow, but the girl demon wasn't there. Their rotten faces were focused on the battle. They stood on the outskirts of the battle, watching and waiting.

"Don't do this!" said an angel close to Alexa, who she recognized as Andy. He was backing away from a mortal woman with a death blade. "Please. I'm here to protect you."

"Protect this." The woman stabbed him in the chest with the death blade, her eyes wide and smiling like she'd just won a car.

Alexa turned to the sound of someone shouting.

"...it matters! You should have joined us when it mattered, Janet!" shrieked a man with red hair. "How does it feel now to be on the losing side!" He let out a cackle of mad laughter as he plunged his blade into her chest.

"The world's gone mad," whispered Lance. "This is Lucifer's plan. Isn't it?" He aimed his question at Milo. "He's made the mortals mad. He's made them turn against us. The angels can't fight back! Can't you see? They're being slaughtered by the very beings they're sworn to protect."

Alexa recognized another angel from the CDD but didn't know her name. The girl disappeared under a group of four mortal men. She heard a muffled scream and then nothing until the triumphant howls from the mortal men.

To her right, a mortal child was beaming, her teeth sharpened into points like that of a fish. The child threw herself at an unsuspecting angel's neck, ravaging him like a vampire. The child's face was wet with blood. Alexa blinked and the two vanished into the crowd.

"This can't be happening," whispered Alexa, looking around frantically, her throat tight. "I thought mortals were protected from demon or supernatural coercion. Don't their souls act as a layer of defense? Aren't souls a protection against that sort of thing? I know some souls are weaker than others, but to have so many compelled by Lucifer at the same time? It doesn't make any sense."

Milo was stone-faced. His grip on his swords slacked, and for a second Alexa thought he was about to drop them. His body shook as he said, "Whatever this is, the only way to stop it—"

"Is to stop Lucifer."

A wave of nausea hit Alexa. Bile rose up her throat. Everywhere Alexa looked, mortals were killing angels at an alarming speed. Hell was staring at her in the face.

She wished the oracle had warned her about this in his note.

"I've lost Ariel," shrieked Lance in a panic. "I can't smell her. I've lost her scent!"

Alexa ran her fingers through the fur on Lance's head. "We'll find her. Don't worry," she soothed as best she could and grabbed a fistful of his fur to keep her fingers from trembling. Was Ariel still alive?

"Give me the note," said Lance urgently.

Alexa's eyes widened. "*My* note?"

"Yes, yes. Quickly. I have a plan."

Alexa reached down and pulled the note from her pocket. She placed it in Lance's mouth.

"What's the plan—"

The air was rent by a scream.

Alexa turned just as a pudgy mortal man came at Lance with an axe.

"This is for Helen, you snitch!" The axe went sailing straight for Lance and Alexa as she stood next to him.

"Move!" she shouted and pushed Lance out of the way. She felt her hair lift as she lowered to a crouch. The axe landed next to her with a thud, the handle sticking out from the ground.

The man never stopped moving. He lunged at Lance, his hands outstretched, going for his neck—

Alexa spun, kicking under him, and sent him sprawling on the ground.

"Stay down," she warned. But the man scrambled up, teeth showing, and came at her swinging.

She ducked and hit him on the side of his temple with the hilt of her blade. His eyes rolled in the back of his head and he hit the ground.

"Alexa! This way!" she heard Milo call.

Once she was sure the man wasn't getting up, Alexa turned towards Milo's voice. She stumbled over a body lying half in and half out of the mud. It was an angel. Light poured from a long gash along his neck. His eyes were vacant as they stared into space. Alexa felt nauseated.

A noise made her scramble to her feet. She smelled the citrus scent of angel blood before she saw it—the shadow of something looming up behind her.

Alexa spun but not fast enough. She felt something tug at her stomach, like a stinging kiss, cold and hot at once, and felt a warm trickle of liquid spill down onto her waist.

When she looked up, she found Milo surrounded by mortals, death blades pointed at his neck. Anger rippled across his body, and his spirit sabers shook in his hands, his knuckles white. She couldn't see Lance anywhere and prayed he'd gotten away.

A tall, broad-shouldered mortal man stood before her, the promise of violence dancing in his dark eyes.

He smiled in triumph and anticipation as he said, "I told you I'd kill you for what you did, Alexa."

CHAPTER 21

TRANSFIXED, ALEXA STARED AT THE STRANGER'S face and at his lips where he'd uttered those crazy words. The clatter of her soul blade hitting the floor was barely audible over the hammering in her ears. She stumbled back, staring at the black hilt of a death blade sticking out of her lower abdomen.

Alexa yanked the death blade from her stomach and tossed it, but she could already feel its poison spreading through her veins. She looked back at the mortal man. Beneath the growing fear she managed, "What did you say?"

The man lifted his nose at her, his features twisting as though he'd tasted something bitter. "Thought you were real clever, didn't you? You think I don't know what you're trying to do with that staff? You think you know more about the world of angels than me? The first creation? The first angel? You're a lesser angel, inferior in mind and spirit. Did you really think you would get away with it? Kill two of my friends and wouldn't suffer the consequences? I warned you'd pay for your actions. Give me back my staff."

Realization dawned on Alexa and she took a step back, staring at the stranger's face. "Nathaniel?" she said in a voice that broke with emotion. "But how? No, can't be. Impossible."

"Yes, it is me, in the flesh, so to speak," said the man who claimed to be the angel Nathaniel. "I'll admit it takes a little to get used to this new body and its *daily* functions. It was a surprise to experience hunger and thirst, but they are nothing compare to all the other remarkable sensations and feelings. This is not an inferior M-suit the Legion forced us to wear. This is a *real* mortal body, not an imitation."

Horror washed through Alexa. "But how? Only demons can possess a human body. And when that happens, there are signs of sickness and disease. The flesh starts to decay on its human host. But you look... you look well."

"Why thank you."

"It wasn't a compliment, you creep." Her voice was ragged with rage, but Nathaniel the mortal dismissed her with a wave of his hand.

"You are sadly misinformed if you think that only demons can possess a mortal body. I can assure you, angels have possessed human bodies in the past, but never indefinitely or quite like this."

"Indefinitely? What do you mean?" Alexa hissed through gritted teeth.

"Again, proof that you lesser angels are being misled by the Legion. Proof of your inferior intelligence and lack of imagination."

One of the mortal men that surrounded Milo snorted. Alexa wished she could smack him with the staff and see what would happen.

Alexa met Milo's gaze, his lips thin and eyes wide with shock and horror and grief.

The air around her still contained the incessant sound of metal on metal, the hacking of flesh, and the pounding of fists, all coming from various directions like a steady rhythm that seemed to vibrate deep in her chest.

Nathaniel caught her looking at the battle. "The angels will be destroyed. All those who dared defy us will be killed here, in the early hours of the morning. It won't take long. They can't fight back. As you know, angels cannot take a human life."

"They can if the mortal *intends* to kill them," said Milo. "I know the code. It's self-defense."

"Perhaps," said Nathaniel. "But by the time it takes the angel to make the connection—that the mortal actually *means* to kill— the angel is already dead."

Alexa's gaze traveled to Lucifer's castle. Somehow, she had to reach it. She had to stop this madness. Remarkably, she still held on to the staff. Her fingers clasped around it, gathering courage from it.

"It won't last," said Alexa, returning her attention to the mortal Nathaniel. "You might not be demon, but eventually the mortal bodies will reject you. You can't stay indefinitely in a human host. You're a celestial creature. These are flesh and blood. And then you'll be fair game for all the demons. Trust me. The Legion won't save you. Not after what you've done."

"These bodies will *never* reject us," laughed Nathaniel. "And before you ask... yes, this body will grow old and weak and eventually die, but by then I will have discarded it and taken another. There are billions to choose from. My choices are endless." His grin widened at the horror on her face. "You see, Alexa," said Nathaniel. "This is not possession. This is *integration*. A union. The binding of two creatures into one. We become them. They become us. It doesn't really matter, as we, the angels, take control of the bodies."

Alexa looked over to Milo, but all she saw was utter confusion on his face.

"I've never heard of integration," said Alexa, as her mind whirled with scenarios on how to reach the castle. "You've made that up. You're a liar."

"Not I," said Nathaniel, his voice full of admiration, "but my lord. He made this happen. He made this possible and gave us the gift of integration. His power and wisdom. Without his skill, his infinite power, this *union* could not be possible. And now, here we are. And here we take."

Alexa was trying hard to see beyond the mortal mask, the costume which was Nathaniel. She had to remember there was an innocent soul in there.

She blinked the sweat from her eyes. "But what about the mortals' souls. What happens to them? The mortal bodies don't function without souls. I know as much."

Nathaniel pursed his lips. "Trapped, I would imagine."

"Trapped?" Alexa was going to be sick. "You mean you can hear them? Like, subconsciously?"

Nathaniel smiled. "It was the only downside to the binding. But with a little practice, it's easy enough to suppress them. I don't hear Henry's voice anymore."

"Henry," said Alexa. "The man you possessed, the man whose life you stole." Alexa frowned, trying to get used to the new face with the familiar voice. She couldn't help but notice that he'd picked a very handsome man to possess.

"I'm not a thief," spat Nathaniel. "You are. This world belongs to us. It was made for us—angels—not humans. We took what was ours. The mortals can stay, as long as we can ride their bodies." He laughed. "As strange as it sounds, we need their bodies as vessels."

"And all these mortals…" Alexa couldn't utter the words. Storms of rage erupted within her. She knew she was looking at all the members from The Order of the First. Her stomach lurched, and bile stung the back of her throat. She clamped down on the horror with all her might, but even the oracle's premonition couldn't shake the dread she felt.

"This is Lucifer's big plan?" said Milo, sounding both surprised and angry. "To merge angels with human bodies?"

"Brilliant, isn't it?" Nathaniel gave Milo an easy smile. "To bring about the cleansing of the Earth without actually killing any of the lesser creations." Nathaniel circled around Alexa and Milo. His mortal body was bigger and taller than the angel one, more like an angel on steroids.

"It's the new and improved apocalypse," said Nathaniel. "What? Did you expect something different? The burning of the world, a giant plague that would wipe out billions of mortals perhaps? Or did you assume there would be a demon invasion, like the rest of the angels? That our lord would open the gates of hell and let them in? No. The mortal world belongs to us, not demons. Our lord discovered a better way to take control, one that we angels couldn't wait to discover, to taste, to rule."

Alexa's knees shook. She'd been so wrong. They'd all been wrong. Even Ariel, the Legion, how could they fight this new threat?

"And once all the lesser angels and the other treacherous angels are removed, and the mortals integrated, perhaps we shall bring back the Spanish flu since the world is overpopulated and all. Then we will have a peaceful, pure world without famine or wars. Remove the will of mortals, and the world will prosper."

"It's never going to happen," spat Alexa.

But Nathaniel only smiled and said, "It already has."

Milo's eyes, intense with loathing, fixed on Nathaniel. "Has my father integrated too?"

Nathaniel sighed impatiently. "He doesn't have to. He's *The Lord of Darkness*. His power is endless. He can do whatever he chooses, and as it so happens, he chooses to remain in his castle."

"Maybe he knows something you don't." Alexa knew she'd hit a nerve at the uncertainty that flashed across Henry-Nathaniel's face.

His face twisted into something ogre like. "You know nothing, you worthless brat!" A dribble of spit flew from his mouth, and his face reddened to an ugly shade of purple. "You lesser angels are insignificant. Too weak and stupid to recognize that you've only ever been slaves to your precious Legion. There will be no more corrupting and polluting the minds of the first creation. You are the Legion's mistake, and you are their downfall. You lot are nothing but filth, stains of dishonor, taints of shame on the first creation. The Legion should never have been allowed to use mortals as angels. You should never have been made angels. You should have stayed dead as a mortal because your angel life is worthless."

"Someone believed in me enough to make me an angel," said Alexa, her chest swelling as she realized the truth in her own words. She smiled at him. "And someone still does." She gave a swing of the staff and regretted it as her wound stretched and burned. "I'd say that's worth something."

Nathaniel looked at the staff in Alexa's hands. "That staff can't harm me or any of us, not while we are *integrated*. Still, it *belongs* to me. And I will have it back."

"It was never yours," said Milo, and Alexa had never heard so much contempt in his voice. "It belonged to the archangel Michael and to the Legion."

Nathaniel moved to stand next to Milo with the grace and supernatural speed of an angel but with a mortal body. It was unnatural, and it made Alexa feel as though she were watching a movie with added visual effects to enhance the character's speed.

"As the only remaining son of Lucifer, I will give you the option to choose. If you choose to surrender, you will be brought safely to your father's castle unscathed. I was told to find you and bring you to him, but he never specified in *what* condition. It seems he still has faith in you. If you were my son, I would have killed you long ago."

Milo smiled. "But I'm not."

"No, you are not." Nathaniel sighed, looking down into Milo's ferocious, anguished face. "I have orders not to kill you, but no one said anything about not killing this one." He turned a little, indicating Alexa. "Kill her. And bring me my damn staff back!"

CHAPTER 22

EVERYTHING MOVED AT ONCE.

Mortals rushed towards Alexa, crowds of them from every direction. Young, old, woman or man, it didn't matter. They all came for her with brutal efficiency.

Alexa hit them with the staff like she was swinging a baseball bat.

"Sorry!" she shouted as she smacked the staff across the chest of an elderly man, knowing the real man was in there somewhere. It was hard enough just to concentrate, let alone, try to wrap her mind around what she was actually doing. She had to keep telling herself that she wasn't killing them. She was making them indisposed temporarily until she dealt with Lucifer.

"Didn't mean that," she cried and knocked an Asian woman down. "Nathaniel made me do it!"

Alexa sensed others behind her. She spun like a top, just in time to see three more mortals abruptly appear. They were racing to join the fight, grinning.

With a backhanded swing of the staff, Alexa sent a powerful blow at the two of the mortals, catching them hard in their chests. The staff reverberated against her hands.

"Can't you people just stay down!" she bellowed.

Without pause, the other mortal, a young fifteen-year-old girl, came at her thrashing madly with two death blades in her hands. The girl ducked and twisted, evading the knock-out thrust of Alexa's staff. But as the girl came around, closing the distance to deliver her own strike, Alexa drew the staff back, thumping it across the back of the girl's head. She cried out once and slumped to the ground.

It worked that way for a while, but after the twentieth attacking mortal, Alexa began to really feel the effects of the death blade's poison. She started to tire. No matter how many she struck down, they were quickly replaced by five others.

A new group of mortals had taken the place of the other fallen. They were standing now, scowling at her, but she had caught glimpses of them smiling to each other, apparently pleased with the way they had been able to draw her into their game.

"I'm going to take my sweet time with you, lesser angel," spat one of the mortal men with black hair and matching beard. "Cut that pretty meat-suit off those lesser bones." He twisted his death blade in the air, mimicking the way he was going to gut her.

"Screw you." Alexa took a step back, the staff held firmly in both hands. It was her only weapon.

She felt the air move behind her, but it was too late.

Something struck her hard from behind and she went down, skidding over a puddle of mud and blood. She heard Milo's voice over the grunts of the mortals, just as something both hot and cold pierced her back.

Alexa screamed in pain as she felt wetness dribble down her back. She had to move. If she stayed down, she was dead.

She bit down on another scream of pain as she pushed upward, her legs buckling as she strained to stand. Using the staff for support, she stood, reaching behind her to wrap her hand around the hilt of the death blade. She hissed as the poison burned her skin and pulled. But the blade wouldn't move. She yanked harder, but it wouldn't budge, it was lodged into one of her ribs.

For a panic-filled instant, Alexa froze.

The world spun black and white and red as hands grabbed her and shoved her against the ground, her face smashing into a stone. When she opened her eyes, the world shifted. Blackness was everywhere, and the death blade's poison was moving quickly through her veins, too quickly.

Two figures stepped into her line of sight.

"Kill her while she's down!" yelled a mortal woman with glasses. "Get the staff!"

"I'm not touching that," said a mortal man with skin the color of oil. "You take it."

"Idiot," hissed the woman, and she knelt down next to Alexa. She reached to take the staff.

Alexa tossed a handful of dirt and mud into her eyes.

The woman screamed as her hands went to her face and she fell back.

The man's face went red. "You're gonna pay for that."

He grabbed for Alexa. She brought her boot up between his legs. When he cried out, she scrambled on her belly, going as fast as she could. But each stroke sent a jarring pain up her spine, the death blade tearing her skin like a hot knife. Sweat beaded on her brow and trickled through her scalp, but she wouldn't give up. Again the pain came as she struggled to her knees amidst another tear at her back. She gritted her teeth against her scream.

"Kill her! What are you waiting for? She's just a lesser angel." Nathaniel's voice sent a new surge of hatred through Alexa.

She pushed herself to her feet, just as she felt movement from behind.

Instinctively, Alexa whirled and cracked the staff across the woman's head. She collapsed into a puddle of mud.

Another mortal with bulbous eyes and a hawk nose threw himself on Alexa, grappling with her and punching her in the ribs. She stumbled back, blinking the black spots from her eyes as he came at her again.

Alexa swung the staff at him, but he ducked, and it caught only his shoulders. His fist in her gut drove her back.

"Your moves won't work on me," said the man. "I trained you. I know what you're going to do before you do it."

Alexa cradled her stomach and stepped back, shaking her head. "Takumi? Is that you?"

Takumi rolled his death blade between his fingers. "You could have joined the order when Nathaniel gave you the chance. Then you'd get to live out eternity back in the place you'd so admired. I know how much you missed being a mortal. But you missed that chance. That was stupid."

Alexa stared at the man-angel who'd trained her at Operations level two. He'd recommended her to Ariel's Counter Demon Division unit because of how fast she'd excelled and how gifted she was in combat training.

Alexa spat blood from her mouth. "I can't believe you'd turn your back on the Legion for a few mortal thrills. I looked up to you, Takumi. I admired you. How could you do this?"

Takumi lowered his body, and Alexa noticed how he had chosen a mortal who had similar traits, nearly the same height, build, and age. She lowered herself in a defensive stance. She knew what was coming.

"Why don't you just give up, Alexa?" said Takumi, moving with the grace of a skilled warrior. He wore his knowledge, experience, and skill like a second skin. "It's over. You're fighting a lost cause. You could have lived if you had surrendered and joined us."

With wind-like speed Alexa remembered all too well, Takumi attacked. It took every bit of strength for Alexa to block his assault. She heaved him over the top of her as she crashed to the ground and then rolled to her feet. As Takumi turned to get his footing, she kicked him in the face.

The air rang with the sound of steel. Nathaniel shouted something, but Alexa couldn't make it out amid the piercing sounds of yelling and roars from the battle.

Takumi cursed loudly. Alexa kept her eyes on him as he sprang up with blood running from his nose. Before he could charge at her again, something grabbed her from behind.

It threw her to the ground, and something sharp ripped at the back of her throat and shoulders. She thrashed. It let go. Alexa rolled over to her knees, cursing as she felt the death blade sink deeper into her back, and blinked into the face of a young boy, his teeth sharped like the girl she'd seen just minutes ago.

He couldn't be older than seven. Alexa felt both pity and anger at the sick angel who decided to use this child's body for play.

He was on all fours, like an animal ready to pounce on his prey. On his hands were gloves with razor blades stitched at the fingertips. He cocked his head to the side, his face stretching into a smile. Her own blood dripped from the corners of his mouth, dribbling down to his chin.

He pounced on her, his claws slicing her flesh, her face. She raised her hand to cover her eyes. He was going to rip her apart. Terror—like she'd never known—took over. Alexa covered her eyes as he clawed at her face, neck, and chest. She swung out blindly.

The staff shook, and she knew she'd hit something. The clawing stopped. Blinking through the wetness from her eyes, she saw the boy on the ground, shaking his head. Blood ran from a large cut on the side of his skull.

She stood over him for a second. Defiance and rage mixed in her soul. Part of her wanted to rip his head off, but he was still a child. Somewhere inside that body was the soul of a child. She couldn't do it. And then she knew the angel had chosen that body for the exact reason; the angels wouldn't dare harm him.

The boy sprung to his feet, licking his lips.

"Don't," warned Alexa and held the staff in both hands. "I don't want to hurt you."

"Why? I *want* to hurt you," said the tiny boy with the voice of a grown man. Alexa's skin rippled in goose bumps.

Another child—the same little girl—hopped over and crouched next to the boy. She too had the same makeshift razor gloves.

"I think I'm going to be sick." Alexa's bottom lip trembled. "This is so wrong. Stay away!"

She swung her free arm, aiming at the girl's face, but missed.

The girl went for her throat, teeth snapping like a piranha. Alexa flung herself backward, only to feel white-hot pain shoot up her back. She pitched headfirst into the ground. Tears welled in her eyes. Her back was aflame with pain. Alexa cried out as they leaped on her.

With a feeling of drowning in dread, she knew her strength would soon give way to the poison that flowed in her. The darkness rippled in her vision. She trembled and sweat trickled down her temples into her eyes. She was cold and hot all at once. The fever from the poison ate away at the last of her strength. How long did she have before another wave of the poison-induced sickness took over her body?

Cold fingers pierced the flesh of her back, neck, and scalp like knives. Alexa screamed and screamed until her voice broke. She slashed blindly with the staff, but they were weighing her down. Her strength was leaving her. She could feel the warmth of her M-Suit trying to heal what it could, but there were too many mouths and fingers tearing at her flesh.

Tears blinded her vision. She wanted to scream, but she could barely open her mouth, too tired to move her head. She'd never imagined that she'd be eaten alive by little kids.

Suddenly, Alexa felt the weight lift from her body. The tearing and biting stopped.

Get up, said the tiny voice inside her head, *the oracle saw you defeat Lucifer. This isn't the end. Get up!*

Moaning, Alexa propped herself up on her elbows.

The two angel-mortal-suit-wearing kids were face down on the ground, their wrists and feet bound and mouths gagged. Lance was sitting on the boy, his tongue lolling out of his mouth.

"Don't know what's gotten into our kids these days," he said and winked at Alexa.

Blinking, Alexa saw Nathaniel and his loyal group of mortals struggling on the ground next to her, a metal net secured around them.

"Keep their hands and feet bound," said a rough voice. "We need to keep them down for as long as possible."

Alexa turned and saw the archangel Metatron, his large frame soaring over the angels. In his hands was the largest gun Alexa had ever seen. It looked like a rocket launcher. Maybe it was.

But as he aimed it at a group of mortals and pulled the trigger, a metal net shot in the air, opening as it fell over the mortals. They stumbled, and the weight of the metal net pinned them to the ground.

Metatron shot a look in Alexa's direction. "On your feet, kid. It's not time for a break!" And then he disappeared in the chaos of mortals and angels.

"I'll help you."

Alexa turned and blinked into Milo's handsome face. He pulled her up effortlessly and with extreme gentleness.

"What's going on?" Alexa managed, using the staff like a crutch, and noticed that all the rest of the duct tape and bag had been ripped off. The staff was glowing dimly in the gloom.

Looking over Milo's shoulder, she could see the blur of bodies as they fought and could hear the clang of metal with the shouts of combat. Disappointment rushed through her as she saw the clear signs that the battle was not over. Angel bodies littered the ground, covered in blood, lamenting their last breaths. Angels ran in every direction, some carrying or dragging other injured angels.

But then she noticed a mortal body tied on the ground. And then another. And another.

Movement caught her eye. A female angel in the black CDD gear tossed a net over an unsuspecting short mortal man. With astonishing speed, the angel had already tied his wrists and feet

266

when she grabbed the net and took off running after another mortal.

Hundreds of mortals were immobile, their wrists and feet bound with what Alexa suspected was the same material the angels had used on her.

"They've tied up the mortals?"

"Yeah, looks like it. I don't know how long it's going to last," said Milo, casting his eyes over the harbor. "But the Legion's managed to come up with a temporary strategy to stop the integrated mortals without killing them."

"Seems to be working."

Milo's eyes went over Alexa's head. "I can see more and more of those integrated mortals spilling through that town. They keep coming. The Legion can't keep up with this forever."

"We need to get to your father's castle—" Alexa made to turn her body towards Lucifer's castle and flinched. "Milo," she said, trying to control the pain from her voice. "I've got a death blade in my back. It's stuck. Can you—"

"I'll remove it."

Ariel had appeared at Alexa's side, and her body tightened as the archangel stepped behind her. Alexa bit down on the scream as the death blade was pulled out. Tears spilled down her face. She couldn't help it. But she immediately felt some strength returning to her body.

Ariel cursed. "They did a real number on your back."

Heat rose to Alexa's face. "How bad is it?"

"Put your arms up," commanded Ariel, and Alexa did what she was told. She was pulled and tugged as Ariel wrapped white gauze around Alexa's middle until she felt like a mummy.

"There," said the archangel and she stood back. "It's not the Healing-Xpress, but it'll keep you from bleeding out."

"Thank you." Alexa felt like she was wearing a metal breast plate.

"Why didn't you show me the note, Alexa?" asked Ariel, as she pulled the oracle's note from her pocket and handed it to Alexa.

Alexa looked over to Lance who was still sitting on the kid. "I didn't think you'd believe me," she said. "I've tried to talk to you before, and I ended up in Tartarus."

Ariel sighed. She watched Alexa for a long moment. "Well, there's no time to get into all that. If we live through this, we'll need to sit down and have a chat about what you two have been doing. Is that the Staff of Heaven?"

Alexa lifted the staff and angled it for Ariel to see. "It is. Do you want it back?"

"It was never mine," said Ariel. "It disappeared so long ago, we never thought someone other than Michael could use it. I can see we were wrong. It won't be the first time or the last. It seems as though it was meant to be used by you. The oracle was right in keeping this from us. With everything that's happened, we wouldn't have listened to him." Ariel wrinkled her brows. "If the oracle's premonition is correct, you, Alexa, must use it against Lucifer."

Alexa's spirits fell at the faith in Ariel's voice. Her palms were moist as she lowered the staff. "But will it work without the blood of a demon? The willing sacrifice?"

"I'm not sure," said Ariel. "I know the archangel Michael didn't need any demon blood to use it. Perhaps we don't either." She gave Alexa a reassuring smile, but it didn't help suppress the growing fear in Alexa's gut.

"But the oracle wrote that—"

The ground shook, and a thundering noise blasted through the air. Forks of green and yellow lightning ripped under the boiling clouds hanging over Lucifer's castle.

Alexa's heart shot up to her throat. "What was that?" Just as the words escaped her mouth, the castled shimmered and then lost its solidity. For a moment she could see the mountains through it on the other side of the river. She blinked, and the castle was solid again.

"That's the sound my father's castle makes before it disappears," answered Milo.

CHAPTER 23

"HURRY!" URGED MILO. "We've got minutes. Maybe seconds. If we're not in it before it leaves," he said panting, "we might never find it again."

"Angels!" Ariel bellowed as she drew her sword. "With me!"

The archangel Ariel and fifty strong angels charged down the lane towards the castle, barreling through the line of mortals and knocking them down like pins from a bowling alley. The mortals scrambled back to their feet, slashing their death blades, but they were quickly flattened to the ground by Metatron's nets.

"Traitors," he spat, his eyes wild as he turned and shot his gun at another group of mortals. "Infidels! Rats! Angel waste!"

"Let's go," Milo yelled. He, Alexa, and Lance gathered themselves and pelted after Ariel, heads down, through the midst of the fighters. They slipped in puddles of blood and mud towards Lucifer's castle.

Alexa's back burned as she ran. Every stride sent a painful jab at her wound. But the others never slowed, so, neither did she.

Determined, and with tears streaming down her face, Alexa pushed herself harder than ever before.

There were more integrated-mortal-angels all along the port. Alexa saw, close to the castle's main entrance, an angel she knew as Mike in combat with a giant-sized mortal man who had a shaved head and was covered in tribal tattoos.

There was another sonic boom, and Alexa looked up to see the castle shimmer into a mist. Then the dark stone walls loomed overhead again as it took solid form.

"Quickly, angels! Hurry!" called Ariel from ahead of them. "It's leaving! Faster!"

Alexa sped behind Milo, Lance and Ariel. As they ran, Alexa saw another group of Higher demons standing just outside the castle, watching them as they approached. Next to them was a group of lesser demons and what she recognized as the rotten cadaver-like figures of belphegors.

She felt her body tighten, and her muscles trembled from the adrenaline at the sight of the demons, but then they just stood there as she and the others galloped past.

The castle loomed before her like a giant skull, black and ominous and angry. It hunkered high on a distant hill, giving the impression of a giant floating head in the sky. She could see the bleak, rain-slicked, stone walls. It was the ugliest structure Alexa had ever seen, carved as though it was screaming in pain.

The four of them sped silently into the imposing maw of the castle as it flickered and became semi-transparent. For a horrible moment, Alexa felt as though she might fall through the floor, but then her feet kept hitting solid ground, and she kept going. They sprinted under the barreled roof of the iron portcullis in the shape of a screaming mouth and flew up the path toward a dark entryway to the top of the stone staircase into the entrance hall—just as Alexa felt a shift in the air. Her ears popped as pressure pushed on her from all sides.

Alexa had felt a familiar pressure like that before—like iron chains tightening around her chest, arms, legs and head—when she had stepped through the portal to purgatory.

The castle had jumped, transported to another place while they were inside.

Having seemingly reached the same conclusion, the four of them skidded to a stop. "We made it," breathed Lance. "We freaking made it. For a moment there, I didn't think we would. But we did it."

Milo smiled, looking at Alexa, but she couldn't smile back. Her face muscles were frozen. Now being inside, Alexa didn't feel so confident anymore. Tingling dread thickened in the pit of her stomach as the small flame of hope extinguished. A cold bead of sweat trickled down her back. What if the oracle had been wrong...

"Alexa? Are you okay?" Milo's eyes were full of worry.

"I'm fine," she lied, and her stomach gave a lurch. "Which way to daddy dearest?" her voice bounced on the cold black walls.

Milo turned his head towards a dark corridor. "This way."

Heart pounding faster than ever before, Alexa willed her body to move and follow Milo. Ariel and Lance flanked on either side of her like bodyguards. Still, the presence of Ariel and the others did little to quell her fears. She was about to face the Lord of Darkness himself, Lucifer.

The whole idea was absurd. The more she thought about it, the more she wound herself up until she was so tight she felt as though Ariel had wrapped her entire body in gauze. How could she, Alexa, ordinary-angel-fledgling, defeat such a foe?

She had met him before, fooled by the boy Markus. But this was no boy. This was the most powerful archangel that ever was. Not only could he not be killed by any means or weapons she possessed, he could only be defeated by sending him back to his prison—purgatory.

Alexa and the others followed Milo through the corridor. The black stone walls were bare of everything but hissing torches in brackets. As they walked, Alexa could feel the dread of each of the others rising along with hers in a collective apprehension.

With every step, Alexa's uneasiness increased. She wasn't ready. She didn't have the blood of a willing demon. What if Ariel was wrong? What if the staff wouldn't work without the demon blood?

The corridors were as harsh as the exterior castle walls. It was more of an armed fortress without the pretension of the comfort of a castle. As they followed Milo, Alexa saw just a few crude wooden chairs and torches set in rusty iron brackets. They met no one as they worked their way into the heart of the castle. They came to a large double door, carved from the same black stone from the walls. Milo pushed open the doors. Alexa glanced at them briefly as she passed through and almost started. The face of a grinning demon was carved into the stone, leering at her.

The room was vast and capped with a huge vaulted ceiling. Paintings hung on the walls, depicting angels, attired in the old style of robes, fighting demons. Alexa's eye went to the largest painting in the room with angels surrounding a glowing figure that looked a lot like Lucifer. His arms outstretched, he looked to be extending his affection to the angels.

Alexa frowned at the painting.

In the middle of the room, above an ornate burgundy patterned carpet, was a massive table that could seat twenty people. Papers and maps of the mortal world littered the long, lustrous tabletop, and at the end of the table sat a woman.

The woman stood up at the sight of them, her delicate features wrinkled in a mask of puzzlement. She wore a white cocktail dress with a halter-like bodice, a plunging neckline, a full pleated skirt, and a waist band amplifying her ample chest. Her short blonde hair was curled neatly in waves against her head.

Even behind the disguise, Alexa knew who she was. Her fears were forgotten as she glowered at the blonde woman whose red lips spread into a false smile.

"Ariel," said the woman. She stepped away from the table and smoothed out her dress. "Never thought I'd see you on this side of the spectrum." She took in Alexa, Milo, and Lance. "How did you get in? And what's that mutt doing in here? I thought I smelled wet dog."

"And I thought I smelled a rat," countered Lance. "Oh—wait—it *is* you. I didn't recognize the backstabbing, tramp, Sabrielle under all those layers of makeup. Word to the wise—less is more.

And who are you trying to be now? Marilyn Monroe? Not even close."

Sabrielle looked to the others, a blank expression on her face. "You're too late. There's nothing you can do to stop it. And why would you? It's the best thing that could ever happen to the mortals."

"What's that?" said Alexa. "Share their bodies with someone else? You know how twisted that is, don't you?"

"You have very limited imagination," said Sabrielle.

"And you can't stand to be the *real* you," refuted Alexa, "so you dress up and pretend to be someone else. What's the matter, Sabrielle? Afraid to show the world what you really look like? Afraid to show how *ordinary* you are?"

Sabrielle's face slacked. "I... I am the Lord of Darkness' most faithful servant," she added more proudly. "His favorite."

"Yes," agreed Ariel, her face darkening. "That you are. You fooled us all with your *charming* ways."

Alexa's face heated at the thought of that woman's arrogance. Sabrielle had thought to have the glory to herself.

"I do whatever he commands me to do," said Sabrielle. "I serve him in his work to make the lives of angels in this world better. The only chance we have to better their lives is to become like the rest of the mortals—to live among them."

"You mean *in* them," said Lance. "Can I *bite* her now?"

"It's a violation!" shouted Ariel, and her sword shook in her hand. "The mortals were never created so that you and the other angels could play dress-up with their bodies."

275

Sabrielle smiled wickedly. "We can do whatever we want with them. We own them. They are ours!"

Before Alexa knew what she was doing, she bounded across the room and pointed the staff at Sabrielle's chest.

"You know what this is, Marilyn?"

Sabrielle stumbled back, her eyes widened in fear at the sight of the staff. "You wouldn't?" she said, her bottom lip shaking as her pretty face contorted in fear causing her makeup to crack.

"Oh, yes. I would."

Gathering composure, Sabrielle smoothed her voice. "I did everything for us—for the angels. Surely you can see that? It was all for *us*. So we can be free at last from the tethers of the Legion. Free to make our own decisions. Free to live how we want."

"Free to kill angels and mortals, you psychotic bitch?"

Sabrielle almost never let emotion touch her smooth features, but it touched her face now as her brows drew together in a murderous scowl.

"Why, you good for nothing lesser angel! I should have killed you when I had the chance!"

The staff was an inch from Sabrielle's face. For a second Alexa really thought she was going to use the staff on Sabrielle. But then she made a fist with her left hand—and punched her across the face as hard as she could.

Sabrielle fell to the floor, stunned and holding the right side of her face in her hands.

"That…is for lying and tricking us into going to purgatory."

Alexa felt immense satisfaction at sight of tears in the archangel's eyes. She had a mean left hook.

"You don't deserve to live after what you've done," said Alexa, pointing the staff in Sabrielle's face, "but I'm not here for you—"

"No, I presume you are here for *me*," a voice behind her said.

CHAPTER 24

THEY ALL TURNED AT THE SOUND OF THE VOICE, but Alexa already knew who it was.

Lucifer sauntered into the chamber. He was clad in the same black armor she remembered moving over him like liquid oil. Taller than his son and heavily muscled, he wore a long ancient-looking sword at his waist. He was beautiful, and she could see the resemblance with his son, but his eyes made Alexa's skin prickle in fear. They seemed to hold both light and dark, and she had to force herself not to look away from them.

"You've come to destroy me, have you not?" Lucifer's striking face held no emotion. His voice was deep and annoyingly charismatic. "With Michael's staff, I see."

Alexa had opened her mouth, but Milo moved to stand before Alexa. "I won't let you harm her, Father."

"Milo, my son," said Lucifer with a slight shake of his head. "Why do you continue to disappoint me so? Have I not been a good father to you while you were in my home? Why did you choose to run away?"

"I'm here now, aren't I," said Milo.

Lucifer halted. "Yes. But not for the reasons I had hoped. I thought I made it clear what would happen if you disobeyed me again. You knew I would kill these... friends of yours, these allies, and yet you chose to bring them here... to my home." His spectral stare moved around Alexa and the others and she swallowed hard. The staff seemingly got heavier in her grasp.

Alexa could feel the tension in the others and could see the slight shake of Ariel's body as she moved to stand next to Alexa. Lance hid behind Milo's legs.

Lucifer's gaze fell on Sabrielle and he took in the welt on her face. "Unless you're here to deliver them to me." Lucifer's smile had Alexa frozen in fear. "Now that is a delightful gift, my son."

Milo's face paled. "Your madness has to stop. What you're doing to the mortals, to children!" his voice rose. "I can't let you do this. I won't stand by and watch you destroy their world."

Lucifer's eyes rested on Alexa. "And you thought what exactly? That you would bring Alexa here and she would use Michael's staff on me? That I would even *allow* her to get close enough to use it? Did you imagine I would puff into dust?"

Milo scowled. "Maybe."

Lucifer's eyes narrowed. "Don't think for a single moment that your arrival here went unnoticed. I *allowed* you to enter. I even waited until you were safely aboard before I moved my home again."

"That's not good," whispered Lance.

Alexa shifted her weight when she realized she was shaking, dread weighing her down.

Milo's voice was cold, but Alexa saw the tension in his face. "Why would you do that if you knew we had the staff?"

"Because I wanted my son back. If it meant letting your friends in with the intention of destroying me, then so be it." He smiled. "Their efforts are fruitless. Nothing can destroy me. Can't you see that now, my son? Don't you want to be part of what I've created?"

"I've never wanted to be part of you," said Milo, and Alexa knew he'd hit a nerve by the look on Lucifer's face.

"What do you want?"

"To put a stop to the angels integrating with the mortals."

"Unfortunately, the only way to stop it is with my demise," said Lucifer simply.

"Exactly why we've come," said Alexa, trying to make her voice braver than she felt.

Lucifer looked at her in surprise. "As I said, I cannot die. Have you not realized what I am? I am the most powerful celestial being that ever was, more powerful than all the gods and archangels combined. Michael couldn't destroy me, and neither can you."

Alexa didn't shy away. "It won't stop me from trying."

Lucifer looked into her eyes a long moment. "You are a very rare person, Alexa Dawson. Not many would stand as you do now, with that in your hand. I will give you one opportunity—one—with that staff. You can use it on me. I won't stop you."

"What's the catch?" asked Alexa.

"I smell a setup," mumbled Lance.

"No setup, no catch." Lucifer's voice purred with malicious pleasure. "If am I not what I say I am, then one touch of the Staff of Heaven will destroy me. Isn't that why you came here? To destroy me? Then go ahead, Alexa. Use it." He stood with his arms wide. "Do it."

"No, my lord!" cried Sabrielle sitting up. But with one look from Lucifer, she clamped her mouth shut and settled back down.

Alexa stood shaking, partly in fear and partly in fury. She scanned Lucifer's face, searching for the glimmer of lies. There was only bold rebellion and arrogance within his gaze.

The entire room was silent. Even Sabrielle's whimpers subsided.

"It'll work, Alexa," whispered Milo. He squeezed her shoulder encouragingly. "The oracles saw it. You were destined to do this. He's not invincible. He just *thinks* he is."

Alexa tried to take comfort from Milo's words, but she had nothing but a deep fear growing in her.

Trick. Trick. Trick.

She thought of the time she'd vanquished the two archangels with the staff. There had been no demon blood, and the staff had worked. Maybe it would again.

It is going to work, she told herself. *The oracle saw it.*

Gathering the only bits of courage she had left, which wasn't much, Alexa moved towards Lucifer. His strange, eerie gaze made her heart pound even faster, louder. But then the staff hummed— not like before but with a pulsing that she felt all the way up to her shoulder. The warmth emitting from it went hot. It was though it were telling her it would be okay, telling her to use it. It *wanted* her to.

Confidence bloomed in Alexa's chest.

The entire room was silent, and Alexa's attention was on Lucifer. Her revelation must have been evident on her face, for he lifted his chin and spread his arms in a silent invitation.

She took another step toward him, and then another.

The oracle is right, she thought. The pulsing increased in the staff as if in answer. *It's going to work. The staff will send Lucifer back to purgatory. The mortal world will be safe.*

But there was a faint smile on Lucifer's lips as she stood before him, the staff in her hand. His arrogance sent hot flashes through her.

"This is for all the souls you took," she said and stabbed him with the staff.

CHAPTER 25

LUCIFER CRIED OUT AS THE STAFF touched the flesh just above his collar bone. White light exploded from the end of the staff, blinding Alexa. The light intensified, and she could still see the burst of its brilliance through her eyelids. Eyes watering, she blinked through the spots in her vision as the light diminished. She stepped back.

For a triumphant moment, Alexa saw strings of light travel over Lucifer's skin and body just as it had been with the other two archangels. Light swirled over Lucifer like a mist. He lurched forward, stumbling. Alexa saw the light inside him, illuminating his eyes and skin and veins, moving just under the surface of his skin.

Lucifer was dying. The staff had worked.

And then he straightened. The light around him vanished. And Lucifer began to laugh. Low at first, and then high and hysterical.

Bathed in darkness, Lucifer slowly rose a few feet off the ground, a satisfied grin on his face and his eyes sparkling with power. His head rolled back in rapture as strings of black tendrils rotated about him.

Alexa whirled around and found Milo staring at her, his face pale and contorted in horror. Ariel had tears in her eyes, out of anger or despair, Alexa couldn't tell. But Lance was snarling. His canines gleamed in the soft light of the room, and he looked about to jump on Lucifer.

"I told you the staff couldn't harm me," said Lucifer, his deep voice belligerent. "For none of you can fight the Lord of Darkness in his place of power, not even with Michael's staff. You assumed that you, a lesser angel could wield such a weapon, a weapon created by none other than the archangel Michael, and that his staff would answer to you? You? A lesser angel? Foolish, stupid little angel."

Alexa was paralyzed in fear. What had she done?

Lucifer moved as swiftly as a lick of flame to seize Alexa by the forearm. She flinched back with a gasp. "What would cause the most pain to my son?" he hissed at her, teeth gleaming, his voice like the crackling of fire. "Your death."

"NO!" cried Milo, fast footsteps echoing all around Alexa.

But she couldn't move. She couldn't even cry out as something far more violent than a bomb hit her. The staff fell from her grasp as she was lifted off the floor with a whip of darkness and sailed across the room to crash against the wall.

Alexa heard something crack as she slipped to the cold stone floor. Searing pain like none she had ever known assaulted her body. Every nerve in her body burned with razor-sharp misery. Her mouth was open, but no scream came out. The pain blacked her vision out. Fire burned through every muscle and bone, consuming her, choking her in convulsing agony.

Her insides burned with a kind of fire that made everything a bit muddled. She was lying prone on the ground, and the cold hard floor pressed against her cheek. Every inch of her ached and burned. *Get up*, she told herself. But her body wouldn't listen. She couldn't move.

A scream reached her ears followed by the horrifying whimper of an animal in distress. Black spots floated in her vision, and she blinked through her tears. Ariel was on the ground, her body still as the dead. Her head was turned the other way and Alexa couldn't tell if she was still alive. A small cry escaped Alexa's lips as she spotted a bundle of white fur lying next to Ariel.

"You choose them over me!" Alexa heard Lucifer shout and her eyes darted across the room.

Milo was suspended in the air by black tendrils, pinning him to the wall. His face was knotted in pain and misery, but his eyes were on Alexa. She read the fear in them when their eyes met. *I'm sorry*, his eyes said. But this wasn't Milo's fault.

"Yield, my son, and you can rule with me," said Lucifer.

"Never," said Milo through gritted teeth, his eyes tearing up in pain.

"The opportunity of surrender I give now carries incentives. You will be able to join me without prejudice or sanctions. I will forget your traitorous behavior because you are my son. I forgive you."

"I won't. I'll never join you."

"Kill him, my lord," urged Sabrielle, her eyes red. "Give me a mortal body and I will give you *more* sons, better sons—"

"Quiet!" bellowed Lucifer, and Sabrielle winced as though she'd been punched in the face again. She lowered herself to the ground, trembling.

Alexa savored the coolness of the stone on her cheek. Darkness played at the edges of her mind. It took every ounce of energy she had left just to keep her eyes open. Death was near. She could taste it. She was hot and cold and hot again. The room seemed to sway, blurring in lines. Her face burned like the heat of a fever or an infection.

Through Alexa's fractured vision, she saw the staff, lying on the ground near the entrance of the room. Even if she could reach it, what good would it do now?

It hadn't worked. The oracle's prophecy had been wrong.

Her eyes settled on Lance, and buckets of tears flew from her eyes. He was dead. He was dead and it was her fault...

"You *will* join me," said Lucifer, turning back to Milo. "Whether it be by force or not, that is up to you. But you will be my first in command, and we will rule... together. I am going to make you pay for your insolence, my son." He snarled. "You did kill all your brothers."

"They weren't my brothers. They were monsters."

"The same essence flowed in you," Lucifer snarled. "Be warned, I intend to wipe the Legion and everything in it. Angels, oracles, every other celestial creature who will not submit—all of it.

Those who are foolish enough to try and stop me—like your friends here—will suffer the same fate. No mercy will be granted."

Alexa bit down as another wave of torturous agony went through her. It was like she was melting from the inside, and soon she would be a puddle of angel mess. Only her eyes could move, unable to out-scream the pain.

"Kill me," said Milo, "because I will never join you."

Lucifer laughed. "I will never kill you, my son. You will join me. You will rule with me."

"Kill me."

"Enough!"

Lucifer sent another blast of tendrils at Milo. They hit him hard, and his head cracked against the stones, his spirit sabers dropping from his splayed fingers.

Stop, Alexa tried to say, but only blood spilled out of her mouth.

"You can't get away with this," said Milo. His eyes met Alexa's. Blood dripped from his nose, his ears. "We'll stop you."

"Who? There is no one left *to* stop me," said Lucifer with a hateful smile. "It was a valiant effort, but you assumed that you understood the contents of the oracle's riddle. You forgot one of the main ingredients," Lucifer mocked. "Blood of a *willing* demon."

Alexa could only wince at her failure. Lucifer was right.

"The oracle filled you with false hopes." Lucifer's eyes danced with amusement. "No demon would ever sacrifice themselves willingly for the things they hate most… for angels."

"I would," came a familiar voice.

Alexa darted her eyes towards the voice.

A girl demon, sucking on a lollypop, stood in the entrance of the chamber. And in her hand was the Staff of Heaven.

CHAPTER 26

ALEXA COULD ONLY WATCH AS Willow strolled into the room, her eyes taking in the scene. The light that shone from the torches lit the top of her bald head in glints of gold. Black blood oozed sluggishly through wounds around her scalp and neck while bones peeked through holes in her clothes and flesh. A severed arm was strapped to her chest. The air stank of sulfur and the unmistakable taint of carrion.

Willow stopped when she saw Alexa.

"You dropped this," said the girl demon and tossed a piece of paper on the ground next to Alexa. Even on the ground, with limited vision, Alexa recognized the oracle's note. Now that she thought about it, she didn't remember pocketing it. She must have dropped it in her hurry to get to the castle.

Alexa looked over to Lucifer. His face was strangely pale, and he stood still. Why wasn't he attacking Willow?

Willow scanned the room again, and her eyes widened when she spotted Sabrielle. She tossed her severed arm across the room and it hit Sabrielle square in the chest.

"That's disgusting! You freak!" shrieked Sabrielle, her white dress smeared in yellow and black pus.

"See this?" said Willow as she closed the distance between them. "It doesn't want to be reattached. No matter what I do, it just doesn't want to hold. Now why is that? If I'm so powerful, why can't I do a simple reattachment? Hmm?"

Sabrielle recoiled in horror. "Get away from me."

Willow sucked on her lollypop. "Can I have my arm back?"

"Get back! Don't touch me!"

Willow shrugged. "You told me I'd be stronger than any angel. I'd be invincible. A goddess. You never said I'd rot and lose my limbs. You never said it would keep getting *worse*." She pointed the staff in Sabrielle's face. "You lied to me. You lied to everyone."

"I don't know what you're talking about. You're crazy," spat Sabrielle, her hair disheveled. She looked like a frightened cat pinned to a wall.

"You had me convinced that I should kill Milo, that he was interfering with the *big plan*. But he never was. I can see it was because you wanted him out of the way. Didn't you? You didn't want to share *your* Lucifer." Willow turned and winked at Lucifer in an overly seductive way. "He's hot. I get it. But he's also very, very, *evil*, isn't he?"

Sabrielle made a face. "And *you*, you couldn't even do a simple job, could you? Couldn't even kill one itty bitty angel boy. You deserve what you get. Filthy demon."

Willow giggled. "Yeah, about that. I've changed my mind. I don't want to keep living like this," she pointed to herself. "Why should I look like a zombie while the rest of you, the rest of the angels, get to roam around in perfect, healthy mortal bodies. Hmm?"

"Who are you?" snarled Lucifer.

When Willow smiled, Alexa noticed only blackened gums. "Willow. And you must be the big bad Lucifer. I like your castle. Very goth."

"You're a demon," said Lucifer. "Getting rid of the Legion is a favor. You should be thanking me for giving you free reign on the mortals now that they can't defend themselves."

"Wrong," said Willow, twirling the staff like a baton. "You think the demons are happy about the angels riding in mortal bodies? You think they want that? No. They. Don't. Why do you think they all sat back and watched while your mortal-angels went to war with the Legion? The demons don't want the angels to take over the mortal bodies, *duh*. What's in it for them? Nothing. *They* want the mortal world for themselves. They want the world like it was—*before* you messed things up."

Lucifer's face slacked, and Alexa watched as his features contorted until he looked truly feral. "You're a demon. How can you handle the Staff of Heaven? Only angels can touch it. You should be burning into cinders!"

Willow gnawed down on her lollypop. "Because I was once an angel. The staff knows that. I can tell. She and I are friends now. That's right. It's a *she*." Willow stepped carefully towards Lucifer, his eyes on the staff.

"I heard a rumor that you can't escape your home when it's traveling," said Willow lazily. "So, if it's true, it means you can't portal yourself out of here. Basically, you're stuck."

The oracle's note flashed in Alexa's mind's eye: *You will need to bind Lucifer. Otherwise the vacuum rift will be useless as he can use his portal abilities and get away unless he's in a closed environment...*

"The things is, I *know* why you haven't tried your dark powers on me," said Willow, with a feral grin. "You can't kill me because we both know what will happen if you do."

"What is she talking about?" Sabrielle's voice hitched in her throat. She held on to the table for support. "My lord?"

"Tell her," drawled Willow. "Tell her why. Tell her what will happen if you spill *my* blood while I'm holding this?" She gave a wave of the staff.

Lucifer's face was thunderous. "I'll give you anything you want. Power? A new body? It's already done. You want to be an angel again? I can make that happen. I can give you anything you want. Anything."

Willow huffed out a breath of laughter. "I made a mistake, see. I wanted out, but I didn't know how I was going to do that. But when I saw Alexa, I knew she was up to something—because she always is. I saw how she was protecting that staff of hers. And when she dropped the oracle's note, I knew what I had to do. What I was *meant* to do. So, I followed her and hid in your castle." Willow looked at Alexa and rolled her eyes. "Of course, Alexa, being as conceited as she is, wanted to be the star of the show again." Willow shook her head. "Having the soul channeling power apparently wasn't enough. She's insufferable, you know. I'd kick her if she wasn't already down. She thought she was the one—the chosen one—but it's me. It's always been me."

"If you do this," hissed Lucifer, his eyes widening in the realization of what was happening, "you will die. You will never be reborn!"

Willow sighed, nearing Lucifer. "Maybe. Maybe not. But it'll be a hell of a lot better than living like this."

With a sweep, the girl demon brought the staff over her head. Her black blood gleamed as she rubbed the top of the staff in it.

"NO!" cried Lucifer as he ran towards the door.

And then with a powerful swing, Willow slammed the staff on the ground.

The room suddenly resounded with a peal of thundering noise. Alexa's ears popped. Shards of stone fell from the ceiling and the walls. Where the staff touched the ground was a black hole.

As Alexa watched, she felt the staff's power rip through every fiber of her being. The hole grew. It grew until it became a black ring, pulling Lucifer and Willow towards it.

Lucifer struggled and shrieked, but the ring bound him. Alexa's hair lifted around her as she watched in wide-eyed terror as Lucifer thrashed on the spot, waving away things she couldn't see. Capering madly, he threw himself from side to side, seeking to cast off the black band that held him but only causing it to grow bigger, wider, until it was large enough to fit two people. It was a distinct hemisphere, as black as coal. Alexa saw a strange smile appear on Willow's face, just as the black ring rose up like a wall.

With a thump and a hiss, the mound of darkness that had been the vacuum rift was gone. The Staff of Heaven glinted as it rolled to a stop on the stone floor.

Alexa felt her death was near. Her last thoughts were of Milo's soft, luscious lips on her and his strong body holding her warm and close.

There was a faint crash and rustle, and then the darkness swept in to tear her apart.

CHAPTER 27

SUMMER SEEMED TO HAVE FINALLY ARRIVED. The evening was warm and full of spices. Alexa sat outside on the terrace of Amore Ristorante, staring at couples and families as they ate and drank happily, a warm breeze brushing against her cheeks.

"I can't believe you did this," said Alexa as she folded her napkin on her lap with trembling hands.

"You don't like it?" Milo's voice was calm, but a muscle jumped along his jaw. He sat across from her, looking like a fairy tale prince with his high cheekbones and golden skin. He looked different without his spirit sabers across his back—softer somehow and less intimidating, surprisingly more like a mortal. Still, before they had made the jump, Alexa had spied two soul blades hidden under his jacket.

Alexa looked at her glass of ice water, wishing her fingers would stop shaking so she could have a sip. "Of course I like it. I'm just... it's just... very modern of you. It's really nice. Thank you."

Her eyes met his. "I can't believe we're out on a *real* date. It's insane."

Milo's lips curled into a smile. "With all the changes that are happening with the Legion, this is the first of many." He began to cut into his filet mignon. "Although we still don't need to eat, it's refreshing that we can at least... pretend."

Alexa stared at her plate of mixed green avocado salad. Two weeks ago, she was lying on the cold stone floor of Lucifer's castle, dying. Even now, she couldn't shake off the shock that she had made it out of Lucifer's castle *alive*. But most of all was the shock of Willow's sacrifice.

"You think Willow's still alive? In purgatory somewhere?" Alexa chewed on a slice of tomato. "I mean, she's not my favorite person in the world, but after everything she did, it would be cruel if she didn't make it."

"I don't know, but if she is, I hope she's giving my father a hard time."

Alexa smiled. During her recovery in the Healing-Xpress, she'd learned from Lance who'd visited every day, that with Lucifer back in purgatory, the angel integration with the mortals failed. Whatever hold he had in the mortal world went with him. The angels could no longer remain in their human hosts and were cast out, to return to Horizon where an army waited to escort them to the newly repaired Tartarus. Nathaniel had cried like a baby all the way. Her only regret was that she hadn't been there to see it.

Alexa's smile grew. "I heard Sabrielle was released into Metatron's care. What do you think he'll do to her?"

Milo leaned forward in his seat, his muscles barely contained within his tight shirt. "Well, for starters, he stripped her of her archangel powers."

"You can do that?"

"He can. And he did."

"What does that make her now?"

Milo gave her a sideways smile. "An angel, just like us."

Alexa sat stunned for a moment, imagining Sabrielle's face when she got the news that she'd be reduced to a mere, unremarkable angel.

"This is the happiest day of my life," she said with a smile.

When Alexa reached out and grabbed her ice water, she saw a good-looking young guy two tables over and wearing a black leather jacket lift his beer to Milo in way of greeting. The young woman sitting with him turned in her seat and waved, a large smile on her pretty face and her citrus scent rolling off her like a sweet perfume.

Milo gave them a smile and returned to his dinner, as if he were a regular at the restaurant.

Alexa put her elbows on the table and lowered her voice. "Who are those angels? I don't think I've ever seen them before." The male angel caught her staring and flashed her a grin. Alexa quickly looked back at her plate.

"David and Kara," said Milo as he put down his fork. "Great guardians, these two. They have the most successful rate of closed rifts and solved demonic cases between them than the rest of the Counter Demon Division combined. David's always been a little colorful in his demon hunting methods… but he's a great guardian. I should introduce you sometime," said Milo. "*She's* a lot like you."

"Hmm." Alexa moved her food on her plate, her eyes flicking back to David and Kara, who were now absorbed in their own conversation.

"I know what you're thinking," said Milo. "Give it time. You'll break some records too."

"Now that I've been pardoned and reinstated in the Counter Demon Division," said Alexa. She thought to lower her voice at the strange look she got from the mortal woman sitting at the next table to her right.

"How's your mom? You didn't tell me about your visit."

"She's good." Alexa took a sip of water, careful not to spill any. "Well, she thinks I'm her long lost cousin, thrice removed. I told her I was researching my ancestry and found out that we both lived in the same city. Anyway, she bought it. I asked her if I could come and see her sometimes, and she said yes. It's a really nice change, the Legion allowing us to visit our families."

Milo's stare cut into hers, and he smiled. "And allowing us to have *real* relationships."

Alexa's face flushed. "That too." She felt as though she was about to burst. She could feel Milo's nervous wiggle across from her.

They could be together. Finally, together.

Shivers raced along her skin. Milo was here with her, and she wasn't delusional. They'd come through death and fire and shadow and found each other again.

"Well," said Milo, his voice soft. "We better get used to it because it's happening. And we're never ever going to be apart. You're mine, *fledgling.*"

Alexa reached out and grabbed his hand, holding it tightly. She would never let him go again.

ABOUT THE AUTHOR

KIM RICHARDSON is the award-winning author of the bestselling SOUL GUARDIANS series. She lives in the eastern part of Canada with her husband, two dogs and a very old cat. She is the author of the SOUL GUARDIANS series, the MYSTICS series, and the DIVIDED REALMS series. Kim's books are available in print editions, and translations are available in over seven languages.

To learn more about the author, please visit:

www.kimrichardsonbooks.com

Made in the USA
Middletown, DE
07 January 2023